HEAD
in the
GAME

REBECCA RATHE

Cover design by: JG Designs
Editing by: Book Witch Author Services

For my mom,

Because Luke's coming out story was my own, and I know how lucky I am that you always accepted me for exactly who I am.

I love you.

HEAD IN THE GAME

Groveton College Series

Rebecca Rathe

AUTHOR'S NOTE

Head In The Game is a dark MM sports romance. While the main story and relationship is strictly MM, there are some graphic descriptions of MF and MFF pairings within the story.

This story contains dark themes and potential triggers, including but not limited to: coach/player forbidden relationship, age gap, dubious consent, degradation, praise, voyeurism including recording of sexual situations, rough sex and scenes that may contain dubious usage of proper lubricants, discussion and imagery regarding alchoholism and addiction, explicit language and sexual situations, and more.

There are many references to homophobia throughout the book, including homophobic language used by both the main characters and outside influences. There is a brief mention of suicide and conversion therapy.

Please keep these potential triggers in mind, as your mental health is of the utmost importance.

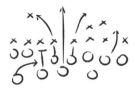

PROLOGUE- BRYANT

How is it that the fate of my career depends on some hotshot spoiled brat with a cocky attitude?

Okay, I admit it. He's good. Really good. Too good to still be available to pull out from under a big conference school's nose.

"What's the catch?"" I ask bluntly, eyeing my assistant offensive coach and scout we sent out to find new talent. Tucker Sanders, aka Tuck, has a good eye for talent, and he's been helping me build a championship worthy team over the past season. It's a hard job, considering the Groveton College Jackals haven't won a championship since my days of playing on these historic fields.

With all the money that flows into this school, the dean had high expectations when he hired me. He overlooked a lot of problematic gaps in my resume to offer me a job here, but he made no bones about what he wanted from me—a championship season. We'd been able to pull off a decent season this year, falling just short of the playoffs, and I'm proud of the team. The dean, however, doesn't give a fuck what kind of feat it was to pull off every win. All he cares about is a championship, and he's made it very plain that if I don't bring home the title in the next coming season, I'll be back out on my ass.

"Kid's a little problematic. He stirred up some trouble and got kicked off the team. There's some scandal involved, but no official charges filed. Now he's about to lose his scholarship and his draft potential, so I'm hoping he might be desperate enough to come and play nice."

I pause and zoom in on the footage of the kid. "What's his name again?"

"Jack Perry. Junior. Six foot two, two hundred pounds. He's got the most receiving yards on the NCAA books right now. Great hands, and he's fast. His forty-yard dash time is close to a four point three."

"No shit?" *Jack Perry.* "Looks like a cocky little sonofabitch."

Tuck laughs. "That he certainly is, but to be fair—he's got the goods to back it up. Just a matter of reining him in a bit."

"Taming I can do. What exactly did he get in trouble for?"

"The usual—partying, not showing up to classes, starting fights on the field. There's some concern about one of his teammates ending up in the hospital. Rumors say Perry put him there, but again, no charges have been filed, so we can't say for sure." He passes me some of the information gathered about the incident. The kid that got put in the hospital isn't likely to play again. Damn, Perry really fucked him up. "Oh, and there's the small matter of getting caught fucking the coach's daughter on his desk."

I raise an eyebrow. "Bold of him."

Tuck chuckles uncomfortably. "Yeah, that's not all. Turns out he recorded it and decided to do a little showing during an aftergame recap meeting, did an override of the game footage and showed the whole room a video of the coach's little girl shouting, 'Jack's my daddy now'."

"Jesus."

"Yeah."

"So what you're saying is I'm going to have my fucking hands full."

"Without a doubt. But he's also crazy good. You don't see talent like that often."

I grunt and start the footage over again, effectively dismissing Tuck.

What he said is true; I have to admit that talent like Jack's is rare. He could have a future if he straightened his shit up. And I could help him make that future happen. I'm good at making men out of the scrawny, spoiled dipshits that saunter through these doors hoping to walk in the shoes of their father's glory days. Hell, in just one season, I turned a losing team around and gave us a fighting chance. It still hasn't been enough. Putting together a decent offensive line with a top-tier quarterback, who I trained personally, will never be enough if there isn't someone good enough to catch the fucking ball. We need hands, and we need speed.

We *need* Jack Perry.

CHAPTER 1–JACK

I watch through the chain-link fence as my former teammates fuck up another play, my replacement tripping over his own feet and fumbling an easy catch. I laugh as the other team easily scoops up the ball and gains thirty yards before the clock runs down. These assholes are nothing without me.

I'm not here because I'm feeling sorry for myself and wishing I was out there with them. I'm here to watch them lose and get their asses handed to them; waiting for the moment that the coach throws a tantrum so I can revel in his misery. Fucking asshole got what was coming to him. They aren't shit without me.

I catch his eye and give him a knowing smirk before looking behind him. His daughter, Millie, stands on the sidelines, and I shoot her a blatant wink before turning on my heel and walking away. I don't have to look back to know that the coach's face is so red he's close to turning purple. Millie's probably going to end up in a nunnery after what we did, but it was her idea. She wanted to get her asshole father back just as much as I did.

He was already threatening to kick me off the team under false pretenses just because he didn't like that I put his good for nothing, date raping, smug asshole of a nephew in the hospital after I caught him putting something in Millie's drink. Dude was fucking obsessed with his cousin and wouldn't leave her alone, but daddy dearest doesn't believe her. He keeps saying she's being dramatic or jealous that the twerp gets more attention than her because he's a football star. He always wanted a son.

So, I bent her over his desk and we pressed record.

I groaned as I lifted the back of her tiny cheerleading skirt and pushed two fingers into her hot, wet cunt.

"God, your pussy is tight. I hope that pervy ass cousin of yours knows what he's missing. Damn."

It was directly after a game, and I was still streaked with dirt, sweat dripping all over her back. Millie and I had fucked around before, and I knew she liked it down and dirty. I grabbed coach's discarded tie and wrapped it around her pretty throat, pulling her head back and forcing her to look into the camera when I shoved my dick into her so hard, she let out an animalistic grunt as the breath pushed out of her. She was always down for some kinky shit.

"Yeah, you like that, don't you Millie? You like taking my fat dick while you're bent over your daddy's desk?"

"Yeah," she moaned, her pussy tightening. "Yeah!" she

mewled, her voice going up an octave every time I slammed my cock into her dripping pussy. "Oh God, yes!"

"Too bad your daddy is such a fucking pussy, isn't it, little girl?" I didn't wait for an answer, driving into her at a faster pace. This video could only last so long, and I needed to cram as much disrespect into it as possible before I made Millie scream and come all over my cock.

"I think you need a better daddy, baby. What do you think?" Millie was moaning so loudly, I was worried the coach might walk in and find us before we were done with our little performance. Not that she was faking. I could tell by the way her pussy walls were rippling around my cock that every moan and cry was real.

Just when I felt her clenching down on me, ready to come, I slammed her face down onto the desk, making sure she was facing the camera, and fucked her savagely. Her whole body lurched with every thrust.

"Come for me, little girl. And tell everybody who your daddy is now."

"Jack!"

"Louder baby," I growled, licking my finger before shoving it in her ass and making her scream.

As she clamped down hard around me, she sobbed, "Jack Perry is my daddy!"

Then I pulled out and forced her to her knees in front of me before I blew my load all over her face.

I grin at the memory. God, that was a good fuck.

I'll never forget the way his expression morphed from

confusion to mortified rage when the game footage cut out and the pornographic noises started. Watching his little princess taking my dick like a fucking porn star was a shock to his system, and he looked like he might have a heart attack when she shouted that *I* was her daddy now.

That's what you get when you're a shitty-ass father.

Fuck, I'm almost hard just thinking about it. If I thought that Millie would ever be let out without supervision again, I'd call and see if she wanted to suck me off. She's the only person I'm going to miss at this shithole. This so-called Christian college is full of nothing but preppy assholes and posers. Millie is the only one here that isn't a fake bitch just living off their rich parent's success, waiting for shit to be handed to them on a silver platter. She's already applied to law school at Columbia, and plans to transfer there next year. Otherwise, I'd be worried about leaving her to the wolves. Now that her cousin has been put down, she can take care of herself. We parted on good terms, helping each other out one last time. We made a fool out of her idiot father and showed him just how much respect he was owed.

Fuck this school. Fuck this team. And fuck their chances for a championship. They can't play worth shit now, especially without their first-string quarterback or a decent wide receiver.

I don't need them to achieve my goals. I'll find a rec league to play on, send some tapes to scouts, and find an agent. There's more than one way to the NFL. I've only got one more year before I'm eligible to be drafted. That's plenty of time to come up with a game plan.

My bags are already packed. Pretty much everything I own is inside my large, army-style duffel bag. I pull the strap over my shoulder and grab the small box of books and other crap I'm taking with me, and I leave without saying goodbye to even one person. I wasn't here to make friends, and I'm not crying on my way out.

The cab home hurts my wallet, but I've got a job lined up starting Monday. As long as I have enough to pitch in for bills and feed myself, Mom won't mind that I'm home earlier than expected.

When I walk in our single-wide trailer, I see her passed out on the couch, still in her stained uniform from the diner. There's a bottle of cheap whiskey next to her that I grab and take a deep swig, wincing at the burn. This is the shittiest booze I've had since I left home, and that's saying something, considering most college parties are fueled by warm beer and cheap liquor. Fortunately, there were enough spoiled rich kids on the football team that I drank the good stuff most of the time.

I consider if I should wake Mom and tell her I'm here so she doesn't worry someone's broken in, but I figure I should let her sleep it off. She works hard and means well, but she can be a mean drunk. I leave my shoes within eyesight so she knows I'm here, and head to take a shower. The small trailer is dingy and old, but it's clean enough, if a little dusty. Mom isn't here very often, and when she is, she's usually passed out drunk. It's been like this as far back as I can remember.

The water is cold when I step into the spray, but I welcome the jolt to my system. What's that quote? *I've got miles to go before I rest.*

CHAPTER 2–BRYANT

Jack Perry is a work of art. His strong back muscles ripple through his thin t-shirt as he picks up boxes that easily weigh more than he does, carrying them across the floor and arranging them on the proper shelves. His sun-tanned skin is glistening with a layer of sweat, and his closely buzzed dark hair and strong jaw make him look tough and weathered. I get the impression that his shitty habits and attitude were hard earned by a rough life. Football was probably all this kid had to raise him out of this shithole Alabama town, but now look where he's landed himself.

I watch him from the shadows as he unloads boxes in the old warehouse, and briefly wonder if this place is a legit operation or if they're hocking stolen goods, but I shrug it off. It doesn't really matter either way, and sometimes those shady jobs pay more. I've been there.

At least he's keeping himself strong. All of this lifting is certainly helping him maintain all that lean muscle.

Just as I'm considering what his body fat percentage might be, he speaks.

"You gonna stand there and stare at me all night, or are you going to get on with it?" His southern drawl is more subtle than the Texas twang I've become accustomed to.

I can't help but chuckle a little. "On with what?" My voice feels too loud after standing here quietly for so long. How long have I been watching him? And how long has he been aware of me?

"I dunno," he says with a shrug. "I figured you're here to rob me, but the way you've been watching me thinks maybe you're tryin' to fuck me. And no offense, man, but I'm not into either of those options."

Now I'm really laughing. He's so casual about the statement, all but ignoring me as he goes about his business. You'd think he thinks he's invincible. Maybe he does. His cocky attitude both amuses and perturbs me. Every time this kid turns his back on me, I want to thrash him for being such an idiot. Maybe he could take some rando, but he couldn't hold me off if I wanted something from him.

"And what would you do if I wanted either of those things?"

"I'm sure I'd figure it out, I'm pretty scrappy." It's a thinly veiled threat that he can take care of himself, but the way he delivers it is smooth, nonchalant, like he couldn't care less.

My chortle is accompanied by an amused nod of appreciation. "Yeah, you certainly seem like you would be."

"Where're you from?" He asks, giving me a quick once over before picking up his next box.

"Originally? Small town in the midwest. But I've been in Texas for some time. That's where I drove here from."

He gives me a proper look now, his eyebrows pulling together like I might be familiar, which I might be if he were a little older.

"Didn't think he had it in him," he says, his mouth turning down in a strangely appreciative frown of complete acceptance for whatever he thinks is happening here.

"What are you talking about?"

"I'm assuming Coach Worth sent you to *teach me a lesson* or something like that." He emphasizes the words, so the meaning is clear: he thinks I'm here to rough him up, or worse. But he still looks unconcerned. He's too cocky for his own good.

"And why would he do that?"

A salacious grin spreads across his face, and it does something to me that I'm not quite ready to acknowledge. "Because I deserve it. But for the record, so did he."

"Nobody sent me," I say, trying to hold in my laughter. "But now I'm curious about what you did to Tim Worth to warrant him sending someone so far to *teach you a lesson*." I use the same inflection on the words that he did.

"I maimed his quarterback and fucked his daughter," he says with a shrug, returning to his work. He doesn't let much distract him from his job. He's focused, I have to give him points for that.

"Bit more than that, from what I heard."

Jack looks over at me with a hint of surprise on his face before his features smooth into a self-satisfied leer that I want to wipe right off his face. "Yeah, maybe."

A difficult box, heavier and too long to be handled by one person, grabs his attention. I move closer to pick up the opposite side, helping him lift the box. He looks at me curiously, but doesn't tell me to fuck off.

"Are you gonna tell me what you're here for, then?" he asks as we heft the heavy box onto a loading platform.

"I have a proposition for you." When he raises his eyebrow, I bark out a laugh. "Not *that kind* of proposition," I say, although there's a voice in the back of my head that thinks otherwise. "I came to see if you might be interested in continuing your college education and trying out for another football team."

He scoffs arrogantly, and I have little doubt the accompanying eye-roll is because I mentioned trying out. Truth be told, I have zero doubts he'd be first string and a star player immediately. The team, along with every girl on campus, will probably flock to him like flies on dog shit, but he needs to know his place.

"Every player on my team earns their place. We don't have room for cocky showboats and jackasses that don't follow the rules. I know exactly what kind of trouble you've gotten up to, and I won't have that bullshit from my players. I'm prepared to make it worth your effort, but the moment you step onto my field, I *own* your ass."

"Yeah... that ain't gonna happen. I've had enough of self-righteous old assholes bossing me around."

"I've seen your footage, and I know what you're capable of—" I cut him off with a raised palm before he interjects with any of his cocky bullshit. "But you could be better. *Can* be better. And I can make things happen for you."

He raises an eyebrow and gives me a look like I must be joking. Don't I know that he's God's gift to mankind?

"Your receiving skills are near perfect, but your ball security needs tightening up. You're fast, but you could be faster if you worked on your form—your posture is sloppy, and you're not taking advantage of your stride length."

I eye his long, strong legs and imagine just what he could do with them. I have to blink myself out of my thoughts when the image of his corded muscles and how they would feel under my hands fills my mind. I don't know where these types of thoughts are coming from, but I'm going to chalk it up to exhaustion from the thirteen-hour drive, and my hopefully unnoticeable desperation to get him on my team. There's something about this kid, something more than the winning season a player like him could bring us. I can see the determination in his eyes, but there's also a weariness that I recognize, and I don't want to see him give up. There are very few truly special talents out there. I want to see him succeed. The strength of my desire to turn this kid's life around is almost as shocking as the gutter path my thoughts have taken.

Jack Perry is special. Unfortunately, he knows it.

His gaze is narrowed as he considers my words. "What school did you say you're from again?"

Now it's my turn to give him a cocky grin. This is one of two cards I'm holding that I know will tip the scales in my favor.

"Groveton."

Jack snorts. "Groveton. You're fucking kidding."

"Nope, and I'll tell you something else," I say, leaning back casually on the platform. "I think Tim Worth is as much a piece of shit as you do, and I'd get personal satisfaction out of tearing his championship prospects out from under him."

"Well, you're welcome, then," he says, winking. "I've already done that for you."

"You think Tim fucking Worth doesn't have more money and resources than God, and isn't already actively recruiting the best replacements from across the country? Because my scouts are working the same circuits, and you can guaran-fucking-tee that there isn't a bribe he isn't capable of making to build the best team in the conference. There's only one thing that can come between him and a national championship."

"Oh yeah? What's that then?"

"You."

His eyebrow raises, clearly interested but not sold.

I continue before he has a chance to interrupt. "With my

help, I can not only make sure that you have a chance to rub it in Worth's worthless face, but I'm your best chance at being a first-round draft pick after one season. Your stats are good, but I'll make them better. I'll turn you into the kind of player that the NFL will start a bidding war for."

"The NFL wants talent. I can give them that without another year of bullshit."

I shake my head. He's in for a rude awakening if he thinks being good at catching a ball is all it takes.

"You think the NFL is going to pick up some trouble making nobody from bumfuck Alabama after the mess you've made of your reputation? Tim Worth will make sure no other college will touch you, and your shitty academics are going to hold you back even more—you couldn't get a scholarship to a community college, and I know that this dead-end job isn't paying you enough to make tuition even at the cheapest schools. Maybe you think you can just skate into the NFL with old stats and a gap in your playing career, but you're even dumber than I think you are if you really believe that."

"And what do you get out of it?" Jack asks combatively.

"A championship," I answer honestly, shrugging. "But don't think that you're a shoe in because you can catch a ball and run fast. If you want what I have to offer, I need a commitment from you. It'll be a hot, hard summer. You'll spend it training even harder. I'll push you until you break, tear you down piece by piece, and rebuild you into the best version of yourself. And that's all before the season even starts."

I extend the envelope with his offer, like it's some kind of bullshit olive branch. Inside there is a bus voucher, my card, an explicit contract where he's going to more or less sign his life over to me, and an offer for a full ride scholarship.The dean wasn't happy about that; charity cases aren't his thing, apparently. But he'll do what it takes to win, so he signed off on it.

"My card is in there if you have questions. But I expect to see you on the field on the first Monday in June. Check in with me the moment you arrive."

I get a sick sense of satisfaction watching the way Jack's mouth turns down in a frown at the mention of summer training.

"We'll get you down to less than ten percent in no time," I say, openly raking my eyes over his muscular form to guess his body fat percentage. If I can get him down to the eight percent range, he'll be lightning on the field.

I don't wait for Jack to respond further, turning on my heel to leave.

"I'm tougher than you think I am," he calls out after me.

"I'm counting on it."

CHAPTER 3–JACK

The fourteen-hour bus ride to Texas affords me plenty of time to rethink all my decisions. At every stop, I consider getting off and hitching my way back home.

I mailed in my acceptance letter for the scholarship weeks ago, but I still haven't signed the contract. There's no way this thing is legally binding. It's insane. He's asking me to sign away my autonomy. Give him full control of my life—from what I eat, to what I wear; and when and how I train.

I did my homework, looking up who he is and the team he's building. Bryant Nicks. First pick of the NFL draft after his senior year. He led Groveton College to three consecutive national championships back when he played for them. Spent the next decade trading up and living the dream as a three-time Super Bowl champion until a bad hit put him in the hospital with a concussion and torn rotator cuff. It was a career-ending injury for the once great quarterback.

I couldn't find anything on him for years until I came across a news article announcing he was stepping in as Head Coach for the Groveton College Jackals. After almost two decades of losing seasons, Bryant Nicks stepped in, gutted the staff, and turned the team around. They actually made it to the playoffs last season, which is an impressive turnaround for one season coaching.

Local forums are excited about the new coach; many are even reminiscing about what he was like when he played for Groveton. Apparently, he was quite the ladies' man, and cocky to boot. Not everyone was a fan, though, and some still seem to hold grudges. There was more than one person that mentioned the way he seemed to drop off the earth, some of them suggesting that he'd gotten addicted to painkillers and spent a year in a swanky rehab before coming back to Groveton as a favor to the dean. I don't know what's true, but I can tell, just on paper, that he knows what he's doing.

I'm willing to give this a chance. I'll do *anything* to make my dreams happen, to live exactly the life he had before it was all taken away from him. That won't happen to me, though.

Coach Nicks wanted me to report to him when I got

here, but I'm not ready to talk about the contract and his unrealistic expectations. Instead, I check in to my dorm and drop off my things. Just like the last place, I don't bring much. Just a duffel full of clothes and a box of other random shit, mostly books. I throw it all down on the bed and it's then I realize that I don't have any sheets or a bedspread for the twin loft bed. But at least I don't have to share with anyone since it's a single room. It's not as swanky as the room I stayed in when I was playing for my last team, but it's good enough. Aside from looking a bit like a prison cell, and having to share a communal bathroom with the whole hall, it's not terrible. Pretty fancy for what are clearly the poor people dorms.

After I check out the dorm, which is mostly empty since the semester doesn't start for another two months, I take a walk around campus. It reeks of old Texas money and people who think they're part of the elite. Even the dining hall looks like a restaurant you might be required to dress up for. Hopefully that isn't the case, because I don't dress up for shit. Pretty much all I have are athletic clothes, a couple pairs of jeans, and an assortment of sports and band t-shirts. I actually even own an almost vintage team shirt for The New Orleans Saints, the team that Coach Nicks played for when he was drafted to the NFL.

There aren't any cars in the sports complex, so I figure it's safe to poke around. I'm surprised to find the doors are unlocked, and I'm able to walk right in. I let out a low whistle of appreciation as I walk around. This place is swanky as fuck. Groveton has a pretty good sports medicine study track, so there are all kinds of amenities available to players to act as guinea pigs for the students. There are physical therapy stations, a sports massage office, and a number of other facilities that might be useful down the line. The best part is that all of their services are free, since you're being worked on by students, but you still have a professional supervising.

I find the football locker rooms and walk around, running my fingertips over the metal lockers and gleaming wood benches. The lockers are all engraved with the last name and numbers for each of the players. Well, all except one. "Perry" is scrawled in black marker on a piece of masking tape on one of the lockers, probably waiting until I sign the damn contract before they'll give me a fancy engraved name plate.

The showers are gleaming dark green tile stalls with three shower heads each, and there are two rooms for ice baths and a huge sauna. I wouldn't mind slipping in there for a while to relax my travel weary muscles, but I don't know where anything is and I still want to do a lap around the stadium. As I'm walking towards the tunnels, where the players run out on game days, I hear the clink of equipment. I follow the sound, interested in seeing what kind of gym facility this place must have.

The room is mostly dark. Whoever is in here only has the recessed lights on, which casts a comfortable glow over the room. Sure enough, the gym is state-of-the art. There are enough machines and equipment that the whole team could probably work out at the same time, although typically the groups are divided into days.

I slip into the room silently, not wanting to bother anyone but also wanting to get a closer look. There's a man at the bench press, lifting an impressive amount of weight, especially considering he doesn't have a spotter. His richly tanned arms are bulging, veins popping almost menacingly, as the man raises and lowers the bar without much difficulty. His shirtless chest is toned and gleaming with sweat, grey streaks swirling through the smattering of dark chest hair. His pecs flex, and my eyes are drawn to his nipples. I can't say that a man's nipples have ever turned me on before, but I can't help but stare. And I'm forced to swallow as my eyes trail down his ripped stomach and notice the shape of his dick through his gym shorts. Curious at my own reaction, I marvel that I can make that much out when he doesn't seem to be hard at all. His dick is definitely bigger than mine, which, while it's not a competition, is impressive. That's probably why it's capturing my attention the way it is.

The man lets out a low grunt of effort as he lifts the bar one last time and settles it back on the rack. I pull farther back into the shadows, not wanting to get caught ogling. If I were staring at a sexy woman, I wouldn't be as shy. I'd probably set up right across from her and squat thrust until she came and sat on my dick.

I harden at the thought of it. Definitely not because I'm looking at him. I mean, it's perfectly normal to admire an athletic form. I know how much work he must put into his body. Being an athlete is kind of like being an artist in some ways, our bodies are our canvases and it takes a certain amount of cultivation to get our bodies in the right shape. Admiring another artist's work, that's all I'm doing.

And then I notice *who* I'm admiring.

Coach Nicks sits up on the bench, swinging and stretching his arms in front of him. I pull farther back in the shadows, because I don't want to get caught watching my new hard-ass coach, especially not with the raging boner I can't seem to get to go down. Quietly, I slip my hand into my track pants and pull my hard dick up under my waistband. Hopefully, the elastic is strong enough to keep it back. You'd think the fear of getting caught would deflate the fucker, but it's having the opposite effect.

Nicks walks to the other side of the gym to grab a towel, and I take the opportunity to slip out as quietly as possible.

My heart is beating like mad as I jog out to the sports complex main atrium when a gruff voice stops me.

"Perry!"

I groan and turn around, assuming an irritated demeanor to cover my nerves. "I'm checking in. You weren't in your office."

"You could have called when your bus pulled in four hours ago."

"What, you're following me?"

"I keep track of my assets." He looks me over, his hazel eyes assessing me. "You hiding a contract in there?"

For a moment, I stumble, thinking he's referring to my still hard cock that is pressing against the bottom of my stomach. But he's looking around me, not at my crotch.

"I haven't signed it yet," I say boldly.

"Why the fuck not?"

"Because that fucking contract is insane. You can't control me like that."

"I can, and I will. It's part of the deal. No contract, no draft prospect, and no scholarship, so you can fuck off back to Alabama."

My face heats and my fists clench. He's not going to get away with this. "Fine." *But I'm going to make your life a living hell.* Good luck taming this dog.

"Let me grab something from my desk and we'll get going then. I'll help you unpack and see what we're working with." Nicks says, turning back towards the hallway.

What is he even talking about?

"Can't I just bring it to you later, or like tomorrow?"

"I've got time, and we need to go over your schedule and details. "

"Like when I'm allowed to piss?"

"Precisely," he says, turning a menacing grin on me.

I'm almost embarrassed when we walk into my small dorm room. All that I have in the world is sitting on the bare bed in a dusty duffel bag and a cardboard box that came from a liquor store.

"This it?" Coach Nicks asks in his gruff voice. It seems more like a simple question than a judgment, but my hackles raise anyway.

"Yeah, what of it?"

The coach turns to me and crosses his arms over his wide chest. He's a big dude, wide across the chest and shoulders, tapering to a lean waist. His dark hair and short beard make his hard, hazel gaze feel almost menacing. The room gets considerably smaller and warmer with his influence, but I'm not about to let on that I'm intimidated. Not backing down or shrinking even a millimeter, I raise an eyebrow at him.

"When you're answering me, you'll do so respectfully and intelligently, and refer to me as coach or sir."

I snort. "Yes, sir," I say sarcastically. I turn away to pull a few books out of the box and come across a small football trophy I've held onto all these years. It's dumb, and pathetic, but football was the one good thing I had going for me back then. This is the last trophy that hasn't gotten ruined by a random drunken purge of my things when my mother would decide to kick me out again. I push it to the side of the box and pull out an old, faded football.

"Game ball?" Coach asks, grabbing it and turning it in his hands, my disrespect momentarily forgotten.

"Yeah."

He glowers at me, a stern darkness in his eyes that

would definitely intimidate a weaker man. My issues with him aren't that I find him intimidating on an authoritative level, it's more that standing next to him makes me feel warm. Too warm. It's confusing, and it's starting to piss me off the longer he's in my personal space.

With a deep, angry sigh, Coach Nicks tosses the ball back in the box and gets right to the point. "Where's the contract?"

Narrowing my eyes, I pull the creased papers out of my duffel. I've read everything he handed me that night so many times that I've memorized it all. Which is exactly why I'm so apprehensive about this contract.

"Is this even legal?"

"It's enough to make sure that you couldn't sue us if you got injured or got your panties in a twist. We have good lawyers," he says, and it sounds like a warning. "But what's more important is that when you sign your name on that line, you know exactly what you're in for. There are no surprises, and I don't beat around the bush. I'll tell you exactly what I want from you, when I want it, and how I want it. I tell you when to jump and how high. You either don't speak or you say 'yes, Coach,' and you fucking do it. Simple as that."

"And all this bullshit about what I eat and wear, what I do with my free time?"

"Watch your mouth, boy."

"I haven't signed shit yet," I challenge him.

He doesn't look impressed, but allows me my moment

of victory. I'm sure I'll pay for it later. *Why does that prospect feel exciting?*

I think I just want to prove that he's not as tough as he thinks he is, that I can't be broken in the way he expects. We can both pull a win out of this. We share most of the same goals. But this battle of wills between us? I'll give him a hell of a lot more fight than he is expecting.

"You need to give yourself over to me entirely so I can shape you into the kind of man that will thrive in the environment you think you're destined for. It's not an easy road—it's hard fucking work, every single day, and there are expectations of how you carry yourself if you want to be truly successful. Nobody wants to interview an idiot or an asshole, and no one is going to pay to sponsor or endorse someone they don't respect. Good looks and decent stats are only going to get you so far before the system spits you out on your ass."

"You think I'm good lookin'?"

Coach Nicks smacks me on the back of my head, but I can tell he's trying not to crack a smile.

I'm going to break you, old man.

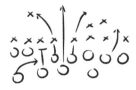

CHAPTER 4–BRYANT

After a tense afternoon of explaining that nothing in my plan is negotiable, I finally got that hot-head to sign my contract. I walked out of there more satisfied than ever before. I'm raring to own his ass.

There's something about this kid that gets under my skin. I feel like he knows whenever my thoughts start sliding sideways, which is happening way more often than I want to admit to even myself, and he's feeling cocky about it.

It's the first day of training. All one-hundred-and-ten players and around fifty support staff are milling about the field, shaking hands and introducing themselves. They're all in their practice gear and ready to go, most of them sweating in the already uncomfortable Texas heat. But it's early and we're just getting started. They're going to have to get used to it real fast. I've got a full class of sports medicine students and a bench full of water and sports drink dispensers, cooling towels, and whatever else we might need to combat heat stroke. But it's time to man the fuck up, and they know it. The second I start walking out to the field, everyone stops talking and turns their attention to me. The coaching staff joins me at midfield, forming a line behind me.

This is my least favorite part of the job. I never was one for public speaking, so I keep it short and sweet.

"Listen up, Jackals! Today, we embark on a journey. It won't be easy. It won't be fun. But it will be an accomplishment that you will carry with you for the rest of your lives. Today we start the hard climb to a championship season!"

The players let out whoops and cheers, the coaches behind me clap. I start to walk amongst the crowd as I talk, searching out the opportunity to look each player in the eye, if only for a moment.

"If you were with us last season, you know what you're in for. Summer training with me makes boot camp look like a vacation. It's going to be hot, and it's going to hurt. You're going to arrive here every morning at the crack of dawn and you're going to bust your asses until you are dismissed, well after the sun has gone down every night. You will have no social lives outside of swatting each other in the locker rooms. You will eat training and you will breathe football. And you'll come out of it ready for the best season this team has played in twenty years."

I give each player my most intimidating stare down, daring them to oppose me or punk out.

"I demand sacrifice, discipline, and unwavering

commitment. I won't listen to your bitching and moaning, and I don't give a fuck who your parents are and what they think of my methods."

Finally, my eyes land on Jack, standing towards the back in his white and green practice uniform. His dark buzz-cut makes his jaw look more square, his cheekbones chiseled. The jersey he's wearing is cropped above his waist, showing off his cut abs. His grey eyes watch me intently, and I see something there that both irks and pleases me—determination. *Hunger.*

"I will push you to your limits. I will knock you down again and again, until the only thing you recognize is my voice telling you to get the fuck up and get back in the game."

I tear my eyes away from Jack and walk back to the front of the crowd.

"Embrace the challenge. Embrace the pain. And eventually, you'll embrace victory."

I don't stand and wait for them all to finish cheering before I turn around and gesture to my coaching staff.

If the players thought they were going to get a moment to fuck around on my time, they're about to learn differently.

Tuck Sanders takes over and yells out assignments. "Alright! Shut up and listen! We're going to split up into five groups—freshman offensive and defensive lines, you're with Coach Mans, follow him and he'll explain your schedule to you. Second string offense, you're with Coach Lee, defense with Coach Blane. First strings, you're with me and Nicks."

There's a moment where no one is moving, so I pull my whistle and blow it hard. "What the fuck are you standing around for? You're burning training time— let's fucking go!"

I notice Jack marches right up to the first-string group as Sanders gets them started on stretches, not even questioning that he'll be a starting player. First string has the run of the field every morning at the beginning of practice while the other groups are getting in their gym time and agility training. Then after lunch we switch it up, and at the end of the day we'll run scrimmages until I'm satisfied. I expect improvement every single day, and no slacking.

We run the players through the schedule while they stretch, and then I call out to Jack, who is chatting with Lane Masters, the first-string quarterback, while they stretch. Neither of them looks happy about whatever they're discussing.

"Yes, Coach?" He says, jogging over to me.

"That's not the uniform I gave you yesterday," I say, looking down at the exposed skin on his stomach.

"I thought you said you weren't going to pick over my workout gear," he says, trying to throw our conversation from yesterday in my face.

"When you're wearing my jersey, you're representing me. Fix it or take it off. And then you can start running laps, get those legs moving."

With his eyes boring into mine, Jack pulls the shirt over the back of his head and removes it. He throws it at my feet, quirking an eyebrow before he jogs off towards the track.

By the time we have the rest of the first-string players joining him, he's been running for well over half an hour. He's drenched in sweat. We all are—it's only just past nine o'clock in the morning and it's already close to ninety degrees out. To his credit, he doesn't complain or slow his pace. Other than the sheen of glistening sweat over his body, you wouldn't know he was working at all. It doesn't take long before he's not the only shirtless player running, although he's the only one I notice.

After a few miles of running, I have them all take a water break and request the student equipment managers spray down the shirtless players with sunscreen. I watch a little too closely as the young woman helping Jack smiles and runs her hands over his shoulders to rub in the sunscreen. He seems to be enjoying the attention. I think a few sprints would help him warm up, and when the same student manager brings him a cooling towel, I assign her elsewhere. We don't have room for distractions, and I want to watch him struggle before I let some simpering girl coddle him.

We spend the rest of the morning doing strength and conditioning exercises before it's time to go inside to eat. The sports complex has its own cafeteria, and it's the only place these players will be eating their meals for the next eight weeks. Even if they were leaving for more than just sleep at night, nothing else on campus is open yet and they're all under strict orders not to leave. The last thing I need is my players filling up on greasy fast food and stopping by the liquor stores.

Jack jogs by me as if he hadn't spent the last five hours doing strenuous exercises in the blazing sun. I grab his arm and pull him to the side.

"I've gone easy on you so far, son. Don't test me and do not disrespect me in front of my team ever again."

"Yes, sir," he says in a way that heats my blood. His eyes watch my throat bob when I swallow, and his lip quirks. "I'll make sure to keep that for our special alone time." I don't even get a chance to knock him over the head before he's running off to eat.

I don't typically join the team for meals, and today is no different. My lunch times are my hour of silence that I get in the middle of the day, where I get caught up on my emails and eat whatever lunch I brought from home. Instead of opening up my email, however, I find myself opening my access to the security cameras and watching Jack join the throng of players that are loading their plates with sandwiches, potato salad, and chips. I roll my eyes at the offerings. Menu options were something I had to give up control on in exchange for taking a firmer hand with workouts. My staff felt I was being a little too controlling, and providing three meals a day without a full staff was already hard enough. So I let go, mostly. I'll be making some firm suggestions about chips and desserts.

Jack picks up a couple sandwiches, and I mutter to myself as he moves through the rest of the line to make his selections. We have a meeting later to go over more specific guidelines for his training, and I have a full dietary schedule for him to follow as well as a study routine so he can stay on top of his classes. He'll have no time for anything outside of football and studies for the year that he is here, but for what he's receiving in return, he should be grateful. He doesn't seem to have made any friends yet. I sensed some thinly veiled animosity from the other first stringers during their training this morning, and Jack has chosen a seat at the end of a table of freshman players. He doesn't seem to be attempting to converse with them at all, and I don't notice how long I've been watching him eat until he stands to throw his tray away and stalk out of the cafeteria. There's almost a full hour before the next leg of training begins for the day. Where could he be headed?

CHAPTER 5–JACK

I can't decide if I want to tell Coach to fuck all the way off, or push myself even harder to prove myself to him.

The dynamic between us is shifting as the weeks go on, and I no longer feel like it's all about football. It's like there's a game of cat and mouse between us, and I'm enjoying it more than I'd ever admit. Coach Nicks tells me what to wear, what to eat, how long to study and when to sleep—and it pisses me off to no end. I'm finding tiny ways to assert myself around those guidelines, though, and I'm not ashamed to admit I'm getting a sick joy out of it. My favorite way to push back is with my clothes, often choosing to remove my shirt or wear shorter shorts than he's prescribed, just to get a rise out of him. Whether it's out of pure frustration or something more, I can feel his eyes on my bare skin and it gives me a thrill knowing I've thwarted him.

The controlling bastard even prepares my meals for me, expecting me to eat stuff like unseasoned grilled meat and spinach instead of what the other players eat. I signed the contract, begrudgingly because I had no actual choice in the matter, so I eat what he gives me. But I'll grab a handful of grapes and eat them while looking dead into the camera, letting him see. Letting him know that I know he's watching me like some kind of stalker. He punishes me by making me workout harder, do more reps, run more sprints. Joke's on him though, I like the pain of pushing my body to its limits.

If anything, our back-and-forth gives me something to focus on while Nicks runs us through his grueling training sessions. In the Texas heat, these workouts feel ten times harder, but he's relentless. He wasn't lying when he said he'd make boot camp look like a vacation. I've never been more exhausted than I am every night when I walk my aching body back to my dorm room. I've also never slept better, and more nights than not I go straight to bed without even looking at the books Coach gave me to study before classes start. I don't understand why he didn't sign me up for the easiest classes since I'm only here to win him a football championship, but he seems to get off on making me struggle. Maintaining a B average is going to be difficult with the advanced course load he's piled on me. I'm not stupid by any means, and I got high scores on all of my testing, but I've never maintained a great grade point average. I skipped most of my classes, to be honest. I preferred to sleep in, recovering from the most recent game or party.

Once the semester starts, Coach will have to loosen the reins. He won't be able to keep me on a twenty-four-hour lockdown anymore. I'll have more free time to get to know people and enjoy myself, and I've overheard some of the team talking about the crazy frat parties that happen here. I'm not exactly making friends on the team yet. The QB, Lane something, and his buddies barely acknowledge me when they aren't openly ridiculing me for being Bryant Nick's *charity case*. Though, the more points I score us every scrimmage, the less they have to say. I'm hoping that by the time the season starts, they'll at least accept me enough to make some decent choices on the field so we can win a damn championship. For now, they're enjoying finding ways to take me down and pitting the whole team against me. The last time I ended up under a pileup after an unsanctioned hit, I blew my top in Coach's office, because I know he sees what's happening and he continues to let them skate by with their shit, choosing to punish *me* for *their* bullshit plays. Nicks looked positively menacing when he grinned back at me and told me that a little hazing would toughen me up, and I realized then that he's a fucking sadist.

I'm exhausted and miserable, and every day I consider giving up and going back home, but I won't give him the satisfaction. I'm just biding my time until school starts and I can take a breather.

Once this season is over and the championship is won, I'll be on my way to realizing my NFL dreams. This summer will be nothing but a blip in my history when I'm climbing the ranks. When it gets to be too much, I close my eyes and imagine what it'll be like to dig my toes into the turf of the Superdome, to hear the crowd screaming my name, to run a game winning ball past that white line.

Steeling myself, I step out onto the field, looking up

into the rapidly darkening sky. The pressure in the air is oppressive, and it's been hotter than hell all day. I feel a headache building in the back of my head and chug some water to try and stave it off. Like every day these past few weeks, we've been pushing ourselves through the heat and exhaustion. No matter how much water I drink, it's hard to stay ahead of dehydration when you're sweating this much. At least it's looking like a storm might cut our scrimmage time short today, so I might be able to lie down and get some real rest.

The other players run out of the tunnel entrance to the locker rooms, many of them purposefully shoulder checking me on their way to line up. Every night, Coach has first and second-string players scrimmage against each other. The second string is almost as good as the first string, but that might be because they play better together. First string is too busy one-upping each other and trying to knock me back, instead of using my position and speed to their advantage.

The coaches are starting to get pissed off, and keep telling them to run plays and to use me, but Lane keeps coming up with excuses not to. For the past few weeks since training began, Coach Nicks has sat way up in the bleachers, watching stoically until he's had enough. But tonight he's on the field, and it's making everyone a bit jumpy. I grin to myself at how intimidating they all find him. He's like a shark circling and they're all on their periods. *Bunch of pussies.*

"I've sat back and watched, waiting to see some improvement that tells me I can pull back on the intensity of your training before the real heat sets in, but you've continuously disappointed me. You're not playing like a team and I'm not having it on my fucking field." He levels a look at Lane. "You're supposed to be the leader of this outfit. If you don't get your shit together, I'll bench you and put Kiff in instead." Lane opens his mouth to protest being threatened with the second-string quarterback, but Nicks cuts him off with a scathing look. "At least he's playing to his team's advantage and knows how to utilize his assets."

"You're talking about the charity case?" Lane jokes, but it sounds whiney as fuck and no one laughs.

"Why the fuck do you think I brought him here?" Nicks bellows. "I don't give a fuck if you don't like it. We play as a team so we can *win* as a team. This is your senior year, Masters—your last chance to bring home a title. Do you want it?"

"Well, yeah."

Nicks glares at all of us, a thick vein throbbing angrily on the side of his temple. "Do you want it!?" he yells to the team.

"Yes, sir!" they say back, still unconvincingly. I don't say a word, already hating the target he's hanging on my back. As if there wasn't one already.

"DO YOU FUCKING WANT IT!?" Nicks barks out.

"YES SIR!"

"Then get your heads out of your asses!" A murmur ripples through the team as he gestures for the ball, palming it like it was custom made to fit in his hand. I notice some of the other support staff and any remaining players have filed out onto the field to see what the commotion is about, looking on with interest and excitement when he sets up to throw the ball.

"Perry!" He calls out. "Fetch."

The ball flies through the air in a perfect arc. For a split second, I want to refuse, but the allure of showing these assholes up is too great. I take off like a shot, running faster than they've seen in any of our sprinting exercises. They know I'm fast, but when there's a ball in play, I'm a heat-seeking missile, honed in on my target and more determined than ever. Despite the ball being near halfway over the field before I even started, I manage to catch it cleanly and sail over the end zone. I smirk at the few gasps and a murmured, "no way" from one of the second-string players.

Nicks throws me more increasingly difficult passes, some of them near impossible, but I catch every single one. He even tries to get me to slip up a few times, testing me, but I don't falter. At one point, I even think he's starting to enjoy himself, judging by the sadistic grin on his face.

Before long, lightning cracks across the sky and huge, fat raindrops fall from the ground in a sudden torrent.

Coach dismisses the rest of the team to go home early, but makes me hang back. "Stay," he says, pointing and looking me hard in the eye.

My teammates on the first-string bark as they make their way off the field. Nicks continues to throw me the ball, until the wind and rain are impossible to see through, and I'm slowing down, my growing headache getting increasingly harder to ignore. Finally, he gestures for us to go inside, and I swear I hear a mumbled, "good boy" as I pass by him on my way towards the lockers.

I spin around to tell him off, but I'm too exhausted to deal with it. I wince at the pain in my head when I clench my jaw, and decide to head off to the showers.

CHAPTER 6–BRYANT

"Damn, his hands are like magic," I hear one of the rookie players mutter as the team jogs off the field and out of the rain.

I chuckle to myself. *He's not that good.*

Okay, the kid is better than I give him credit for.

No matter what I throw, he catches it. I keep him out in the raging storm, testing him, trying to trip him up, but he's infallible. It's like the ball is attracted to his hands. The rain is too heavy for me to see through before he fumbles even once, and honestly, it's my throw that causes it to be off enough for him to miss. He doesn't balk or protest, continuing to run down the field again and again until I call it.

I'm... *proud* of him. Excited for the prospects his talents will bring to the team, once the rest of them get their heads out of their asses, that is. I've been lax with them, letting the assistant coaches manage their training while I've focused my attention on our new recruit, but it's time I focused some of my attention back on the team as a whole.

Whether they like what side of the tracks he comes from or not, Jack is the new star wide receiver for the Groveton Jackals, and he's going to pave our way to a national championship. It's time they got comfortable with it.

I hear the taunts they throw at him, and I've noticed during the end of day scrimmages that they are gunning for him. Up until now, I considered it yet another part of the process. He's followed through with most of my strict instructions, but his will is still too strong for my liking. As well as he's doing, I still have the intense urge to break him. He's got more mental fortitude than I gave him credit for, but that just makes me want it more.

The way he bristles at my praise sends a delicious shiver up my spine, and I wait, holding my breath, for him to lash out. I want him to rage at me so I can knock him down a peg, put him in his place. I've found myself waiting in anticipation for his little acts of defiance. They make me feel alive, and I get the most intense pleasure from punishing him, pushing him to the limits. Truth be told, maybe too much pleasure. I find my dick growing hard every time he grunts with the effort of another deadlift, every time a bead of sweat rolls over his temple when I'm spotting him at the bench. I've had to start wearing a jockstrap to conceal my unusual reactions to his pain, to the effort he puts in to prove his worth, to meet my standards, to *please* me.

Surprisingly, he lets it go. For a moment he looks like he'll bite, but then he just drops his shoulders and turns around towards the locker room. It's unlike him to roll over so easily, but I did notice him rubbing his temples earlier, and the storm pressure is pretty intense. It's definitely not helping the ache in my rotator cuff, nor did over two dozen long passes in a row while I tested just how magical Jack's hands were.

In my office, I dry off my hair and face with a towel and shirk off my sopping wet clothes to pull on a pair of track shorts and a t-shirt from my gym bag. After shaking a few ibuprofen into my hand, I consider that Jack could probably use some pain relief as well. I'll throw him a bone; I'm not *that much* of a sadist.

The locker room is empty when I open the door, but I can hear the shower running. I walk over to where I can see Jack's gym bag, intending on leaving the bottle of ibuprofen on the bench next to his things and leaving.. But a deep sigh pulls me towards the door to the showers, and I find myself frozen.

Jack is at the back of the room, the curtain to the shower stall wide open, exposing himself to what I'm sure he thought was an empty room. He knew I was still in the building, and I often come into the locker room to discuss things with the players or tell them to hurry their asses up. *Did he want me to walk in on him like this? Want me to see him in all his glory?*

Glory is the right word for it. He's turned toward the wall, his hands bracing on the wall while the water beats down on his head and back. I watch, transfixed, as the water flows over his suntanned skin, flowing over the globes of his firm ass and down his muscular legs.

I take a step back.

This is fucked up. I'm not attracted to him. Not like that. He's my student, and half my age. *This is fucked up.*

Punishing him, making him work hard for my approval, does do something to me, though. I can't deny it.

As much as I enjoy denying myself, I also really enjoy dangling things I won't let myself have right in front of my face. Like a bottle of good Scotch, or my favorite dessert, Jack Perry has somehow become something I crave.

From the shadows, I watch Jack turn around, his eyes closed against the spray of water. He reaches for the body wash, lathering up a body sponge and rubbing circles on his smooth, muscular chest. I watch the rivulets of soapy water rushing over his body and between his cut abs, my eyes tracing the body sponge as he scrubs it over his entire body. The spicy, musky scent of his body wash permeates the steam building in the room, lulling me into a trance, hypnotized by the way he washes himself. Time feels stalled, his movements slow and fluid. I jerk in surprise when water splats against the ground, Jack wringing soapy water from the loofah. He hangs it back on the hook with his shower bag, then runs his hands over his body, sluicing off the bubbly remnants of his body wash.

When one of his hands reaches down to grip his cock, I suck in a breath. So far, I'd been able to train my eyes away from the appendage, denying my curiosity about his body. But I can't tear my eyes away now that they've followed the path of his hands down to his thick, hard cock. My mouth fills up with saliva, and I forget how to swallow. I forget how to breathe. I forget how to do anything but watch, frozen, as Jack starts to stroke himself.

The way he handles himself is slow and purposeful. He strokes languidly from base to tip, squeezing at the end. My own cock, standing at attention in my gym shorts, twitches when my eyes lock on the drop of pre-cum Jack forces from the tip before fisting over the end and slowly spreading it down the shaft. His strokes pick up, and the wet sounds of his hand working his dick echo over the spray of water and the thudding of my heart.

At some point, my own hand finds its way around my cock, stroking up and down my hard length in time with Jack's strokes, but I stop when I get close to release. Instead of climaxing with Jack, I squeeze firmly around the base of my cock and watch, enraptured, at the expression on his face as streams of white erupt from the end of his cock, shooting across the shower room. I squeeze harder to stave off my climax, my balls clenching painfully. My eyes are locked on the way his cock jerks with each spurt of cum, ending with a slow drip that Jack squeezes from the tip. My tongue darts out to wet my lips, salty with the sweat that pours down my face in the humid room.

A low chuckle makes my heart seize in my chest. My gaze darts up, making direct eye contact with an unsurprised Jack Perry. His cocky grin lets me know he knows exactly how long I've been here, and that, no matter how far back into the shadows I am, he knows exactly what I'm doing.

My student just caught me watching them shower with my hand in my pants.

CHAPTER 7–JACK

Coach hasn't talked to me much since I caught him watching me in the shower. No matter how many times I've stayed late, purposefully and obviously leaving the door open, he hasn't been back. I'm not even sure why I'm doing it. Is it to taunt him or invite him in?

I...*liked* knowing he was watching me. It excited me in a way I've never felt before. It was even better than publicly shooting my load all over Millie's face to spite her asshole father. It was heady, and the moment he backed away, wide eyed and terrified of what he'd been caught doing, I'd had to lean back against the tile and catch my breath before I got dizzy.

I wanted to watch him come with me, but he hadn't. I'd waited, trying to extend every moment of my orgasm, but then I realized he was holding himself back. Then, for no other reason than I'm a sick asshole, I made sure he knew that I'd seen what he was doing. Now that I've realized I want him to come back and do it again, I regret my impulsivity.

We're a month into summer training, marking the halfway point. As hard as training has been, as pissed off as I've been about Nicks trying to control every aspect of my life, I'm actually starting to enjoy it. It's almost freeing, not having to make these decisions for myself. For the past week since the shower incident, I've been sticking to the routine he prescribed. Not that he seems to have noticed, he's turned his targeted focus from me to the rest of the first-string offensive line.

He's determined to make us work as a team, and it seems to be getting through to the rest of the guys that we're all actually pretty damn good for each other. We're starting to pull off seamless, perfect plays, and I'm feeling more confident than ever that this championship is definitely going to happen. Lane Masters and his ass kissers are coming around to not openly hating me, and even invited me to a team party for July 4th. There's supposed to be a barbeque, a pool, and plenty of beer flowing. I was even told some members of the dance and cheer squads would be there, which means I might get the chance to work out some of this tension on a warm body instead of my hand, which has recently become less satisfying now that I've experienced what having an audience feels like.

The night of the party arrives, and I'm feeling exceptionally well rested. Today has been our first day off since summer training started, and I slept far past when I'm "supposed" to wake up for training, choosing not to go in today at all.

After staying late last night, running sprints and

hitting the weights without Coach's instruction or notice, I'd once again showered alone, and it pissed me off more than it probably should. I mean, *how fucking dare* he perve on me and then back down like a fucking pussy? If he's going to watch, if he's going to get off on torturing me, then be fucking honest about it. Don't pretend you don't want my cock.

Fed up, I'd stormed out of the locker room, still soaking wet with only a pair of gym shorts thrown hastily over my raging erection, and taken out my frustration on a punching bag. For a moment, I'd thought I felt that prickle of awareness I get when he's watching me, but I turned around and found nothing. I'd even rushed through the room, making sure he wasn't hiding in the shadows anywhere. And then I got a good look at myself in one of the floor-to-ceiling mirrors.

When did *I* become such a fucking pussy? I'm not even gay, but for whatever reason, I want that man salivating over my balls. And I've been doing everything he asked, like a fucking puppy, hoping to be rewarded for being a *good boy*.

I stormed home last night with a new resolve. I'm fucking done playing his game. I'll give him a winning season, because it benefits me, but fuck his schedule and fuck his rules.

I slept like a baby with my new resolve, thinking about how hard I was going to get my dick sucked by someone at the party. I don't even care who. It's never been hard for me to find a willing mouth or pussy, and I don't expect that to change now. No matter how much of a charity case I may be, I'm about to be one of this team's star players and a shoo-in for the NFL draft. They *all* want my dick, and tonight I'm going to give it to them.

An actual cheer goes up when I walk through the backyard gate of the huge frat house, which is surprising. Most of the first-string players live here, members of one of the oldest and most elite fraternities on campus. I grin at the reception, secretly glad that they've put their bullshit away. Most of them still think of me as a charity case, but they've come around to treating me like a human being now that we're working together as a team.

I hold up the two bottles of Jack Daniels that I picked up before coming here. "Where do I put this?" I'd had to take a bus into town and used my very meager savings to buy it, but I didn't want to come empty-handed.

"Magic Jack brought Jack! Nice!" Exclaims Masters, pointing to the back door. "Toss it on the counter inside for now and come jump in the pool once you make yourself a drink. It's too fucking hot for anything else."

I laugh and agree, once again thankful that we have this short reprieve from practice due to the holiday. Well, I was supposed to go in today even though the team wasn't, but I didn't show up. Coach texted once, but I turned my phone off. I'm not dealing with his bullshit anymore, hence me leaving campus and attending a party as a special fuck you to his rules. I hope his stalker ass watched me walk off campus.

He'll figure out real quick I'm not going to be his obedient little puppy. I've proven I can do the work, and this team is better than ever now that I'm here, so I'm still upholding my end of the bargain. The rest of it is just his perverted bullshit, but he's not man enough to admit to it.

It only takes me two drinks to catch a buzz, and by the time the party is in full swing, I'm feeling damn good. The girls all arrived in the skimpiest bikinis known to man, and by the time the fireworks are lighting up the sky, most of them are topless. There are more than a few couples making out under the lights, and I've got two hot mouths servicing my dick as I watch the colorful explosions overhead.

As they work me over, I find myself thinking of Bryant Nicks; the image of his stern gaze on me as the blonde pulls my balls into her mouth, swirling her tongue around them. His heated eyes boring into my hard cock as the other girl, brunette with bleached highlights, licks the shaft like an ice cream before closing her mouth around the head. She hollows out her cheeks and bobs on my dick, but despite the two mouths on me, it isn't enough to make me cum. I grip the second girl's hair in a tight fist and force her head down until her lips are almost kissing the blonde's. She gags, and when I pull her off again, a long stream of drool falls on the other girl's face. They give each other a look, and the blonde releases my balls to lick up my shaft, meeting the other girl's lips just above my cock. They make out, taking turns to slurp and lick the head of my cock. The interaction between them is fake as hell, almost as fake as the blonde's big tits, but that doesn't make me want to fuck them any less. I need something more than this to get off, though.

"How about we take this inside, and I can paint those tits?" I say huskily. They grin at each other and nod, and the three of us slip inside. There are no free bedrooms, but most everyone is busy elsewhere, so I direct them to the living room couch. "Take off your clothes," I tell them. They both comply quickly, pulling the strings of each other's bikinis and slowly stripping each other. I'm not here for a show, though. "You," I point at the brunette.

"Aniyah."

"Whatever. Push her tits together," I say, moving my finger to point at the blonde.

"Tammy, but you don't have to remember that. As long as I get to feel that fat cock," the blonde purrs. I manage to avoid rolling my eyes. I couldn't give a fuck less what her name is. I just need to get off.

I arrange the girls so the blonde is sitting in front of me with the brunette behind her, pushing her tits together while they make out. The blonde's legs are spread, her fingers working her clit while I slide my dick between her firm tits, slick with suntan oil. I rub myself through them, gritting for the brunette to squeeze them tighter, all but stabbing the blonde in the throat with my hard cock as I thrust into her. Finally, I can feel my orgasm building.

In my drunken haze, I have a last-minute idea and I pull my phone out of my pocket, starting it up to press record just in time to paint the blonde's big fake tits with my cum. I spray it all along her neck, covering her tits, down her stomach, and all over her exposed pussy. She looks right into the camera and moans loudly as the brunette rubs my release into her boobs, massaging it into her skin. I'm still pumping my dick. The little red dot reminds me of just what I plan on doing with this video, keeping me hard and ready.

"Lick her pussy clean," I tell Amy, or Annie, or whatever the brunette's name is.

She kneels in front of her friend and does what she's told. She seems a little unsure of herself at first, but gets comfortable, making the blonde lay back and widen her legs, holding her head just where she wants her to lick. I know it's all for the camera, but I also know how to get a real reaction from them. Scooping up some of my cum from the blonde's tits, I kneel down behind the brunette and set my phone against the nearby chair to keep it pointed at the action.

I angle the brunette's ass where I want it, and show off my messy fingers to the camera. I'm sure she expects me to fuck her, but I'm not interested. Instead, I move my fingers down her ass crack, and she flinches as I rub my cum covered fingers over her puckered hole. She moves, ready to protest, but I move my other hand around her front to rub her clit and she moans, grinding into me. She cries out when my finger breaches her asshole, but I don't relent, increasing the pressure on her clit. I pump harder with my finger, adding a second one, while my fingers rapidly bring her closer to an orgasm.

The big-titted blonde brings her hand down and plays with her clit as her friend whimpers and cries against her pussy. The fireworks display is ending, judging by the sounds of the finale ramping up, multiple explosions echoing loudly against the outside of the house, illuminating the depravity happening inside.

"Now," I command, looking directly into the camera,

and both girls tremble with their release. The blonde shrieks, coating her friend's face as she cums. The brunette screams just as the fireworks end, her orgasm loud against the silence following the deafening booms. Hot liquid squirts across my hand. I look into the camera and purposefully flick the wetness towards the lens.

Pulling back from the girls, I give the brunette a smack on her ass before I pick up my phone and walk away. I clean myself up and pull on my clothes while I wait for my message to load. The little ping that tells me my video was sent makes my dick hard all over again. That gives me an idea for the next message I want to send, but there's too much commotion in the house for that right now. I slip out the front door unseen, grinning as I see the *sent* notification turn to *received.* I've got more pep in my step than I have in over a week as I walk towards my dorm, knowing that he's watching my handiwork.

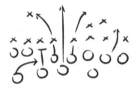

CHAPTER 8–BRYANT

"What the fuck was that shit?" I ask Jack when he meanders into training, late.

He's supposed to be here at 6AM, two hours before the rest of the team arrives at 8AM. Yet he's casually walking in here at 7:45, without a care in the world. The others will be here soon. Most of the staff is here already, and I can't lay into him the way I want to in front of everyone.

I knew he was at that party. When he didn't show up to practice yesterday and my calls went straight to voicemail, it didn't take me long to figure out he wasn't coming. I thought I was pretty clear when I said that he wasn't getting the day off with the rest of the team, but not only did he ignore that, he directly disobeyed me. I watched him leave campus, returning with a bag from the liquor store. My car was down the street when he walked into the party.

Maybe I should be glad that the team is finally treating

him like one of their own, but I'm not. I realize that not allowing him to socialize with them hinders his ability to grow close to the rest of the team. But Jack is willfully disobeying me and that makes my blood boil.

Late last night, when my phone pinged, I'd been sitting in the dark, staring at an unopened bottle of Macallan. I saw that it was from Jack and immediately my insides clenched like I knew something was wrong.

At first I hadn't been quite sure what I was seeing, but then I looked closely and realized it was a cock thrusting between two breasts, which became even more clear when said cock erupted all over the girl. There were two girls in the video, both of whom I recognized as being on the cheer squad. The brunette, Aniyah, looked upset, but did what she was told, while the blonde girl covered in cum performed for the camera like a bad porn star. I looked away from the girls, both uninterested and terrified at the trouble I could get into for just possessing this.

I barely registered most of the video until the end, when Jack was looking directly at the camera. It felt like he was looking directly into my eyes, and the moment he commanded those girls to come, my cock jerked and splooshed into my pants.

I knew then that he'd sent this to me purposefully, to get some sort of reaction from me. What exactly was he expecting?

Jack flashes me a crooked grin. "Seems like you might like watchin'. Thought I'd do you a favor."

"Were you fucking drunk? You can't send that shit to

me. Or anyone else. If you got caught, getting kicked off this team is the least worst of your worries," I hiss at him.

He shrugs. "I had a few."

"I don't know who the fuck you think you are–"

"I'm *Jack fucking Perry.* And I'm tired of being bossed around by a pussy like you."

"You are nobody, and you're not going anywhere or doing anything if you don't get with the fucking program," I growl.

Jack squares up to me. He's only a few inches shorter than my six-foot-four frame, but I'm quite a bit wider than his lean body. I feel the warmth of his chest pressing against mine, both of us breathing heavily.

"You're like a baby bulldog, Jack. All that pent up aggression and anger, with no real outlet. I'm trying to turn all of that into something useful. As long as you're out there being an idiot hothead, you're going to fail."

"And you're a fucking pussy, hiding in the shadows while I show you again and again that I can do anything —handle *anything*—you throw at me. So if you're not fucking man enough to do anything about it, why should I bother?"

Seething, I grab his hand and place it on my cock, half hard and growing by the moment. "Is this what you're trying to get to, baby bulldog? You couldn't fucking handle this. You can't handle me."

"Bullshit. You're just too much of a pussy to show me what you're made of. And I'm not fucking gay, you fucking pervert."

I know he's goading me, and I know I need to back away, but a mixture of rage and arousal is lighting up my veins, and if I don't do something, I'll combust.

With a growl, I wrap a hand around Jack's throat and back him into the wall. I loom over him, meeting the challenge in his darkening eyes with one of my own. Swiftly, I open the supply room door next to us and push him inside, slamming the door behind me. The fluorescent lights come on automatically, casting an eerie, almost clinical glow over the polished cement flooring and walls of shelves with equipment, cleaning supplies, and stacks of extra towels and practice jerseys.

"Your hair is too long," I grunt, fisting the ends that haven't been trimmed since he arrived. I haul his body back against mine and feel his erection hit my thigh. Reaching forward, I run my hand along the length of it, squeezing hard. "Is this what you want, baby bulldog?"

Instead of answering, his tongue lashes out and licks my bottom lip. I grit my teeth and force him to his knees.

I know what he wants, what he *needs.*

"You need to learn your place, Jack," I grouse, pulling out my painfully hard cock. I smack him once across the face before pumping myself. In two quick strokes, I grunt my release, spurts of cum splashing over his face. He blinks and sputters, struggling in my hold, but I tighten my hold on him until I'm finished.

I release his hair with a push, making him stumble back, catching himself on his hands and knees. His eyes are wide and incredulous, mouth open in shock, face dripping with my cum. There's a moment of silence where we both consider what just happened here, and my heart beats even more frantically. Jack's tongue darts out, tasting the cum I painted his mouth with, and I decide I need to leave before I do something worse.

I throw a towel at him. "Clean yourself up and get to practice. Expect to stay late to make up for this morning." Opening the door, I listen for anyone in the hallway, but I think they've all made it to the locker room. The coast is clear.

"And Jack?" I say, turning back to him.

He doesn't respond, but looks up at me with narrowed eyes. "You're supposed to say 'Yes, Coach?'," I prompt him, trying to keep my cool demeanor.

"Yes, Coach?" he repeats, and the way he grits out the words makes my cock twitch. I'll need the strap today for sure.

"Be a good boy and we'll see what kind of reward you can earn."

I'm more than a little worried when I walk out onto the field and Jack isn't there yet. Did I go too far? He could go to one of the staff, the dean, the police... Am I about to lose everything because I lost it?

It takes a lot for me to lose my control. I've had a harsh grip on myself for five damn years, only to lose it now? I'm supposed to be helping this kid, but who is going to be here to straighten his ass up if I'm fucking homeless because I lose my job? And who is going to keep me from drowning in the bottom of the bottle again?

Jack finally makes it out onto the field, shouting a quick, "Sorry, Coach!" as he joins his teammates. They're all slapping him on the back, no doubt congratulating him on his escapades yesterday and last night.

"Don't let it happen again," I respond, trying to act normal. Jack turns and looks at me, his eyes seeming to search mine for any signs that I mean what I say.

Will it happen again? It *shouldn't* happen again, that's for damn sure.

Most of the players are sluggish today, probably hungover from their long day of booze, sun, and sex. I'm too tired and busy overthinking the predicament I've gotten myself into to have it in me to be too hard on them today, and as another storm starts rolling in just after lunch, they get even more of a reprieve.

"Two hours in the gym and then get home and rest. I expect every single one of you in top form tomorrow," I order, and they run off the field.

Jack hangs back, watching curiously as I walk past him and towards my office.

"Four hours for you," I say before I close the door behind me.

CHAPTER 9–JACK

I push myself through my hangover all day, and by the time the other players are leaving, I'm feeling weaker than the puppy Coach accused me of being earlier today.

"Yo, Perry!" Masters calls out. "You getting out of here? Some of us were going to head out to the burger joint downtown. A good greasy meal to help kick this hangover."

"Thanks, man, I'm good. I have to make up for this morning or Coach is going to kill me."

"I don't understand why he rides you so hard," he says with a scowl. My crotch gives an odd lurch at the visual those words bring.

Fuck. *Do I want Coach to fuck me?*

I've never even *considered* being with a man before. But the idea of Bryant Nicks fucking me puts new thoughts in my head.

Would it hurt? Would I mind if it did?

I shake my head of the thoughts and grin up at Lane. "I'm a charity case, remember?"

He furrows his brow. "You work twice as hard as anyone on this team. You've proven you belong here."

How heartwarming. I scoff. "And I need to keep proving it. There's also the chance that I might have recorded certain things that occurred last night and maybe... sent them to Coach Nicks."

"Why the fuck would you do that!?" The quarterback all but screeches, his eyes wide like he's surprised I'm still alive.

"I was pretty fucking drunk and feeling a bit full of myself," I say honestly. "If I don't want to lose my place here, I'm going to have to do a lot of work to make up for that little oversight. He nearly kicked me off the team this morning. That's why I was late."

The thought of what really happened has my cock growing. *What the fuck is wrong with me?*

"He won't kick you off. He knows we need you to win."

"Maybe, but better safe than sorry. Besides, sweating the liquor out works best for me," I say, assuring him.

"Yeah, you're like a health food junkie, right?" He says, alluding to the strict diet that Coach Nicks prescribed me. If only he knew that everything I've done so far has been because of our coach. Hell, even me stepping out of line yesterday was inadvertently because of him. I wanted so badly to get under his skin, to piss him off and see what happens when he cracks. *I suppose I succeeded.*

My cock twitches and I look down at it, confused by my reaction to Nicks' treatment and what I think I want out of this. I never in a million years expected distant, controlled Bryant Nicks to cock slap me and cum on my face before walking away like I was nothing.

It was humiliating. Demeaning. Degrading. *And I've never been harder in my life.*

Masters and the rest of the team clear out, and for the next hour and a half, I push myself through each exercise with an added layer of anticipation. What will happen now that the dynamic has changed between us? When he doesn't show up, I think that maybe he's waiting for me in the showers. I move to the treadmill, pushing myself to run twice as fast, as if it could wind the clock down faster.

But he isn't in the shower, and when I finally get dressed to leave for the day, he isn't even in his office. He left without saying a word to me.

Is that supposed to be a reward or punishment? *And why the fuck do I care so much?*

The next day, I show up early for my warm-ups. Coach Nicks works out in the room with me, silently pushing me to do more, lift heavier, run faster, just to keep up with him. For an older guy, he's in damn good shape. His big muscles are dusted with hair, like a big, burly bear. That makes me laugh, because aren't bears a gay thing? I need to remember to look it up to be sure, in case I decide to use it to taunt him.

Nicks looks over at me with an eyebrow raised. So far, the only thing to break our silence has been the whir of the machines or clink of the weights setting down. His expression makes me want to laugh more, but I press my lips together instead. He might not appreciate my bear thoughts.

Hell, I'm not even sure I do. Because if he's a bear, what does that make me? A cub? That's not much better than a baby bulldog, and I don't want to encourage that shit. Nor am I really ready to think about myself in terms of whether I'm gay or not. I don't think I am, but also... My thoughts towards the stoic beast of a man are confusing at best.

He looks like he's about to say something, but the first few second-string players walk in. Neither of us realized the time. I walk past him, intentionally brushing his shoulder on my way out, just to see what sort of reaction I get. He gives me nothing.

The rest of the day, Coach puts me through my paces. He yells at me to run harder, faster, jump higher. With every instruction he gives me, I yell out, "Yes, Coach!", just waiting for a reaction from him. He seems pleased during our end of practice scrimmage and dismisses us, but I know he doesn't mean me. I stay for two more hours, once again with anticipation, only to find he's left again.

For three more days, I do everything he says and wait for him to so much as even acknowledge my presence outside of practice. But I keep getting fucking *nothing*.

I don't know what I want from him, what kind of

treatment or attention would satisfy me, but this isn't it. I want to see the man that cracked in the hallway, that held me down and came on my face.

I want to see him lose control.

It's time to start pushing back again.

CHAPTER 10–BRYANT

I've had to step back. Being around the kid is too much. I was way over the line the other day, and it could have cost us both everything. There's no way I could keep my job or ever get another, if Jack had told or we'd been caught. And there's no way the dean would keep Jack on the team if I was gone. Not least of all because it would imply things about his sexuality that aren't considered acceptable in Texas football society. But also because the dean has a severe disdain for people he considers low class, and would look for any excuse for Jack to leave if he embarrassed him at all.

Jack shows up early and leaves late every day. I know because I check the cameras nightly, watching him arrive each morning and then as he walks to my office before he leaves the building at night. I'm confused by the way he watches me, the way he comes to my office every night after his extended workout, the way he leaves the door to the locker room open so the steam from the showers filters out into the hallways. It's almost as though he's seeking me out, looking for my attention.

I'm curious, but not enough to ask him about it or do anything. I barely pay him any attention at all outside of what I absolutely have to say to him at practice. Every time he says "Yes, Coach," my cock gets hard. The jock strap can only do so much, and I go home with a raging boner every night. I don't allow myself to do anything about it, but I've woken up more than one morning with a sticky mess on my stomach.

The dreams that plague me are both erotic and terrifying. One moment, I'm licking the sweat from his naked spine as he bends over the leg press machine, or looking down into his grey eyes as I force my cock into his mouth, and the next I'm standing before a judge, who looks exactly like Jack, holding an open bottle of whiskey.

He's become an obsession that I can't seem to shake. It's worse than the struggle I've had with alcoholism since my NFL dreams went up in flames, the constant reminder that I'll never be the man I once thought I'd be. Maybe that's why he calls to me, because I know I can help him achieve those same dreams and he could actually live them for longer than a blink of an eye.

I've been watching him closely, and he's doing well. There's no reason to change or push anything while he's succeeding the way he is. I've got him exactly where he needs to be, and if he keeps pushing himself the way he is, he'll be a new NFL recruit by this time next year. I gave him a warning, and as much as a big part of me wanted him to continue pushing back, it worked well enough for him to get his head back in the game.

Or so I thought.

I look down at my watch. Practice started nearly five minutes ago. Jack didn't show up for his early morning workout, nor did he respond to my texts when I asked him where the fuck he was.

I sense movement in the tunnel that leads to the locker room. Jack is there, leaning against the wall, looking at his watch. I look down at mine, curious about what he's looking for, considering he's already late for practice.

At exactly five minutes and one second past the time the rest of the team started their practice, he starts walking out onto the field.

"My bad!" he calls over to me, lifting his hand in a wave, before heading onto the field to get stretched out. My jaw ticks.

The rest of the morning, Jack puts less effort into his training. He runs slower, talks more. I even catch him flirting with the water girl again. *Who the fuck let her back on this field?*

When the team jogs off the field for their lunch break, I try to pull him aside, but he bypasses me. The chicken and brown rice I left in his locker is sitting on my desk when I get back to my office. Through the cameras, I watch as Jack fills his plate full of pasta.

"Fine, be a brat. That's going to hurt later when I make you run wind sprints," I whisper to the camera. Just before I switch it off, Jack looks directly up at the camera, like he knows I'm watching him.

For two days, Jack purposefully shows up exactly five minutes and one second late, doesn't eat the meals I continue to prepare for him, and fucks around on the field. The last straw happens when I can't find Jack before we start our scrimmage. Jogging off the field, I'm expecting to find Jack bent over a toilet because he's been putting trash into his body that it isn't used to anymore, but he isn't in the bathroom. Instead, the door to the supply closet is ajar and I find him in there getting his fucking dick sucked by the water girl.

"Oh, hey, Coach. I'll be right out," he says, holding down the poor girl's head when she panics, realizing they've been caught. She gags in his harsh grip.

"Let her go," I say, rage seething beneath my calm surface.

Jack throws both of his hands up, and she falls back, coughing. Jack's cock bobs, glistening with spit. I fight to tear my eyes away from it.

Turning towards me, her eyes watering, the girl chokes out a cry and stands to leave. I hold my arm out to stop her before she can pass through the door and give her a stern look.

"Don't come back," I warn her. "I'll sign off on a transfer to the girls' softball team, but if I catch you here again, you'll be expelled." Nodding through her snot and tears, the girl runs off.

I turn my gaze to Jack. "What the fuck is your problem?"

"You are," he says lazily before he brushes past me and

walks out of the closet.

I'm trying to relax in the sauna, immersed in the thick steam, heavily scented with eucalyptus that I brought from home. Everyone has long since left the building, so I'm surprised when the door clicks open. I can't see who walks in at first, but I can sense him.

Jack walks into the room, wearing nothing but a pair of low-slung workout shorts. He looks like he's been working out, or running, even though he wasn't working out in the building or on the field.

"What are you doing here, Jack?" I demand, exasperatedly, trying not to show him how glad I am to see him. My cells react to his presence.

"Why aren't you punishing me?" He asks bluntly.

"What?"

"I'm assuming your so-called reward was leaving me to my own devices, but I got bored."

"Ah, I see," I say, feigning calm. "Baby bulldog needs a firm hand with his training?"

Jack squeezes his fists, and my lips quirk. He doesn't like

that at all, yet he's still here, waiting for me to punish him. *But punish him how?*

"And exactly how is it that you want to be punished?" I ask, eyebrow raised.

His eyes shift down to my lap, where my cock is stirring beneath the towel around my waist. Feigning more confidence than I actually have, because honestly, I'm freaking out and way too excited about the prospect that Jack might actually want my cock. I throw back my head and bark out a laugh. "It's not much of a punishment if you want it, is it?"

Jack continues to say nothing, his jaw clenched and flexing as he grits his teeth. I continue talking, both a play for more time and to understand Jack better. *Does he want me to fuck him?* I thought I'd been so over the line, expecting him to either quit or report me, but he... *liked it?* My cock twitches almost violently at the mere thought.

The steam from the sauna is oppressive, the effort to breathe through my arousal even more difficult. I can feel the warm wooden bench bite into the back of my thighs as I hold myself as still as possible. In this little room, surrounded by the thick cloud of steam and low lighting, I can almost make myself believe this might be a dream or fantasy.

Jack's dark hair is wet with sweat and the mist from the sauna, and his light grey eyes bore into mine. Imploring me, tempting me, *daring* me. He sits down opposite me, close enough that I could reach out and touch him. His legs are wide, elbows resting on his knees, so he can continue to stare at me. The silence and his lack of movement might suggest patience, but the look in his eyes is anything but.

I hold his eye contact for a while before slowly unwrapping the towel around my waist, letting it fall open. My cock juts straight up, throbbing in time with my violent heartbeat. Jack's gaze leaves mine, settling on my hard length, his eyes tracing over every inch.

My voice comes out raspy and gruff. "Get on your knees."

His eyes flash back up to mine before darting around the room, clearly trying to decide if this is what he really wants. But he fucking asked for it, and he's going to get it.

"I said on your knees, Jack. Don't make me wait."

He shifts forward, like he might comply, but the effort is too slow. One or both of us could lose our nerve at any point, but I'm too far into this to back down now. I won't be made a fool of.

He wants to be taught a lesson? I'm going to do just that. The next time he wants to disrespect me, he can remember what a bruised throat feels like.

I launch off the bench and crowd his space, my fingers raking over the back of Jack's head and gripping the hair tight, pulling so he's looking up at me.

"From now on, when you disobey a direct order, I'll make you regret it."

"And if I'm a good boy?" His question is sarcastic, but the way my cock twitches, popping him under the chin, gives me away. We both know how much I like hearing him challenge me with those words. The little shit smirks.

"Then I suppose we'll have to figure out a reward that you find acceptable, but it would be very, very hard to earn."

Jack's voice is husky, straining with the effort of pulling back against my hold. "How hard?"

A fucking rock-solid steel pipe, that's how hard.

"Don't test me, Jack." I'm barely holding myself back, still giving us both an out.

"Or what?" he challenges, eyes darkening.

My chest rumbles, my composure close to snapping. I'm already far past my threshold. I intended my threat to be a warning, assuming he'd back away from the idea of taking my cock.

My grip on his hair tightens, my other hand coming up to cup his jaw. I rub my thumb against his bottom lip, stretching it to open. He complies, and I shove three fingers in his mouth, rubbing against his tongue and hooking his bottom teeth. I pull his face towards me before grabbing my cock, spreading his saliva down my shaft before lining it up. My eyes stay locked on his as I slide my cock past his lips. I start slowly, tentatively, giving him his last opportunity to protest, but he continues to challenge me with his eyes. Once I'm about halfway in, I slowly pull out, but then pitch forward, giving him another few inches. Thrust by thrust, I give him a little more each time, keeping a close hold on my control.

When my cock hits the back of his throat, he gags. The sound revs me up even more. I expect him to start pulling back, but he doesn't, and for some sadistic reason, this disappoints me. My thrusting increases, abusing his throat until he's struggling, tears streaming down his cheeks as I use him for my pleasure. When my balls tighten and my release is close, I pull out just long enough for him to get a breath before driving back inside, holding him all the way down on my cock. His throat contracts around my cock, protesting the intrusion and being cut off from air. Jack's fists hit against my thighs, not trusting that I'll let him breathe.

Good. I want him afraid.

I can't hold back a grunt as my climax washes over me. My cock pulses, shooting streams of hot cum directly in the back of Jack's throat, and he has no choice but to swallow everything I have to give him. Only when the last drop is spent do I pull out to let Jack breathe. He sputters and coughs, leaning over like he might be sick.

"Don't you dare throw up," I warn him. "Or I'll have to fill you up all over again."

His face is deep red, almost purple, and it's hard to say if it's because he was just fighting for oxygen, the heat of the sauna, or embarrassment. Maybe all three.

Jack groans, and I don't know what to make of it. It almost sounds like arousal, but that could be my post-orgasm brain speaking. A quick glance down is all it takes to see that Jack is definitely sporting a large hard on. *Yeah, he liked choking on my cock.*

He fucking liked it.

Before Jack can do more than adjust his erection, I give him a new instruction. "If you want to cum, you'll have to earn it. Don't be late tomorrow," I say, picking up my towel and leaving Jack reeling in the sauna.

And this is how I rationalize what I've done. As part of the process, to encourage him, incentivize him.

To make him better.

CHAPTER 11–JACK

There is something wrong with me.

After I'm sure that Coach has left the locker room, if not the building, I leave the sauna and head to take a shower. I step into the spray, letting the cool water calm my overheated skin. Tilting my face up, I let the water fill up my mouth and gargle, soothing the ache in my throat. No matter how long I stay in the cold water, though, the one thing I can't seem to soothe is my raging boner.

Through all of my taunting, I don't know what I expected. It wasn't this, that's for sure. Coach held me down and fucked my face like I was nothing but an object, a tool to be used to get off with. He wasn't exactly gentle, and for a minute there I definitely panicked that I wouldn't be able to get a breath.

Still, I somehow know it could have been worse. I also know that I liked it. A lot more than I can fully process.

My thoughts are a jumble of confusion, warring between anxiety about what I've done, fear over my unexplainable reaction to it, and a desire to know how far I can push this.

I'm not sure anything has ever given me more pleasure than pushing Coach to the edge and then watching him lose that carefully crafted mask he puts up. I want to see what makes him tick, and I'm curious about the consequences.

Hand wrapped around my cock, I pump slowly, giving in to the arousal coursing through my body after the way I was just used. He said not to cum, but how would he know? My eyes flit around the room, not seeing anywhere that he could be hiding or sensing any disturbances.

He can't fucking keep me from coming whenever and wherever I want. My mouth twitches up into a grin, an idea coming to mind.

Cutting off the shower, I dry myself as quickly as possible, throwing on my shorts, still damp from the sauna. After shoving my feet into my sneakers, I go to Coach's office, and sure enough, he's gone for the day. I know that maintenance keeps a spare key in the supply room, so I run in there and find the cabinet where they hang the keys. Behind the inside of the cabinet door there are about a dozen different keys, all neatly labeled. I grab the one with "HC" written on the ring and use it to open his office door.

I turn the lights on and look around, worrying my bottom lip. Where to leave my little message? I want him to know I was here and that he can't control me the way he thinks he can. However much I might let him dominate and punish me, I'm still in charge of me.

The smell of him—fresh laundry, musk, and the faint edge of muscle rub—affects me more than I want to admit. Taking out my dick, I stroke myself as I look over the coach's office. Just like his overall persona, everything is meticulously clean and organized, and it makes me itch to mess it all up. I eye the way everything on his desk is perfectly lined up, waiting for him to start his workday in the morning. He's going to lose his mind.

I swallow, and I barely get a second to reconsider before the soreness in my throat reminds me of my task, sending a jolt of arousal right to my dick, and before I know it, I'm painting Coach Nicks' keyboard with streams of my cum.

"Fuck yeah," I groan, imagining the look on his face when he sits down at his desk tomorrow.

For good measure, I swipe his meticulously lined up pens onto the floor and steal a clipboard.

I slept like a fucking baby last night, waking up early

this morning with a refreshing sense of glee. Even my sawdust protein shake tasted delicious this morning, and I made it to the sports complex in record time, arriving before Nicks himself.

The expectation of what's to come makes me hyper aware of every movement and every sound in the building. I nearly lurch off the bench press when a maintenance person comes in, which startles the poor man into dropping a load of laundry.

"That's okay, Frank. Jack here will take care of refolding those," a deep voice comes from behind us as I help the older man pick up the towels. "Won't you, Jack?" The man side eyes me before muttering his thanks and skittering out of the room. Bryant Nicks has that effect on people, I suppose. I'd be lying if I said I don't feel it too, but I'm fucked up to the bone, and instead of frightening me, it excites me.

I look up at him with a little trepidation, searching his face for any sign of how pissed off he might be. All he's doing is staring back at me expectantly, and I realize then that he hasn't been to his office yet. He's waiting for me to answer him about the towels.

"Uh, y-yes Coach," I stutter a little, trying to hold back my smug grin.

It's no use. I've been smiling like a crazy person all morning, relishing the soreness in my jaw.

He looks confused, but pleased enough, and moves towards a treadmill. Does he not normally go to his office first? Or maybe today he decided to check on me first? That thought gives me a jolt of happiness.

Not that I care if he thinks of me. Because I don't.

The hour before the other players arrive is too quiet, too tense. Every time I think he's about to leave the room to go to his office, my stomach clenches, but it's not until the team is filing out into the field that he separates from the group. Chatting and laughing with the guys as we get stretched out, I am all but holding my breath, watching the tunnel. I want to see the look on his face, the stiffness in his shoulders, when he returns. I want to know how he's going to punish me, and the thought of it has extra saliva filling my mouth. Every swallow stings and reminds me of my last punishment.

We're already jogging around the field by the time Coach joins us. His countenance is definitely stiffer than usual, his mouth set in a determined grimace, but that's pretty normal for Coach. It's not until I feel his eyes on me that I know he's seen my little gift for him, and it's impossible not to break out in a grin, laughing at my own joke that no one around me is in on. When everyone finally stops looking at me, like I might need special help, I blow Nicks a kiss. The angry, throbbing vein on the side of his head mimics the angry, throbbing vein that runs up the underside of his massive cock.

Fuck. My already half hard cock continues to inflate, making it harder to run. I have to deal with it, though, trying to force away any thoughts that will make it worse. I focus on the workout, pushing myself harder than ever.

All day, I keep pushing, every dark look from Nicks encouraging me to work harder, faster. I beat my forty-yard sprint record and run circles around the opposing team during our scrimmage.

By the time the training day is over, the tension radiating off Coach is palpable. He's been quietly seething all day, and I know I'm in for it. As excited as I've been all day, nearly euphoric with the little trick I played on him, I'm feeling anxious about what he'll do.

Will he fuck my mouth harder? Will he fuck my ass? Do I want that? Am I ready for that?

I'm honestly not sure. The prospect of letting someone put their dick in my ass was never something I'd considered before. The prospect of Bryant Nicks doing it is both terrifying and exciting. My trepidation definitely outweighs my curiosity. I have zero doubts it'll hurt, and only a tiny part of me considers the possibility of pleasure.

Again, there's definitely something wrong with me, because the idea of him hurting me, tearing me open with his huge cock, makes me tremble with anticipation. The half-chub I've been fighting all day is winning, and I walk into the gym for my one-on-one training with a massive boner.

Finally, Nicks joins me, slamming the door shut and locking it behind him, which sends a shiver of fear and excitement down my spine. I sit up on the bench, watching him warily as he stalks menacingly towards me. He doesn't say a word, only gestures for me to lie back and grab the bar. I'm vaguely aware of more weight being added to both sides of the bar before he helps me lift it off the rack. The weight he's added is significant, and I can barely get through three reps before my arms are shaking.

I manage two more before nodding to him that I'm done, but he doesn't reach for the bar. Instead, he pushes it down on my chest, locking me beneath the heavy weights.

Kneeling down near my head, he lowers his mouth to the shell of my ear. When he speaks, his voice is low and gravely. Fear pools in my belly, and my cock weeps.

"I guess I was too gentle with you yesterday. I held back, worried that you got yourself in too deep. I won't make that mistake again."

The bar is bruising my chest, and it distracts me from what else is happening in the room. Before I know it, Coach has pulled down his pants and is pushing his cock in my mouth. He leans over my body, his hands on either side of the bench, and thrusts into my face. I quickly realize just how gentle he was yesterday, how much time he'd given me to get accommodated. This time he is merciless, fucking my face with hard, quick thrusts that push the air and odd sounds out of me as I gag around his thick cock.

I resist at first, trying to push up against the bar and thrashing my head for a reprieve, but eventually I relax and lie there, mouth open wide as he uses me. The angle he's at makes it a little easier to take him without gagging, despite feeling him farther back in my throat. My lips are stretched to capacity, my jaw aching. I take short breaths of air through my nose and will my eyes to stop watering. I don't want him to think I'm crying, but I can't stop the tears trailing down my temples whenever I blink my eyes open. Not that I can open them for long, as his balls are hitting against my forehead as he thrusts into me.

I feel like I'm floating a little when I give myself over to be used, and I like it more than I'll ever confess out loud. I'm so deep in my head that I startle when I feel his hand push beneath the waistband of my shorts. My cock jerks as he takes it in his hand, pumping it forcefully in time with his thrusts. My orgasm builds quickly, and I moan around his cock, my hips thrusting into his hand. I'm just about to come, teetering on the edge, more ready for release than I've ever been in my life.

I'm coming... and then it stops.

Nicks squeezes hard around the head of my cock, painfully and effectively stopping my orgasm as he pumps his down my throat. He keeps his hand tight around the head of my cock as he pulls out of my throat. Once again, I'm sputtering and coughing, but this time I'm trying to yell through my raspy, abused throat.

"What the fuck!?"

"I told you, if you want to cum, you have to earn it. You'll learn to obey or I'll be the only one getting off around here."

With one last hard squeeze, Nicks stands up and re-racks the bench press. He walks past me, my body still laid out on the bench, coughing and rubbing my sternum.

"Next time you disrespect me, I'll fuck your ass so hard you'll bleed. Do you understand me, Perry?"

Everything fucking hurts. But nothing hurts more than my balls, straining from lack of release. I'll play it his way this round, see what kind of reward it gets me, and hopefully avoid escalating this to a point where it really hurts me... even if I am a little curious.

"Yes, Coach," I rasp out.

CHAPTER 12–BRYANT

This is working.

It's beyond fucked up, I know that. I'm a terrible human being that is most definitely going to burn in hell. I'm teetering on the edge of my control, and I'm probably one wrong step from losing my job or worse. *But this is working.*

Jack showed up to practice early, looking a little more tired than usual, but he's playing better than ever. He's running faster, jumping higher, and working well with the whole team. When it's time for lunch, I pass him a container of pureed corn chowder, which he accepts thankfully and sips it gingerly.

"Dude, what's up with you?" I overhear one of his teammates ask him.

"Just a sore throat," he answers. I can tell he's purposefully avoiding my gaze, but when he thinks no one is looking, I see the way one side of his mouth turns up in a grin.

I also see the way he looks up at me every time he makes a good play, or makes a great time on his forty and hundred-yard sprints. Like a puppy, he's desperate for my approval. I keep my features schooled and indifferent, but inside I'm perhaps a little too pleased with myself.

He's so eager for a reward, and I'm just as eager to give it to him.

It's almost the end of the day before it occurs to me that he played just as well yesterday, when he was anticipating his punishment. That thought makes it hard to walk around for the rest of the scrimmage.

"Perry!" I bark out. "My office when you're done with your workout," I instruct him.

"Yes, Coach!" he answers, turning back to his friends on the team a little too casually. But another quick glance over his shoulder shows me how eager he is. His tongue darts out and licks his lips, and my rapidly hardening cock twitches.

At exactly one minute after the end of his scheduled workout, Perry knocks at my door. I call for him to enter, and he automatically closes and locks the door behind him. I quirk an eyebrow, but decide not to tease him about his eagerness. He's still in his workout shorts, no shirt. His body is still slick with sweat from his workout, abs glistening, making me want to run my tongue over them. I fight not to stare, finishing my email to the softball coach.

"Come," I say simply, pushing my chair out from my

desk and angling towards him, but keeping my eyes on my computer screen.

Jack walks around the desk to stand next to me.

"Take your clothes off and get on your knees," I say quietly. I pretend not to watch from my peripherals as he cocks his head curiously before obeying. He steps out of his shoes and shorts before pulling his socks off and tossing them on top of the discarded pile. I'll have to teach him to be neater, but his obedience is enough for now.

"Good boy," I murmur as I exit out of my emails and finally turn my attention to him.

"You did well today," I tell him, my hands splayed out over my thighs. "But you fucked up big yesterday. You directly disobeyed me and came without my permission. I had to request a new keyboard from maintenance and make up an excuse for why I couldn't turn in the one I had. Tell me, Jack, did you come after I left last night?"

He shakes his head. I watch him and wait for an appropriate answer.

"I didn't," he says, defensively. I raise an eyebrow and run my eyes down his naked torso.

"Oh. Um. No, Coach. I didn't come without your permission."

"And how are you feeling?"

"Sore," he says honestly. "My balls ache." His hands squeeze the tops of his muscular thighs, like he's trying not to let himself react. His cock, on the other hand, twitches and bobs, dripping pre-cum onto my carpet.

"Would you like to come?"

"Yes, Coach," he answers, without hesitation.

I rub my thumb over my chin, considering him. I like him like this; down on his knees and waiting. For me.

I reach for my belt, watching how Jack's abs clench with anticipation. I imagine he's wondering if I'm going to bend him over and fuck him. Tear his ass apart like I threatened him with. I imagine he wants me to.

But I'm not going to fuck my student. What I've done already, what I'm about to do, is bad enough. Not that I can seem to make myself stop. I've always had ironclad self-control, aside from a short stint after my career-ending injury that resulted in me getting addicted to prescription painkillers and booze. I've been sober for almost seven years now, but what's happening here with Jack is worse than any drug I've ever come into contact with. As soon as he's in the room with me, taunting me, teasing me—it's like I have no willpower at all. All I can think of is making him submit to me. The punk kid that nearly turned me down out of spite has come a long way, and I think that's something—maybe something good is coming from the very wrong things that I'm doing.

Nevertheless, nothing is stopping me from pulling out my hard cock and running my fist down the length of it. And nothing is stopping Jack's hungry gaze as his tongue drags over his bottom lip.

"Suck me, Jack. And if you do a good job, I'll let you touch yourself while you do it."

A sound caught between a whimper and a grunt of frustration leaves Jack's lips, and I give him a look. But he's not looking at my eyes, his gaze is locked on my hard cock. He shuffles forward and I part my thighs so he can fit his body between them. He grips me in his fist, slowly stroking his hand up and down my length, almost like he's familiarizing himself with it. I stay stock-still, doing my best not to give into the urge to slam his face down and choke him with it.

I'm about to admonish him for not taking me in his mouth yet, but I have to suck in a breath as I watch Jack run the flat of his tongue from the bottom of my balls, all the way to the tip. He follows along the thick vein, and then circles the head, swirling his tongue over it. When he finally closes his mouth around the top, sucking and twirling his tongue around, I can't stop my hips from bucking into his wet heat. I want so badly to plow into his throat. As excruciating as it is, this is *his* reward, so I clench my fists and let him do his thing the way he wants.

Pulling himself up taller on his knees, Jack begins to take me deeper into his mouth, experimenting with how much he can take, even though we both know very well that he can take it all. I suppose his throat must be bruised, having taken a beating two days in a row. My hand brushes his jaw and gently rubs against his neck, feeling his Adam's apple bob as he swallows down a gag.

"Relax your throat," I tell him. "That's it. Just open up and let me in."

Jack moans, and the vibrations create another layer of sensation that makes my cock pulse. He hollows out his cheeks and bobs more forcefully, taking me deep enough that his nose touches my pelvis.

"That's good, Jack. Just like that."

Fuck, his mouth feels good. I almost don't want to come, to keep prolonging this as long as I can, but then he looks up at me with pleading eyes, and fuck, if that doesn't cause me to almost lose it.

"You want to touch yourself now, Jack?" He nods, nearly coming off my dick. I grip his hair and hold him on me. "Don't stop," I command. "You're doing so good. Keep sucking me just like that and stroke your cock." I take control of his head, gently guiding him up and down my shaft.

The wet noises coming from Jack's throat and mouth on my cock, and the skin-on-skin sound of him jerking himself off, are too much.

"Fuck, Jack," I groan, my release filling his mouth. He swallows me down, licking up any last remnants from my cock before he releases me with questioning eyes.

"Sit back and let me see how you work your cock."

Jack does what he's told, falling back on his ass and leaning back on one arm as his free hand strokes his shaft, fisting and squeezing the head at the top. Pre-cum is streaming from the tip, and my mouth waters, wondering what it would taste like. I almost consider having him stand up and letting me have a taste, but I don't want to ruin the power dynamic that I've cultivated. That, and despite all the things I've done to Jack—despite the way my cock seems to stand at attention every time he walks by—I'm not actually attracted to men. I was quite the player back in my day, and after I joined the NFL, I married a beautiful woman. After finding out I wouldn't be able to play again and my first stint in rehab, she left me.

I suppose this makes me gay? I don't know. I know I like having control over Jack. I like the way he's looking at me right now, as he squeezes and strokes his dripping cock, silently begging me for permission to let him finish.

"Come for me, Jack."

A choked moan leaves his open mouth, and his cock erupts. My eyes don't know where they want to be most, which part of the action they want to see the most. The way his cock pulses and jerks as it spurts thick ropes of cum. Or the way the cum splashes on his defined abs. Or the look of ecstasy on his face as he finally gets his much needed relief. I soak it all in, my cock attempting to twitch back to life, my heart beating wildly. I'm too old for this shit.

"Good boy," I praise him.

CHAPTER 13–JACK

"Come in," Coach Nicks calls when I knock on his office door. It's lunchtime, and not the time that I normally see him. For the past three weeks, he's made me wait until the end of practice, then he teases me through two more hours of workouts before he finally gives me what I want. Not that he's giving me everything I want, but at least I get a release out of it. Whether or not it's right, I like being under his control.

I crave his cock jamming down my throat, the way he holds me against the tiled wall of the showers as he fucks my face after stroking my cock until I'm so close it hurts. I'm desperate for those four words that precede oblivion just as he's filling my mouth: *Come for me, Jack.*

I didn't get my taste last night after practice. Instead, he'd pressed our cocks together and wrapped his hand around them. We thrusted and rubbed ourselves together until I was gritting my teeth and near tears trying to hold off. Nicks lasts forever and always makes me wait for him, but when he said those magic words, we both erupted all over each other.

Then, most surprisingly of all, Coach lathered up a sponge and washed my body, head to foot, before he stroked me hard again. Then he pressed my face against the tile and jerked me off while his other hand teased my ass. I was tense, afraid—but also excited. When he pressed a finger into my virgin hole, I expected to hate it, for it to be painful. It was foreign, and the stretch did burn a little, but once he got me stretched out enough, he was pumping two fingers into me, pressing into some insane spot inside me that had me painting the wall in no time at all.

"Sorry, Coach." I'd had the wherewithal to realize that he hadn't told me I could come again, but it happened so fast I wasn't ready for it.

Coach only pushed his fingers deeper inside me, milking my orgasm until the aftershocks wore off.

"Hmmm. I'll give you this one," he said, pulling away from me and washing his hands under the stream of water. I leaned back on the wall, my bones barely solid enough to hold me upright, and looked at his half-erect cock. Jesus, even only half hard, it was intimidating. Would that thing even fit if I decided I wanted to try to take him? His fingers had made me think it might not be so bad, but up close and personal, I'm pretty sure that monster would split me in two.

"Quit looking at it like that or it's coming for you," Nicks said, chuckling when my eyes went wide. Then he left, and by the time I finished showering and dressing, he'd left the building.

I thought it might be fun to surprise him, and I'm starting to squirm with memories of the shower last night, which is why I'm here so early today.

"Jack, is everything alright?" Coach Nicks looks up at me over his reading glasses. Other than his insanely fit body, he actually looks his age right now. I sometimes forget how much older he is. It's another reminder of how fucked up I am, because the way he looks at me over his glasses is kind of doing it for me.

I pull the door closed behind me and reach for the lock.

"What do you think you're doing, Jack?"

I shrug. "I came to suck your dick," I say nonchalantly, pulling my hand back from the doorknob.

His eyes flash and dart towards the door.

"No. That's not the arrangement. You get your reward after training, when you behave. There are too many people here. You need to go. Behave."

I give him a salacious grin and cup my erection through my pants. "Come on, Coach. You can't tell me you don't want me to choke on your fat dick at all times of the day." Instead of waiting for his answer, I walk around his desk and drop to my knees, pulling my dick out to show him what he does to me. "I just need a little taste to get me through the rest of practice, Coach."

The telltale bulge in his pants is enough to tell me he wants it. There's no denying I've gotten good at sucking his dick these past few weeks. I know just how he likes it, and he fucking loves my mouth on him. It's a reward for both of us.

I scoot forward and run my hands up his thighs. My fingers are on his belt buckle when someone raps on the door.

Fuck. I didn't actually turn the lock. My eyes meet his, and while I know my expression is one of terror, his is pure vitriol. He's *pissed.*

Kicking me underneath his desk, he clears his throat and calls for whoever it is to come in. His chair pulls up tight, and I fall back against the metal sheeting that hides me from view.

Coach Nicks' voice is calm and patient, like there's nothing out of sorts. "Tuck, what's up?"

"Hey Bryant, you got a minute?"

"Of course, whatcha got?"

Coach Sanders is discussing the defensive lineup and some ideas he wants to try at today's scrimmage. They drone on and on, and I'm getting irritated because I'm missing my entire lunch break, cramped under a desk, waiting to get my ass torn up for almost getting us caught. I know what would happen, and it wouldn't only be Nicks that would be fucked. I'd lose my scholarship and my ride to the NFL.

I know how pissed he's going to be when Coach Sanders finally leaves, and I know my punishment is going to be more than taking a throat beating. This is a real offense, not just leaving a cupcake wrapper in the takeout container he always brings me for lunch. I like finding little ways to get under his skin and rev him up, but this is something different.

But as long as I'm here—in for a penny, in for a pound, right?

Slowly, quietly, my fingers touch the inside of his thigh. He doesn't so much as pause his conversation, giving nothing away, but his cock twitches and swells the closer I get to it. When I reach his belt buckle, he shifts, trying to covertly push me away, but he ends up inadvertently giving me more space between his thighs. He tenses as I get his belt open, and even coughs to cover up the sound of his zipper, seeing as he can't exactly slap my hand away. I'm able to pull his cock out beneath the desk and start sliding my hand up and down his shaft in slow, tight strokes. When I lean forward and lick the little drop of pre-cum that trickles from the slit, Coach actually jumps, but the movement gets covered up by his phone ringing.

"Shit, I need to take this, Tuck. This all looks good, though. I'm looking forward to seeing how it plays out. Would you mind pulling the door behind you?"

He looks down and gives me a death glare. "Fucking stop," he hisses before picking up the phone.

"Bryant Nicks," he says tersely into the phone.

"Yes sir, I have time." I only know of one person Bryant Nicks would call sir, and that's the dean. He moves to start tucking himself back in his pants, but I lunge forward and take his cock in my mouth before he can.

Nicks lets out a puff of air and rakes a hand through his hair. "No sir, all good here. Just pulling out my file for the donor brunch. We have an impressive list this year."

There's some chatter through the receiver, and Nicks diligently makes understanding noises as if he's listening. Meanwhile, he sits back in his seat and fists my hair, moving my mouth on his dick. I do just like he's taught me, relaxing my throat and letting him position me, and he takes control. While he's on the phone, discussing plans for some fancy brunch event, he keeps my movements pretty slow and light. It's almost relaxing. But when he hangs up, he all but growls in my face.

"You fucking brat," he spits between gritted teeth. His grip on my hair, which has grown considerably since I got here, is punishing, to the point I am sure hair is being pulled from my scalp. He thrusts into my mouth without mercy, holding me down as he pummels my throat. When I start sucking air through my nose, he plugs it with his other hand, leaving me without any air at all. My hands pull at his hips and thighs, nails raking at his exposed flesh, pushing and pulling, doing anything to fight my lack of oxygen. Nicks doesn't relent, though, continuing to fuck deep into my throat and looking at me with murderous intent. He's fucking pissed and out for blood.

Just when spots are starting to form before my eyes, Nicks grunts and empties himself into my throat. I force myself to swallow, desperate for breath. He doesn't hurry, making sure I get every last drop before he pulls out of my mouth and smacks me across the face with his wet, flaccid cock before throwing me to the floor.

"If you ever pull that shit again, I'll fucking end you. Do you understand?"

I'm too busy wheezing air into my lungs and coughing to answer.

Through everything I've gone through with Coach Nicks and our arrangement, I've never once actually been afraid of him. Until now. Even so, my dick has never been more alert.

CHAPTER 14–BRYANT

Jack stomps across the field, his baby bulldog out in full force. I've punished him with wind sprints and burpees, weights, and even set him up with some extra tutoring sessions since I'm pretty sure he hasn't been doing the assigned studying I've given him. All the punishments I know he *doesn't* want, frustrating him with my lack of attention. I can tell that he's very close to doing something stupid again. He's right that it'll get my attention, but if he puts my job in jeopardy again, I'll end this little deal of ours in a hurry.

He's been working hard, I'll give him that. And as good as he was before he came to Groveton, he's gotten better. He's stronger, leaner, faster. He's easily the best wide receiver in our conference, if not in the nation right now. I'm looking forward to what kind of stats he can put up once the season begins. I'm proud of the work he's put in and his progress.

I guess it shouldn't surprise me that a twenty-year-old man is motivated by sex, but the circumstances are definitely surprising. I'm nearly fifty years old, and Jack Perry is a good looking, excessively fit star football player who could get any girl he wants. In fact, if his reputation was even close to accurate, he did, and often. The reminder of that video makes me clench my fists, but it just goes to show the power and influence of being Jack Perry. And he is fucking sexy as hell. I'm slowly coming to terms that I'm attracted to him, and not just the dynamic between us. Or to his body, at least. His attitude still needs an adjustment.

When he gets to the point that he'll drop down on his knees and apologize for being a fucking brat, I'll go back to giving him what he wants. For now, I keep my mask of cool indifference and tell the team to huddle in.

"Alright team, you all know we have the donor brunch coming up next week. It's how we officially start our season every year. A few of you are newer, so let me explain some rules. This is a high-class shindig, so you're expected to show up in your Sunday best. When you're speaking with the men and women whose donations made sure you are training in a state-of-the-art facility that rivals some NFL teams, I want you to remember that you are representing me and this school. If I witness or hear of any misconduct or anything but perfect behavior from any of you, I'll bench you for the first game of the season. I don't care who you are. Does everyone understand?"

"Yes, Coach!"

"Good. Now get the fuck out of here. I'll see you bright and early in the morning."

The team jogs off the field, but Jack stays back. I hold up my hand before he can open his mouth.

"I don't want to hear it, Perry. I'm still too pissed to deal with you."

"It's not that, sir." His use of sir gets my attention. I know he's a good ole southern boy like most of these guys, but it's not an honorific that I'm accustomed to hearing from him. He usually sticks to "coach," and his use is sarcastic at best.

"It's about the donor brunch. I'm getting the impression that this thing is mandatory?"

"Is it on your schedule?"

"It is, but—" he cuts himself off, realizing his mistake before I have to correct him. He looks down and nods his understanding. His expression is not one I've seen on him before. It's not just contrite, it's... embarrassed?

"What's the issue here, son?"

He clears his throat and lifts his chin. "I'll need permission to leave campus to find something appropriate to wear. Please," he adds on hastily. The fact that he's trying so hard makes my lips quirk, and I have to purse my lips not to grin. I enjoy seeing him squirm.

My eyes trace down his form, getting an estimate of his measurements. Nothing I have will fit him, that's for sure, but I know someone that might help.

"We'll get your measurements after practice today and I'll have something delivered."

"I can't pay for anything too–"

"I didn't ask for money. It's not a gift or charity, either. It's a necessity to be part of this team. There will be more than one event that you'll be expected to attend, and I expect my players to look and act the part of perfect gentlemen."

This time he's the one trying to hold in a grin.

I roll my eyes. "Get inside. I don't feel like getting caught in this rain that's about to start falling."

His brow furrows, and he looks up. There's nothing but darkness, especially as the stadium lights start to shut off, but you can't see the stars through the clouds.

"How can you tell?" he asks.

"Pressure build up," I explain.

Jack rolls his lips together and turns around, walking towards the locker room.

"What's so funny?" I ask incredulously.

He shakes his head, refusing to look at me.

"Jack..." I warn.

He chortles. "I'm sorry, Coach."

"Fucking what, Perry. Spit it out." By now, I'm more annoyed than curious.

"I just forget how old you are sometimes," he says, almost apologetically, as his eyes water with the effort to not laugh.

"What the fuck is that supposed to mean?"

"Your old football injury acting up when it rains?" His

eyebrows lift as his grin spreads.

My eyes roll, and I huff out a laugh. "Listen, kid. I'll bend you over my knee—"

"Promise?" His eyes glitter with mirth, showing me the playful puppy I've come to know.

I give him a warning look, but I can't help but let go of some of my anger. Truthfully, these past two months have made me forget how old I am.

"I think you owe me chin-ups today," I tell him, trying to get back to business. Chin-ups are his least favorite, which makes them my preferred choice for torturing him. Without realizing, I swat him on the ass as he turns towards the gym.

"Put that thing away," I tell him as I bring the measuring tape to the crux of his thighs to measure his inseam.

"Sorry, Coach. I can't help it," he answers, maintaining a straight face.

I make a noncommittal hum of disapproval. I know he's full of shit. He's having the time of his life standing up on the bench so I can get his trouser measurements, putting his groin closer to my face than it's been before.

Jack sucks my dick, not the other way around.

"What? It's the truth. It's been days, and with all due respect, I was getting used to getting rewarded for good behavior."

"Well, you fucked up—"

"I know I did, and I'm sorry. That's not really how I saw it all playing out, and I see now how stupid it was. We both would have lost everything."

I nod, glad for once that he seems to understand the gravity of the situation rather than just being angry about having blue balls. I stop and consider that thought for a moment. "When was the last time you came?"

"That time in the showers," he answers, his cheeks reddening.

My surprise overshadows my own memories of that night. Caught up in the moment, hypnotized by watching him in the shower, I'd gone a bit overboard, turning our strict exchange into something a little more personal. Before I knew it, I'd stripped down and joined him. It took everything in me not to brace his hands on the wall and lick him from balls to spine before impaling him on my cock. I desperately wanted to know if his ass was as tight as it looks, but I also like to deny myself. So I fingered him the way the hot nurse at my last checkup did me, finding that soft spot that I knew would tip him over the edge again.

Fuck, that was hot.

"That was really the last time?" I ask him, looking him sternly in the eye and challenging him to lie to me.

"Yes, Coach." I actually believe his sincerity when he answers me.

I look up at him and huff. "Get down from there and let's discuss how the rest of this is going to play out. With classes starting soon, we'll need to lock down a new schedule, anyway."

He hops down with enthusiasm, all but bouncing on his toes. "Calm down, pup," I say, to his chagrin. "Let's go talk in my office, where we can look at your class schedule."

I can tell he's disappointed that I've turned the conversation back to business, but I have to draw the line somewhere. He's becoming needy and expectant. This isn't a relationship, it's a reward system for hard work and perseverance, albeit a really fucked up one.

It takes nearly an hour to write out a new schedule. Between classes, tutoring, and studying, he's going to have to cut back on his practice and workout time, but I've still given him a pretty grueling schedule there.

He won't have time to get in any trouble, won't have time to fail, because I have every minute of his day planned out. He doesn't know it, but I'm going to begin pushing his boundaries a little, too. Because while I actually care very little about what he wears on a daily basis, I do like how pissed off he gets when I tell him what to do with his life outside of training. The food thing got less push back because his diet affects his performance, but if I'm going to be able to change him into the person he needs to be, if I'm going to make a real difference, he's going to need to commit and submit all the way.

That's what I tell myself, at least.

Jack looks tired by the time we're through, and part of that might be realizing how much work is ahead of him. Summer training was easy compared to the mental load he's going to have to carry to maintain good enough grades to keep his scholarship and my approval. I'm not like other coaches that'll make deals with teachers to get players special treatment. I know many of the students on my team get special treatment by default, or through their own methods—rich kids are brutal fucking manipulators—but I have no part in it.

I expect nothing but the best and as much as I've gotten my kicks ignoring and punishing Jack, he's given me the best, so I suppose he deserves some reprieve.

"You look tired. Why don't you go home and get some rest? I kept you late, so just show up with the rest of the team tomorrow."

A look of disappointment, and maybe even hurt, darken his grey eyes. "That's it?" he asks, standing to follow me to the door.

I pause with my hand on the doorknob. "What were you expecting?"

"I've done everything you asked," he says in a low voice.

"Ah, I see. Well, you have my permission to get yourself

off as long as you continue to behave accordingly. If you slip up, I'll take it back." I start to pull the door open, but Jack shakes his head.

"What is it that you're asking for here, Perry?" I say, using his last name to create some distance between us. "What reward would you be satisfied with so I can go the fuck home and ice my *old man* injury?" Jack ignores my attempt at humor, staring at me and worrying his bottom lip as he contemplates something.

Just as I'm about to lose my patience and kick him out of my office, he takes three long steps forward and pushes the door closed. Crowding me against the wall, Jack suddenly presses his mouth to mine. The kiss, or rather the stiff press of our mouths, seems to startle him as much as it does me. He pulls back quickly, eyes wide as he stares at my mouth, like he can't believe what he just did.

I can't believe what he just did, either. What's more surprising is how I feel about it.

Grabbing Jack by the front of his shirt, I pull him against me and then turn him around so his back is against the door. I stare at his lips for the briefest of moments before I take his mouth.

This time, our lips move against each other, albeit not softly. I coax his mouth open, dipping my tongue in to lick against his. We're all teeth and tongues, hands pulling at each other's clothes, the energy between us crackling.

I whip Jack's shirt over his head, and he loosens the drawstring on my track pants. Grabbing his hips, I grind my erection into his and Jack moans. Pulling him against me, I turn us around and walk him to my desk, pushing his shorts and boxer briefs down as we go. He steps out of his shoes and clothes before I push him to sit on the edge of the desk, my eyes raking over his form. After two months of nonstop training and mostly eating only foods I've approved, his body is chiseled like a marble sculpture. From his shoulders down to his calves, every muscle ripples with the force of his heavy breaths. His cock, an alluring angry shade of purple and weeping with his need, juts out of his lap. I quickly move some of my things to the side so he can lean back, and then I direct his feet to the edge of the desk. He's splayed out before me like an offering.

I remove the rest of my clothes and stand between his spread legs, examining the prize before me. His cock is throbbing, and it feels as though my own heartbeat skips to match its rhythm. Like I did before, I press our cocks together and wrap my hand around them, stroking them. Jack's head falls back, and he moans. I know he won't last long, but I plan to wring more than one orgasm out of him.

"Come for me, Jack," I tell him, and it's like he was waiting for my permission. His hips buck into mine and he cries out as his cock jerks and spurts.

Hot, sticky fluid splashes against both of our stomachs and coats my hand. I spread it over my erection and use it to stroke myself, rubbing the dripping end of my cock against his asshole. Jack tenses at first, but then relaxes and keeps his legs wide, accepting me.

"I'm not going to fuck you, Jack. But I am going to

make you cum again before you clean me up." He almost whimpers, and I push his chest to direct him to lie back on the desk. Grabbing his legs just behind his knees, I push them up on his chest and instruct him to hold his legs. His cheeks spread wider with the position. Standing between his legs, I give my cock a few more strokes before I shoot ropes of cum all over his ass.

Trailing my fingers through the mess that is dripping over his ass, I rub it around the tight ring of muscle before pushing my fingers inside. I start with two, and he hisses out a breath. The pants of pain quickly become moans as he begins to stretch, his body accommodating to the girth of my fingers. I add another, and Jack gasps. His cock is hard and ready again.

Wrapping my fist around his stiff length, I stroke him while pumping my fingers into his ass. Every time the pads of my fingers hit the soft, spongy spot inside him, he lets out a groan. When I can feel him getting close again, I push my fingers inside and massage his prostate while I continue to stroke his cock in my tight fist.

"Fuuuuuccccckkkk," Jack moans, his body tensing and shaking. The tight ring of his ass begins to pulse and his cock jerks wildly as he ejaculates.

Thank God there's no one in the building this late at night, because Jack shouts loudly with the force of his orgasm, nearly lurching off the desk.

"Fuck," Jack repeats, laying boneless across the desk, trying to catch his breath.

He looks so fucking good splayed out and covered in cum, both mine and his, that I nearly reconsider fucking him. I want so badly to sink my cock into his ass and feel him squeeze around me the way he did my fingers, to see my cum dripping from his gaping hole when I'm through ruining him.

Instead, I grab a towel from the shelf where I keep my extra gym clothes, and wipe the cum from his body, and notice some has dripped onto the dark green carpet. I wipe at the mess, but it leaves a small white stain behind.

I start to clean myself up, but Jack sits up and grabs the towel from me. He wipes the cum from my chest and stomach, bending forward to take my lips in a light and experimental kiss.

I blink rapidly, not sure what to think. It was different when the kiss was passionate and carnal, but this tenderness is not something I'm expecting or even looking for.

He pulls back with an expression that looks just as confused as I feel, before shuffling off the desk and dropping to his knees to clean me up, just like I told him to.

CHAPTER 15 JACK

I open my small closet and look over my new wardrobe. Coach didn't just buy me a new suit. There are two full suits, a vest, two pairs of slacks, five button-down shirts, six ties, and several collared shirts that are meant to be "casual."

First of all, none of this is me. Second of all, I'm starting to feel like some kind of secret whore. I'm okay with him telling me what to eat and how to workout, but controlling what I'm wearing off the field? I'm certain this must be a test. I just haven't decided how I'm going to take on the challenge.

For today, though, at the fancy donor brunch, I'll wear the light grey suit, white shirt, and dark green tie that he has instructed me to wear. I also, with his permission, went into town and got a haircut yesterday. Normally I just buzz my head myself, but this time I did something a little different, and it's more stylish than I'm used to. The sides are cut short and faded, but I had them keep the top long so Coach can have something to grip onto.

I don't know who I am anymore.

It's been a little strange between us the past week. After the hot make-out session in his office that led to me lying spread eagle on his desk and almost begging for a dick in my ass, he seems to be pulling away from me. He's still rewarding me, feeding me his cock on an almost daily basis, and when I'm really good, he does that thing with his fingers that blows my fucking mind.

But he hasn't tried to kiss me again, and I haven't tried either. I'm a little intimidated by the fact that I want him to kiss me. Hell, I might even want his mouth on my lips more than I want it on my dick. Well, *almost.*

The walk to the sports complex is hot, and I'm glad it's going to be an indoor event. I feel like I'm about to sweat through this suit and look like a slob, despite all of my efforts to look presentable.

We're supposed to meet in the locker room and walk into the cafeteria together, which has been decorated to look like a fancy restaurant. There was a whole interior design team here all day yesterday, and we couldn't use the field because they redid all the lines so it would look shiny and new. Luckily for us, that meant a half day of practice and our first chance for some time off since July 4th.

Unfortunately for me, it meant an afternoon of assessments with my new tutor. She's nice enough and is apparently a teaching assistant for someone in the English department. I'm strangely not distracted by her tits, but I wondered fleetingly if Coach knew who he was setting me up with for tutoring. Not that every girl wants to jump my dick, but I do have a tendency to weasel my way into a lot of girl's panties.

Or at least I did. Fuck, it's been a month and a half since I fucked around with those girls at the party. I'm not sure I've gone this long without a piece of ass since I hit puberty and started playing football.

I suppose I *am* still getting some action, just a different kind.

My eyes follow a few of the cheerleaders and dates that came here with the other players. I definitely still appreciate a tight ass and a pair of tits. I've never looked at a dude and thought, damn, I want a piece of that. That is, until that day I walked in on Coach working out. Although, I suppose I refused to acknowledge any sort of real sexual attraction before the day he came on my face and left me on the floor of that supply closet.

Since then, he's all I think about. I eat, breathe, and dream Bryant Nicks on an almost obsessive level.

Surely it's just the dynamic, right? He's figured out that I'm motivated by orgasms, and he's obsessed with making me the best.

But if that's true, why do I crave the taste of him, or the look in his eyes when I'm swallowing his cock whole?

Groan.

I need to redirect my thoughts. Buttoning my suit jacket, I walk into the locker room where the other players are waiting for all the guests to be seated.

Nicks warned me yesterday that we're essentially going to be paraded around like prized pigs, and since I'm a scholarship student, they'll be especially interested in checking me out. He made it sound like they could get really intrusive with their questions, and it irks me to no end that a bunch of rich assholes think they own me because I play for this team. They're the ones that need *me* to win this thing.

"Get used to it," Coach told me while we were resting in the sauna, after he'd bent me over the bench and rubbed his cock between my ass cheeks until he came all over my back. "When you're in the NFL, the sponsors do own you. I had more than one rich sponsor's wife cop a feel and proposition me, thinking they were owed a performance other than what they got on the field."

"None of the husbands?" I asked before I could stop myself.

He wasn't mad though, he just chuckled. "No one's ever been brave enough to try, and there wasn't any interest on my part before," he'd told me, answering my unspoken question.

"So you don't normally..." I trailed off, not sure how to word my question.

"Don't normally dick my players into submission? No," he said, shaking his head. "This is a, uh... new development. Very new, for me."

"For me too," I admitted, and we fell into somewhat of an awkward silence until I was feeling overheated and left for the showers. Nicks didn't join me, and he was gone by the time I emerged.

I think the kiss was too much. Somehow, just wanting to get each other off feels a lot less intimate—and a lot less gay—than kissing him did.

Coach's eyes follow me into the room. I can feel them boring into the back of my head, watching me greet and shake my teammates' hands.

"Looking sharp, Perry," the running back, Grant, says. "You clean up nice."

I'm sure the compliment is underhanded, Grant is kind of a douchebag and seems to think my presence on the team takes away from his position. But instead of taking his bait, I turn it around on him.

"Not so bad yourself, Gipson."

Only then do I turn around and face front, where Nicks and the rest of the coaching staff are mulling about. As soon as I make eye contact, he looks away, and I know it's immature, but it bothers me.

I don't have time to mull over it, though, because the coaches are having us walk out single file, in order of starting players. Since I'm firmly on the first string, I'm one of the first players to enter the room, maybe five people behind Lane Masters, who of course leads the charge as quarterback, with Grant Gipson right behind him.

There is a polite round of applause, and we file along the stage that's been erected on one side of the cafeteria. The rest of the players stand around their tables until everyone is in, and then we're allowed to sit. I'd much rather be at a table than up on this stage, being gawked at.

Coach Nicks introduces himself, which he doesn't need to do, seeing as the polite applause became almost raucous when he entered the room behind the team. He's hot shit around here, leading this team to success despite its embarrassing history of failure. Not everyone likes him as a person, but everyone respects him and the title they know he's capable of bringing home for Groveton College. After introducing himself and discussing some of the training we've been going through over the summer, he introduces the full starting line, beginning with Lane Masters. Each of the players on stage has family in attendance, and Nicks asks them to stand up while he discusses the many qualities that make each player a "fine sportsman".

I don't hear any of it. He goes through the full offensive and defensive lines before he comes back to me, and I nearly miss my opportunity to show my teeth and wave when he starts talking about the final addition to his all-star starting lineup. Nicks gestures for me to stand, and I try not to wonder if anyone will notice I don't have friends, family, or even a date here to support me.

"Now, most of y'all aren't going to know this young man. He's here all the way from Alabama, where Tucker Sanders and I pulled him out from under the Crimson Tide's nose before they could get their paws on him. He's got better stats than more seasoned players, runs faster than lightning, and I'm pretty sure the refs are going to want to check his hands for magnets, because he doesn't miss a thing." The crowd chuckles, beaming up at me like I'm something special. "Jack Perry is a good kid, and he's the player that is going to make our offensive line impossible to beat. I can guarantee you we'll have more points on that board than you've seen in years."

"Since you were on the field!" some ass kisser yells, and the room goes wild—the players whooping, guests standing to applaud.

Coach has us all stand up so we can snap a few pictures, and then releases us to sit down at the tables when the meal is served. It's a never-ending trail of mini courses that are based on real food, from tiny waffles topped with a few berries and swipes of sauce across a plate that is far larger than the food, to finger sandwiches that take less than two bites to eat.

It all tastes alright, but I'm not sure I understand why it's all miniature. I find myself craving Coach's sometimes bland, but filling, meals, and wish I'd had more than my double protein shake this morning. I try drinking a lot of water to make up for the lack of food. The last thing I need is to come off uncouth because my stomach growls, but then, of course, it isn't long before my bladder is screaming at me.

I excuse myself to the restrooms, and on the way back, bump into...

"Aniyah," she reminds me.

"Right. Sorry," I say, wincing. I do actually feel a little bad about using her and her friend the way I did, even if the friend obviously didn't mind. Once I was sober again, I realized I might have been a little rough on Aniyah.

Not as rough as Coach was on you.

Aniyah seems to take my brief moment of reflection as interest, because she moves closer, brushing her hand over my shoulder.

"You can really tell how strong you are, even through your suit," she purrs, leaning in a little too close for comfort. I'm not actually interested, but I wonder if I'm going to need to start acting like I am, in the event someone catches on to how little interest I have.

I smile at her, although it might be a bit tight. "You're looking beautiful as ever," I say, as if I've ever noticed her aside from the day she and her bestie licked my cock together. She preens.

She honestly is gorgeous. Honey highlights peek through her thick brunette hair and amber brown eyes look up at me beneath thick eyelashes, and her pink lips are parted coyly. Her body is slim and fit, with a nice curve to her ass and tits that make her trim waist look even smaller. She's wearing a pretty yellow wrap dress that makes her skin glow, and impossibly high, pointy heels.

But when I look closer, I can see that her tan is fake, slightly too orange. Her eyelashes are almost comically long and also obviously fake. And her makeup is so caked on, you can't see the girl underneath. Her bra is definitely padded—I don't remember her tits being as big as her friend's.

She's trying too hard, and it reeks of desperation. Still, she's interested and I might need a cover. Plus, it's been a long time since I sank my dick into a warm body. Like it knows what direction my thoughts are headed, my cock gives a small twitch, which does not go unnoticed by... Anya?

Fuck. If I'm going to make this work, I'm going to have to remember her name.

She lifts up on her tiptoes to whisper in my ear. "I think he remembers me."

"How could he forget?" My dick really starts to take notice when I think about all the ways I can torture Coach with this. What will I have to do to earn permission to fuck a pretend girlfriend?

Her hand slowly moves down the front of my body, tracing the outline of my half-hard cock. "Do you want to get out of here?" she asks.

I clear my throat. "I have to get back to the donor brunch, but maybe some other time?"

Too many long hours later, all the guests have left and I'm finally free of rich, old people that live in a cloud of cloying perfume asking me questions about my height and weight—like I am indeed a prized pig. Nicks wasn't kidding.

Speaking of Nicks, I don't know where he's gotten off to. He glowered at me when I returned from the restroom with Aniyah, whose name I am determined to remember. One of the guys at my table corrected me and made a joke that she wouldn't mind if I called her the wrong name as long as she's being stuffed full of cock. Apparently, she's dated a few of the guys on the team. I don't give a fuck, and I'm not about to slut shame anyone, especially considering I've been a bigger slut than most. Before moving here, at least.

I take my time getting ready to leave, visiting the restroom again before I finally give up on waiting for him. I shoot him a quick text before I go, though:

> JP: Didn't see you anywhere, and you didn't say otherwise, so I'm heading out.

The message comes up as read, but there are no little telltale dots to tell me he's going to respond. Shrugging, because I'm not going to sit here and wait like the puppy he thinks I am, I head out into the late afternoon. It's too swelteringly hot to be outside, and a big storm is brewing. My lips quirk, thinking about Coach's shoulder.

> JP: Storm coming in. How's that shoulder, old man?

The three tiny dots that say he's responding flash, then disappear twice before his response comes through.

> BN: You can't fuck her.

My steps falter as I do a double take.

> JP: It's like that, is it?
>
> BN: My game. My rules.
>
> JP: Jealous?

I know I'm baiting him. But he makes it too easy.

The little dots that tell me he's typing start and stop three times before I make it to my room. I pull off the stuffy clothes and put them back on hangers, grabbing a pair of shorts and a t-shirt while I wait for him to decide what to say next. My dick thinks Nicks might be flustered, and we both like that very much.

> BN: You can't afford any distractions.

Oh, so that's how he's going to spin this. I think for a moment before sitting back on my small bed, angling the phone just right. I don't give myself more than a second to rethink my actions before I push send on the picture of my hard cock.

JP: This is a distraction.

The dots appear and disappear again before the phone rings, a video call from Bryant Nicks coming through. I answer, expecting him to lay into me about sending shit like that through text again, and then promising me torture on the field tomorrow. Or he might make me do pushups with him on the phone. He's done it before, but not with video.

What I don't expect is a closeup of Nicks' hard cock, his hand stroking the length in a punishing rhythm.

"Fuck," I murmur, my hand squeezing my cock.

"Come on, Jack. We can take care of this distraction together."

That sounds like permission to me. We spend the next five minutes beating our cocks like we're both racing to the same desperate finish. Despite him clearly starting first, I win. And my prize is being aware enough to watch the thick vein on the underside of Nicks' cock throb and pulse as he coats his hand and lower stomach in cum.

He hangs up without another word, and once again, I'm left reeling.

Aniyah might have a great set of tits and a willing mouth, but she doesn't hold a candle to the man that has taken ownership of my mind and body in the past few months.

CHAPTER 16–BRYANT

It's the first game of the season, and the team is full of energy, ready to go.

"This is it, team! Today is the first day of our undefeated championship season!"

They roar with excitement, slapping each other on the back and shoulders.

"I don't have to tell you what to do, you already know. You've spent the last three months working your asses off for this moment. You have all the tools. All you have to do is get out there and kick some Baylor ass!"

The team puts their arms around each other, jumping up and down and side to side, chanting and whooping. Coach Sanders takes my place, giving them his own pep talk, and next Lane will take his turn as captain and quarterback to get the team excited before he leads them out onto the field. I'm listening to Tuck give the team a play-by-play of some of the opposing team's weaknesses when I see Jack slip unnoticed out of the locker room. Nodding to Tuck to keep it up, I follow him out the door and into my office.

"What's going on, Perry?" I say, pulling the door closed behind me. He smirks, knowing my words are nothing more than show.

"Just some game jitters, Coach," he answers, leaning around me to turn the lock.

"Jack," I admonish in a low voice, "this isn't a good time. You should be with the team."

"Well then, we better make this quick," he says simply.

"There's no time for—" he presses his mouth to mine, cutting off my words. Like the last time he kissed me in my office, it turns heated quickly, and in seconds I have him pressed against the wall, grinding my thigh between his legs.

Shouting from the locker rooms infiltrates my office, interrupting the moment, and we stop, breathing heavily. There's no mistaking the raw look of his lips, and I briefly panic over how we're going to cover it. Jack picks up his helmet from the floor. He leans forward and gives my lips one last lick before pulling on his helmet.

"I'm going to win this game for you, and then I want you to fuck me tonight."

I cough, both incredibly aroused by his words, and terrified he could be overheard. Jack hits his hands against his helmet and slips out of my office, joining the others. I have to take a few minutes to myself, using an ice pack from my lunch cooler on my mouth to lessen the swelling. Then, when it doesn't seem like it's going to help itself, I put the ice pack on my balls to help my erection go down.

Fucking hell, this kid. He's really not what I was expecting, that's for sure.

I walk back into the locker room as Lane is yelling, "WHO ARE WE?!"

"JACKALS!" the team answers.

"WHO'S THE BEST?!"

"JACKALS!"

"WHO'S READY TO KICK SOME BEAR ASS!?" A few players snicker, but still answer enthusiastically.

"JACKAAAAALS!" They all yell before Coach Sanders is opening the door to let them know it's time, and then they're running down the hall and through the tunnel onto the field. Jack winks at me as he sprints onto the field, the crowd screaming for their team.

Because of Jack's little pre-game tease, I'm on edge for most of the game. Thankfully, the rest of the team isn't, and the Baylor Bears don't stand a chance. It's almost a complete shutout, but they manage to put up a field goal in the last minutes of the game.

Jack plays better than I've ever seen him. He is fucking unstoppable, and by the end of his first game, every Groveton College Football fan knows his name. The team carries him off the field on their shoulders, and I smile, knowing that even the holdouts like Grant Gipson are going to have to accept him eventually, on his merit alone. They might think he's just a charity case now, but he'll be making more money than any of them could dream of in the matter of a few years. I'm certain his first contract will supersede what any of them could expect. Jack looks back at me as his team carries him off to celebrate, and I wave him off.

I walk around the field a bit, shaking hands with the officials that I haven't seen since last year. And of course, I have to pay my respects to the dean.

"Team looks great this year, Bryant."

"Thank you, sir," I nod, trying to think of how to escape his irritating presence when I hear someone calling out for me.

"Coach!" Lane runs back onto the field towards me. I turn to nod towards the dean before giving the quarterback my attention. "I thought you'd be inside already," he says. "I'm thinking Perry deserves the first game ball of the season."

I raise my eyebrows, surprised. The entire team played well, and both he and Gipson were partly responsible for the number of points that went up on the board tonight. They played as a team. But I can also see that Lane is being a good captain, and making a show of accepting Jack into this new, winning team.

"You know what, Masters? I think that's a fantastic idea. Might help the rest of the guys come around." I pat him on the shoulder, gesturing him back inside to the team. "But, Masters—keep the celebratory drinks to a minimum, will ya?"

He laughs. "Will do, Coach."

I stare at my phone. Or maybe I'm staring at the $300 bottle of Macallan that it's propped up on. Hell, I'm staring at both. Two things that represent the one thing I can't have—

Oblivion.

I've been sober for almost seven years now, but I keep this bottle to taunt myself. I get a twisted sort of satisfaction out of dangling something I can't have in front of me, and I find myself staring at this bottle more often than not. It's familiar—the pain and the desire. No matter how much I want to open that bottle, to pour myself a few fingers of the amber liquid and roll the flavor around on my tongue, to submit to the numbness it promises, I won't. The strength of my willpower is my comfort, even if the effort is excruciating.

I've let myself indulge in Jack Perry, let myself fall into this ridiculous fallacy of a relationship. He's become a drug, addictive in the same way whiskey and Oxy used to be. The difference being that instead of numbness, the oblivion he promises is chaos and ecstasy. Blood rushing, heart pounding, bone deep lust. He's an upper, and though I've only ever been addicted to downers, that is quickly changing.

Earlier today, he said he wanted me to fuck him, and

it's the only thing I've been able to think about since. I want to fuck Jack desperately. But that desperation is dangerous, as is this game we've been playing.

I've succeeded in making Jack Perry the best college football player he can be, but can I maintain progress without falling deeper into this situation? Is it too late to pull back the reins on the motivation that has worked so well? Now that summer training is over, I should pull back on all of it, expect him to follow through on his own now that I've laid the groundwork.

I've tried creating more distance between us. Hell, we barely spent any time in each other's presence this past week since school started. But when he cornered me in my office with that hungry look on his face? I knew this was becoming more than just a game we're playing.

I jump when the phone rings, a video call coming through. For a minute, I don't move, watching it ring until Jack's name disappears from the screen. Then I get a text notification.

JP: Answer. You know you want to.

It rings again, this time just a phone call. I answer like the weak sack of shit I am.

"Jack," I say expectantly.

"Jack," he repeats in my tone. "I was calling to see if you wanted me to come over and suck you off, or if maybe you'd enjoy a video of someone sucking me off."

I sigh. "You're drunk."

"Eh, not really. I've got this annoyingly gruff voice in the back of my head that ruins everything fun I try to do.

So not only have I said no to keg stands and every shot that's been given to me, I also missed out on naked Jello wrestling with the cheer squad," he says wistfully.

I chuckle. "Where are you now?"

"On my way back to the dorm. The party was getting a little rowdy, and there are some boundaries we need to establish."

"What do you mean by that?" Jack's never been a boundaries kind of guy, so I'm more than a little curious to hear what he'll say next.

"Hold on a sec." I hear his footsteps echoing in what sounds like a stairwell, then a burst of noise. "This dorm is a bit loud now that there are other students here. I just have to get to my door."

Voices call out his name, congratulating him on a great game. I grin, happy to hear the other students accepting him. Even in the cheapest dorms, this university is full of spoiled rich kids who will take any opportunity to step on someone they consider lower than them.

Finally, Jack makes it into his room, switching his call to video. I worry over the notification for a minute, but then accept, propping the phone back against the bottle and leaning back in my chair. Jack plops himself back on his bed and holds the phone above him, so I'm looking down on him. I don't hate the angle.

"What do you mean by boundaries?" I ask, keeping my face indifferent.

Jack's mouth twists, like he's not sure if he wants to have this conversation after all.

"If you like, we can go back to the regular phone. Maybe it'll be easier to spit out whatever it is you want to say?"

He puffs out a breath, the front of his hair pushing up away from his forehead. "Nah, it's good. I just don't know where to start. I'm not drunk enough to be as blunt as I'd like." His Alabama twang sounds thicker than usual, and it heats my blood.

"I give you permission," I say, amused. "Say whatever you need to say, and for the length of this phone call, I won't hold anything against you."

He quirks his lips. "What if I want you to hold it against me?"

"Jack..."

He makes a face, rolling his eyes. *Look at me, not saying a word about this little indiscretion.*

"Alright... If I'm not dating around, or at least *making a show* of dating around, people are going to start talking."

"About?"

"I have a reputation to maintain, Coach," he says with a saucy grin that I immediately want to slap off his face. With my dick.

He sighs and looks uncomfortable. "Tonight someone made an offhanded joke about me not messing around with any of the girls at the party, asked me if I turned gay. It was just a joke, and I played it off, but..."

It's not surprising to me that word of Jack's hijinks from his old school made it to Groveton, and if you add in his

Fourth of July antics, I can see what he means about it being a noticeable change.

"I see what you mean, but what can you do about that? You can't be drinking and partying and getting in trouble here. Is it not enough just to clean your act up?"

"I don't have to be drunk or get in trouble to stick my dick in someone."

"Hmmm," is all I can say.

I don't like it. At all. Not one bit.

But... he's right. People might pay attention if he's not acting like his normal man-whore self and spending all his time with me. Besides, this might be just the opportunity I need to break this link.

"Wear a condom. No drinking. No recording," I say, giving him a stern look through the camera. I don't want to see that.

He chuckles but nods.

"What about video calling?"

CHAPTER 17—JACK

JP: I'm bored.

BN: Aren't you supposed to be studying?

JP: This tutor is a dud.

BN: You're just mad because you chased the pretty one away.

JP: She wanted my dick. It was distracting.

BN: I'm proud of your determination not to get distracted. I'm sorry your new tutor isn't fuckable.

JP: I didn't say that.

BN: Jack…

JP: What?

BN: Get an A on that upcoming American Lit test and you'll be maintaining a solid 3.5 GPA.

JP: And? That's well above the 3.0 I'm required to maintain.

BN: Keep it above a 3.5 and I'll reward you.

Fuck. Yes. Finally.

"Yesss," I hiss out quietly.

I set down my phone, trying not to pump my arms in victory because my football coach might acknowledge my presence by jerking off on my face or whatever it is he has in mind. The last time I tried to get him to fuck me, he backed way off and hasn't seemed interested in our arrangement anymore.

I've been trying to do things his way, maintaining my grades and athletic standards the way he wants, but I'm considering taking drastic measures again. I just don't want to screw up everything I've accomplished so far just to get his attention, so I've been biding my time, hoping I can find a way back in.

My tutor, the fucking nerd, rolls his eyes at me and continues droning on about the fundamentals of different styles of poetry. American Literature is honestly not the worst class, and I actually even like the reading part. I struggle with writing some, but I'm managing. I wasn't sure a tutor was even necessary until we started learning about prose and poetry, which I find to be a complete fucking snooze fest.

Then again, maybe it's just this tutor. Emily made everything a lot more interesting, even if I felt like I was dodging hands pretty often. She got fired after a professor caught us making out in a dark corner on the top floor of the library. I feel *a little* bad, seeing as I brought her up there on purpose, so we might be seen by a few of my teammates. Grant Gipson and a couple of his friends are always hanging out in the library for some reason. They certainly aren't looking at books, but they've always got their eyes on the hot librarian.

Luke gives me an exasperated sigh. "If you're not into this today, I'm just going to pack it in a little early. I have a date."

I snort, because for some reason the idea of him going on a date is funny. Or maybe I'm just being an asshole because I'm not going on any dates. I'm not *interested* in dates. The most action I'm getting right now is sending dick pics to my football coach and having them be ignored. I don't want to hang out with most of the guys on the team, and I'm avoiding Aniyah like she might be transmittable. I'm still a little worried she'll tell someone I got soft when she was sucking me off a few weeks back, but she was drunk and I think she thought I was, too. I managed to redirect her attention to someone else's dick, so for all I know she might have thought he was me.

"Where you headed?" I ask, trying to make conversation since I was so outright rude.

Luke's eyebrow quirks up and then he rolls his eyes. He does that a lot around me. "Monster truck rally," he says, sounding a little exasperated.

Now I'm really laughing. "Doesn't seem like your thing."

He shrugs, because I'm right. "It's his turn to pick."

His turn?

"You're... gay?"

Luke straightens his spine, staring back at me with his chin raised. "Yeah, what of it? If you have a problem with it, you can–"

"Slow down, dude. I have no problems. I just didn't realize."

"Does it matter?"

I think about that for a moment too long. "Nah, man, it doesn't. Have a good time. I'll see you next week?"

It doesn't matter to me if he's gay. It never mattered to me. Only now have I realized that maybe the fact that I never thought it mattered was a sign. I come from a backwoods Alabama town where there is definitely not even one openly gay person, and words like faggot, fruit, and homo are thrown around like fucking confetti. I'd grown up in that environment, and I'd never even considered that it was wrong. It just was what it was. But then when I moved away to college and experienced a slightly more progressive atmosphere, I didn't bat an eye to see a dude wearing a rainbow shirt or two girls holding hands in the quad. Okay, that's not true. I *definitely* thought about what I'd do with the two girls holding hands in the quad... and did them whenever the opportunity presented. Bethany and Cora were *freaks*.

To me, someone being gay was more a novelty than a fact about their lives that had real consequences. I never considered if someone in my hometown might be gay, living their life afraid that someone might find out, or maybe someday being brave enough to stand up for themselves the way Luke just did. I certainly never considered that I might be gay. I'm still not convinced I am—can you be gay for just one person? Am I bisexual if I'm attracted to pretty much all women and one guy?

I have a lot more respect for Luke when I consider it all this way. Part of me wishes I were brave enough to ask him questions, try to learn more about what's going on with me. But I can't risk people finding out, and I don't think he likes me much. Not that I blame him. I've kind of been a dick.

"You seem lost in thought," comes a soft voice next to me. The librarian, Miss Wilson, smiles down at me kindly, concerned curiosity etched in her pretty face. Raking my eyes over her soft features, smooth brown skin, and curves for fucking days, I think I'm wrong about myself. I can't be gay. Because *damn*.

"I guess I was," I say, giving her a flirty grin.

She leans on the corner of the table and looks down at my books. "What are you studying?"

My nose crinkles. "Poetry for American Lit."

"I take it you aren't a fan?" she says, chuckling.

"It's not my favorite. None of it makes any sense to me."

She smiles and nods understandingly, then holds up a finger. I watch her hips swing as she walks away, disappearing into the shelves of books. When she returns, she has a book in her hands. It's a worn paperback with a green cover, gold letters and some kind of design. She hands it to me.

Leaves of Grass

"Walt Whitman is probably one of the most important poets in American history. He was all about celebrating the ordinary, doing things his own way, and free love—

that sort of thing." She shrugs and smiles at me. "You might find it interesting. Or you might not. It's worth a try, right?"

"Yeah, I suppose so. Thanks," I say to her back as she walks away. One of Grant's friends is at the reception desk, watching us with narrowed eyes.

I flip through the book a little, and the descriptions of some things are interesting. I decide to take it home with me when my eyes start crossing. I might as well get some rest tonight. It's my only night off this week with the homecoming game coming up.

I've been keeping a pretty full schedule of practice, classes, games, and study time while still making time to workout every night. At first, I was just doing it to see if Coach was going to come in, but now it's just habit. I've been busting my ass on the field and in my classes, and for the first time, maybe ever, I feel like I deserve the accolades that are being thrown at me. Coach was right. I could be a better player—a better person.

But right now, I'm just tired, more so than usual. I woke up tired, and for the first time since coming here, considered skipping a class. I figured skipping one might lead me back down the wrong path, though, so I made it, but dozed off while I was there. Luckily, my beginner's Calculus teacher is a big football fan and I've been doing pretty well in his class, so he didn't give me too hard of a time.

"You look like shit," Ryan, one of my teammates, says, thumping me on the back.

"Thanks," I say sarcastically. I might be coming down with something, but it's nothing I can't handle. We just have to kick ass tonight, which shouldn't be an issue. Texas A&M hasn't been near as good as us this year, so there's no reason this game shouldn't be a wash. Then we have a bye week before we go on the road for an away game, so if I need to recover from whatever this funk is, I'll have two full weeks to do it.

"You gonna make it to the party tonight?"

I glare at him. "We'll see." *Nice of him to be concerned about my wellbeing.* Ryan is one of the second-string players, and he's a huge partier.

"Aniyah is coming for sure," Ryan mentions.

Well, that settles it. I'm definitely not going.

As we're getting ready to run out onto the field, Coach Nicks pulls me back. My lips twitch a little. "Not the time, Coach. Gotta go win us a Homecoming game."

"You're looking a bit pale."

"I'm good, Coach." Before he can question me further, I wink and run out onto the field, throwing my hands up to get the crowd pumped. Tonight, the whole student body is in the stands, decked out in green and grey, waving flags and signs. I see more than a handful of signs with my name or number on them, and I point to a few of them, hamming it up for the crowd.

Tired or not, I'm excited about tonight's game. I want to enjoy the fanfare, even if the noise of the crowd and the marching band music feels like it's reverberating in my head.

Coach corners me just outside the bathroom during halftime. I wipe my mouth and try to get around him, searching for some gum or something to wash the taste of vomit out of my mouth.

"Perry," he calls after me. "I think you should sit out this half."

"What? No. I'm in the zone, Coach. I'm fine."

In the fourth quarter, we're decimating our opponents; up forty-seven points and they've yet to put even one on the board. It's almost too easy, and I can't help but enjoy the way the other team is getting pissed off. My cocky grin isn't helping much, I'm sure. But they came into our house and started this game talking shit, saying shit like, "we're here to take you rich pussies down."

Well, now all my rich pussy friends and I are going to flat out embarrass them. As fired up as we are, their team can't get the ball more than a couple of yards. I laugh out loud as I see our defense shut them down one more time, giving us possession of the ball. I bend to pick up my helmet and the ground spins, but I right myself and secure it on my head.

"Perry!" Nicks calls out. "I saw that. You're sitting out before you hurt yourself."

I'm so tired, I consider listening to him, but we're halfway through the last quarter of the game. I want to help my team send these fucks home with nothing but shame.

"Game's almost over, Coach. I can make it."

"You look like a gust of wind could knock you over. Sit the fuck down, Jack."

The moment my ass touches the bench, the crowd boos and yells. I make a show out of shrugging my shoulders and pointing to Coach, and they start chanting.

"We want Jack! We want Jack!"

Coach Nicks looks up at the crowd, his eyes wide at the number of students, faculty, and fans that are shouting my name.

"Might as well give them what they want, Coach. It'll be over before we know it." I replace my helmet and tap his shoulder before running out to take my position, the stadium screaming and ready.

Our next play is beautiful. Lane fakes the pass to me and passes it to Grant instead, who takes it halfway down the field before running out of bounds to avoid a hit. We can easily make another touchdown on our next play. We huddle up and Lane calls the play. On his call, I fake a step to my right and launch left. I run through the middle of their defensive line and into the end zone. The ball flies, landing perfectly in my hands. It's a clean catch, and another touchdown! The crowd goes wild.

One moment I'm catching the ball and holding it up to celebrate; the next, all the wind is knocked out of me.

The hit isn't even that hard, I've taken way worse. But the lights in the stadium blur as everything spins when I try to push myself off the ground.

I stumble, and blackness closes in.

CHAPTER 18–BRYANT

This is my fault. *All my fault.*

I pushed him too hard.

I knew I should have benched him, taken him out of the game. I probably shouldn't have let him play at all, considering I knew he was under the weather. But I also know how tough he is and how much everyone was looking forward to the homecoming game.

He played his heart out, never faltering for a moment despite being sick and clearly exhausted.

If he's lucky, he won't have a concussion from that hit he took. A *late* hit—one that earned Texas A&M a fifteen-yard penalty and resulted in us putting another touchdown on the board before the game was over. The player that hit Jack was suspended from their next game, and by the look on his coach's face, that's the least of his worries. As much as I wanted to take him out and rough him up myself, the player is being punished for his actions.

And when Jack wakes up, *he's* going to be punished for his bullheadedness. My resolve was weak, but he also needs to know his own limits.

Jack groans, blinking his eyes open. He only lost consciousness for a minute on the field, but he's been resting since we got to the emergency room. They wheeled him back to get a CT scan earlier, leaving him to rest once they gave him a few pills to swallow and hooked him up to an IV.

"How are you feeling, son?"

"Don't call me son. It's creepy. Especially when you—"

I cut him off with a curt shush just as the doctor walks in. She ignores the way Jack is laughing and gets right to business, which I appreciate.

"How are you feeling, Mr. Perry?"

"Actually, a lot better than I did earlier," he admits, which gets a stern look from me. In the bright fluorescent lighting, his skin is sallow and the bags under his eyes are pronounced. He looks like utter shit, and he's saying he feels better?

"The fluids and vitamins are helping then. You were significantly dehydrated, so we set you up with what we call a banana bag. It's saline mixed with electrolytes and multivitamins."

"Good stuff," Jack says, nodding appreciatively at the already half-emptied bag of bright yellow fluids.

"Your CT scan looks good, no obvious signs of

concussion, but you did test positive for influenza A. You'll need plenty of rest and fluids, but you'll be back to your normal self in about a week or so."

"The flu?" I ask.

She nods and flips his chart closed. "If there's nothing else, you're free to leave as soon as those fluids are through. Rest, hydrate, and come back or check in with your healthcare provider if you have any complications. Headache and body aches can be treated with over-the-counter painkillers every four to six hours. Your next dose can be taken in about three hours." She looks at me, probably because I'm the only one here to advocate for the kid. "CT didn't show a concussion, but I'd recommend he not be alone for twenty-four to forty-eight hours. Sleep is good, excessive dizziness or confusion is not."

I nod. "I'll make sure he's taken care of."

"Thanks doc," Jack says, leaning his head back and closing his eyes. At least now that we're here, he's finally resting.

"Uh, hey Coach."

I look up and see Jack shuffle into my kitchen. He's no longer wearing the shirt I gave him, and the sweatpants are hanging dangerously low on his waist, showing off the perfect v cut of his muscles. Dark hair peeks above the waistband.

Swallowing the saliva that fills my mouth, I greet him and turn my attention back to my Sunday paper, pretending like I wasn't just drooling over his body. "There's coffee. And I got you some sugar-free Gatorade. It's in the fridge."

"Thanks," he says, and grabs a bottle of the so-called sports drink before standing across from me at the small kitchen table. He gulps it down quickly, and I try not to stare at his neck when he swallows. Otherwise, we'll *both* need to stay hydrated.

"Feel up to eating something?" I ask, looking over my reading glasses. "I'm making soup for lunch. Chicken and rice. But not that canned crap." I detest pre-packaged foods. They're full of all kinds of nasty chemicals and way too much sodium.

His lips quirk. "That sounds good, thanks. What time is it?"

"Just after eleven. Doc said you needed your rest," I answer, explaining why I let him sleep so late. I was actually just about to check in on him again. He's been asleep for nearly twelve hours. As soon as we left the hospital, I brought him back to my house. After helping him into the shower—trying my best to keep my eyes above the belt—and shoving a pair of my sweatpants and a t-shirt at him, I led him to my guest room. He was asleep before I returned with water and a bottle of ibuprofen.

"How's the head?"

"Not bad," he says. My eyes narrow and he laughs.

"What exactly is so funny?"

"You worried about me, Papa Bear?"

"Why wouldn't I be? One of my players took a nasty hit."

"You let all your players stay the night?"

"No," I say honestly. "It was late. Everyone else was probably asleep or drunk at the afterparty."

"You could have just taken me home."

"Doc said you needed to be monitored."

"Alright," he says. His little grin lets me know he knows I'm full of shit.

Truth is, I am probably more worried about him than I would be another player. Not that I don't worry about anyone on my team that gets sick or injured. I've definitely seen my share of concussions. Normally, I'd assign a teammate or call the family, but in Jack's case, there's no family close enough to call, and he doesn't exactly have a ton of friends. Or at least not anyone I trust. And I wanted to see to him myself.

I'm about to open my mouth and apologize for pushing him to the point of exhaustion, but he beats me to it.

"I'm sorry, Coach."

"What for? I'm the one that should be sorry. I pushed you too far."

"No, you've pushed me exactly the right amount. I've never felt better."

I lift an eyebrow.

"Well, present circumstances excluded, obviously," he says, laughing. He winces a little, betraying the headache he still has.

"Sit the fuck down, Perry," I admonish him. "Have some soup, and then go back to bed."

"Yes, Coach."

I don't miss the tone of his voice, nor the heated way he watches me mill about the kitchen, but I ignore it. After I get him a bowl of soup and a spoon, I leave him in the kitchen and head to my study. I've been working hard to put some distance between us, and I can't let this mishap bring us back to where we were. Me getting too close to him puts us both in danger, in more ways than one.

The bag that the hospital put all of his stuff in is sitting on a chair on the other side of my desk, vibrating. It occurs to me that he probably has a few friends that want to check in on him, or that he might want to check in with. I pull his phone out of the bag to take to him, noticing he has several missed texts and calls, most of which are from Aniyah. Her name lights up the screen again as I set the phone in front of Jack, who has barely eaten any of the soup I gave him.

"Might want to call your girlfriend," I say. My voice comes out harsher than I mean for it to, exposing my jealousy and making me hate myself more. "Maybe you'd like her to watch over you tonight. Let me know if you'd like a ride anywhere. I'll take you."

With that, I head back to my study.

"You know it's not like that," Jack says in a low voice.

"Maybe it should be."

CHAPTER 19–JACK

I wake up in Coach Nicks' guest room for the second time. The light barely filtering through the blinds and dark blue curtains makes me think it's still pretty early morning. Coach will likely need to leave for work soon, and I should head back to my room to get ready for my classes today. After doing nothing but hydrating and sleeping yesterday, my headache isn't as bad. I still have a backache and I feel a little weak, but it's nothing I can't handle. I'm well enough to go to classes, probably. The nurse said I might still be contagious, but I'm not sure that excuses me from classes, and I can't afford any absences. I have my American Lit test this week, and I want my damn reward.

The smell of coffee hits my nose and I hear shuffling in the kitchen, so I head to talk to him. He's wearing a pair of athletic pants, not unlike the ones of his I'm wearing now, except his are a darker shade of grey and not practically falling off of him. No, they are perfectly tight across his muscular ass and thighs. I watch him cook something at the stove, a little weirded out by how much satisfaction I get out of watching him be so... domestic.

"How are you this morning?" He asks, not looking at me.

"Better now," I say, intentionally flirting now that my morning wood has returned with a vengeance and is aching after staring at his ass.

He ignores my suggestive tone. "Did you call Aniyah back?"

"No."

He looks over at me curiously, to which I just shrug. "I texted her and said I was fine. I'd rather be alone than give her an excuse to try to sink her claws into me."

"I thought you rather liked her sinking her claws into you."

"Not exactly," I say pointedly, not wanting to admit that my idea to date around is backfiring. I'm not ready to face the fact that my dick only seems to get excited about him. "I can head back to my dorm today."

"I'm not implying that you have to leave if you're not ready."

In all honesty, a big part of me doesn't want to leave. I'm curious about what Bryant Nicks is like outside of school and football, but I'm not about to admit it. "I have a tutoring session today at the library," I say.

"I already called the student center. You're excused for today, and you can do the rest of your sessions for this week virtually. I also let your teachers know you might be out this week, but that you'll still be turning in your assignments through the online portal, so make sure you check your email. You should probably still isolate yourself the rest of this week to avoid passing the flu to anyone."

"Aren't you worried you might get sick?" I ask, thanking him as he passes me an omelet. Egg whites only, of course, with spinach and bell peppers.

"Bit late for that now. But I have a strong immune system," he says, and I watch as he mixes some orange powder into two large glasses of water. "Extra vitamin C," he says when he passes me one. "When you're done eating, if you want to grab a shower, I'll get you some clean clothes. I've still got about an hour before I really need to be in my office."

I shove a bite of eggs in my mouth and nod, accepting the dismissal for what it is. I've worn out my welcome, and it's time for me to go home and recuperate on my own.

A few minutes later I follow Nicks down the hall so he can show me where all the extra towels and such are. He walks in to bring me a stack of clothes while I'm getting the temperature of the water right, and I waver a little when I stand up.

"Whoa, you alright?" Coach asks me, steadying me by my shoulders.

The heat of his hands on my bare skin is almost scalding. I'm fine, just stood up too fast, but I seize the opportunity to get closer. I lean into him, and my lips brush lightly against the space where his neck and shoulders meet. He tenses, and I think for a moment that he might push me away, or insist that it's time for me to go home, but he doesn't.

"Still need a bit of help, I guess," he mumbles, and I nod.

It's a lie. I don't, and even he knows it. Yet we both let ourselves believe the lie for long enough to strip out of our clothes. As weak and exhausted as I was feeling before, adrenaline courses through my veins at having him this close. It feels more intimate than the rushed moments in the locker room, or his office, where we are hurried in case we're caught. Somehow, this feels both safer and more illicit. As though by doing this here, we're acknowledging something about ourselves.

Coach holds me beneath my arms and directs us into the spray of the shower. I let him pretend that he is helping me shower, and he washes my hair and guides me beneath the spray. When he begins to lather my body with soap, I decide to do the same to him.

"I already showered," he mumbles, but stops when my soapy hand wraps around his thick cock.

"I think you missed a spot," I whisper, stroking him. His eyes dilate, and the dark ring around his hazel irises grows larger, making his entire gaze darken with lust.

He finally drops the pretense of what he's in here for and captures my mouth, pressing me against the cold tile of the shower wall, and reaching for my erection. Our mouths move passionately against each other, and I grip his hard ass as I pump his cock. He presses his chest against mine and increases the speed of his strokes, squeezing my head. But then he stops and abruptly pulls back, releasing my cock and pulling my hand away from his. He lifts both my arms above my head and pins them there with one hand, before pressing his hips into me and rubbing our erections together. I groan into his mouth and buck my hips forward.

"I really want to bend you over and take that tight ass like I keep promising, but this isn't the right time. Consider this my apology for pushing you too far and not realizing you were sick."

He releases my arms and turns me around slowly, pressing my hands to the wall and then trailing his fingers lightly down my sides. My ass pushes into the hard appendage behind me, taunting, begging for his cock. Instead of getting anywhere near my hole, Nicks rubs his cock through my cheeks and reaches around to grab me. He squeezes and strokes and pumps me into a frenzy, all while thrusting against my ass, sliding his big cock through my wet, soapy cheeks. I let out a choked cry, holding back the climax that threatens.

"Come for me, Jack," Nicks grunts, rubbing against me harder and faster as his strokes match the rhythm of his thrusts, jerking me until I fall back against his chest, shuddering as he aims my release at the shower wall. My back is covered in his hot, sticky cum seconds later.

True dizziness threatens, and I rest on the wall as Nicks cleans us both up. Then he leads me back to the guest room and tucks me in, handing me a glass of water and some painkillers. "Just rest here today. I'll be back later and we can figure out what to do next."

Does he mean my class schedule and tutoring while I'm

sick? Or does he mean us? I'm not sure, but I'm hoping it's the latter.

I'm just out of it enough to admit to myself that I want there to be an 'us'. Will I be able to admit it to him when the conversation comes up?

For now, my eyes are already closing. He leaves to get dressed, and I drift off to sleep. I swear I feel the pressure of Bryant Nicks' lips pressing a kiss to my temple before he leaves for the day.

When I wake up again, it's hours later, and I feel a hundred times better. My head and body don't seem to ache as much as they did before, and I don't feel like I'm going to keel over if I attempt anything physical. Whereas before I had no appetite and have had to choke down a few bites of whatever Coach has made me since I've been here, now I'm ravenous.

After using the restroom, I head into the kitchen, finding it's after four in the afternoon. I slept much longer than I thought, but I suppose I needed it. There's a container of soup in the fridge that even has my name on it. Everything in the fridge, aside from condiments, is labeled. While my soup heats in the microwave, I look around the kitchen a bit, noticing how meticulously clean everything is. You can't even tell that he used the kitchen this morning.

I stand in the kitchen and scarf down the soup, first draining the broth by drinking it right out of the container, then eating all the chicken, vegetables, and brown rice. I find dish soap and a sponge under the sink, and make sure to clean everything I used. I don't know where the dish goes, so I leave the clean container on the counter, thanking him for the soup.

Assuming he expects me to stay until he gets back, I snoop around the house. I've nothing better to do, and surely there's a TV around here somewhere.

I push open the door to his bedroom, and his musky, sandalwood and laundry scent surrounds me. I don't go too far into the room, it feels too much like intruding. I notice how clean this room is, too, and it makes me backtrack to the guest room to make the bed and make sure to straighten everything up. Within minutes, it's like I was never here.

The last room to explore is just off the living room. There is a TV in here, but it's small and mounted in the corner. There's a dark wood desk in the middle of the wall, flanked by floor to ceiling bookshelves in the same dark wood. Degrees and awards hang on the walls, and there are a few trophies on the shelves. There are newspaper clippings and pictures of him in his #88 jersey. And there's his fucking Heisman trophy, which is bigger than I thought it would be. I know I shouldn't touch anything, but it's a fucking Heisman trophy, and I'm so curious.

It's heavier than it looks. I read the inscription.

Bryant Nicks

Groveton College

1993

I do some quick math in my head. This means Nicks is, what... twenty-eight years older than me. Why does that sound like so much, but feel like so little?

I put the trophy down and keep looking around. I notice a fancy, expensive brand of whiskey sitting unopened on the center shelf with a glass next to it. Next to that, there's a small crystal dish with various coins and tokens of some sort. I pick some of them up to get a closer look. They all say things like, "to thine own self be true", and quotes about recovery. Some of them have numbers, and when I study them, I realize they are for a number of months and years. I pick up the one that says five years and turn it in my fingers. The sides are smooth and worn, like it's been rubbed down. Either he got this a lot longer than five years ago, or he touches it a lot.

"The fuck are you doing in here?"

CHAPTER 20–BRYANT

Jack startles and drops the token he was holding. With wide eyes, he drops down to the floor and scrambles to pick it up.

"I'm so sorry, I was just–"

"Leaving. You're recovered enough. Get the fuck out."

"Coach, I—"

"You need to leave."

"Just let me explain."

"There's nothing to explain. It's time for you to go."

"What about earlier, I thought—"

He probably thought what I was thinking, that we should discuss what's happening between us. I can't seem to stay away from him, no matter how much I know I need to, and he doesn't seem interested in maintaining distance. If we're going to keep this up, we need a new set of ground rules.

Throughout the day I realized how absolutely, impossibly fucking stupid that is. Never mind the fact that I'm not gay—I can't have a fucking relationship with a student. He's almost thirty years my junior, and I'm his teacher, his coach. It's wrong, and we could both get in a lot of trouble for this. We could both lose everything.

And it's not as if a relationship could last between the two of us even if it wasn't dangerous, so why even entertain the notion? No, I needed to let him down gently, make him understand and see reason.

That was before I walked in to see him in my private space, going through my things. Specifically, seeing him holding evidence of my biggest weakness, my biggest failure, in his hands.

I feel exposed. Uncomfortable.

"There's nothing to talk about. What happened earlier was a mistake. All of this was a mistake."

I turn on my heel, needing to get out of our shared breathing space. I can't bear to look him in the eye.

"What? No. Coach!" Jack chases after me, reaching out and trying to pull me back by the shoulder. "Look, I'm sorry."

I look at him dead in the eyes, ignoring the pain I see behind his grey irises, and covering the pain it's causing me. He needs to see that I'm serious.

"This has gone too far, Jack," I tell him sternly, leaving

no room for discussion. There's no talking anymore, because I know there's weakness in my resolve, and I can't show him that. "You need to go. I'll call you a cab."

"Don't bother," he snaps.

He picks up his phone from the kitchen counter, and shoves his feet in his football cleats, because those are the only shoes he came here with. I should chase after him and hand him the rest of his things, but I'm worried I'll be too weak in the moment and, in trying to explain myself, give away just how many feelings I have on the matter.

So I let him leave. I watch him walk out the door, wincing as he slams it shut, and continue to stand there, staring at the door, for far too long.

The night grows darker, and I put myself through the motions of all the things I'd normally do after work. I shower, reheat whatever meal I prepared over the weekend, and eat without really tasting anything. I notice Jack found the lunch I left behind for him, and stare at the note he left while I clean up after myself. My hands itch to put the container back where it belongs, but I leave it there to torment myself with. Because that's what I like to do.

To exemplify my torture, the next thing I do is grab my fifteen-year-old bottle of scotch and a glass. I set them on the table and stare at them while I turn my five years sober token in my hand. I haven't been to a meeting in over two years, but maybe now is the time. A glance at the clock tells me it's too late for tonight, anyway.

Truth be told, I'm not sure Alcoholics Anonymous is

what I need, or what I ever needed. I started because it was court ordered, and kept up with it because it gave me something to focus on. I definitely needed to get clean from the booze and pills, and I needed to get my life straight. AA helped me find purpose, although I struggle with the religious aspect of it. Fifteen years ago, I was on a downward spiral. I fell into a deep depression when I was told that I couldn't do the only thing I ever loved, and my football career was wrenched from my hands. I overused my prescriptions, and asked for more, for stronger, and I was given them without question, however much I wanted, but it was never enough to numb the pain. So I started drinking, drowning out my own thoughts.

I'm not sure that I was ever truly addicted to the alcohol itself, but I know it turned me into a different person. It turned me into a sad, pathetic, lazy sap. When my wife left me during my first stint in rehab, it didn't even surprise me. She'd always wanted to be a rich NFL wife, and while I still had plenty of money saved, I could no longer provide her with the lifestyle she wanted. So she left, and divorce papers were delivered the day I checked out. I checked back in about a month later when I found out she was already dating one of my ex-teammates, someone I once considered a friend.

Slowly, I lost contact with every person who ever meant anything to me, squandered what remained of the money that Penny didn't wring from me in the divorce, and I lost contact with myself for a long time. Giving myself over to the oblivion that drugs and alcohol promised, always emerging on the other side in more pain than I was before the bender. I had no prospects, no future. I didn't even have a home, since Penny had won that, too.

Rock bottom hit when the paparazzi took photos of me fucking some random woman behind a dumpster. I wasn't popular enough of a story to be breaking news, but it did lose me my last endorsement deal. I suppose I could think of it as saving me from embarrassing commercials about erectile dysfunction that I clearly didn't have, but whatever the case, I lost the last good thing I had going for me and knew then that I had to clean myself up.

Spending the last of my savings on a crappier, but more effective, rehab facility, I started going to AA consistently just to have something to focus on. I learned that my addiction didn't actually have anything to do with the substances, only with abusing my body, so I took up a new form of abuse—exercise. I started pouring all of my excess energy into forcing my body to go longer, harder, faster. I ran until my legs felt like limp noodles, lifted until I broke blood vessels, and plunged myself into frigid ice baths, not to sooth my aches, but to revel in the feeling of being fucking alive. My new addiction, my addiction to pain, is what really saved me.

Five years later, the dean of Groveton College approached me. His team was the laughingstock of college football, and he remembered the days when I'd brought the Jackals to a national championship. He could see that I was floundering, that I had nothing left to lose, so he offered me a job under one condition: I make the Groveton College Jackals champions. If I didn't, I was on my ass again. He didn't even care about the photos of me with my pants down, even helped cover them up. As long as I won them some football games and did what he said, he didn't care.

What I didn't expect was to love the job this much. As much as I loved being on the field as a player, coaching brought something new out of me. I quickly got a reputation for being a hardass, and for sometimes going overboard, but I knew how far to push my players, taking them to their limits in order to help them strive for greatness.

Unfortunately, I lost sight of limits when I met Jack Perry. Maybe it's because he didn't seem to have them. Or maybe it's the way he challenged me. I knew the moment I watched the recruitment footage that he was something special, but I didn't know that I would feel something for him. It's more than pride. More than something a coach should feel for one of his students. More even than the physical need he makes impossible to ignore.

At first I just wanted to beat him down, make him feel small so I could build him back up again. Then it became an encouragement for him to keep performing, and an indulgence for me. But the day he kissed me, it became something different. Something real and terrifying and far more addictive than the bottle of scotch I like to tempt myself with as a reminder of my own strength.

And that's why I don't think alcohol was ever my issue. Because I don't crave the burn of the scotch anywhere near the way I crave Jack Perry.

He dominates my every thought, and the only comparison is my need to dominate him. I want to hurt him and soothe the pain in the same breath, own him and set him free at the same time, push him away while pulling him so close we merge into a single being.

Unlike the stupid bottle of scotch that my reflection mocks me through, he's a true addiction that I can't seem to let go of.

In a fit of rage, I roar my pain into the empty room and throw the bottle as hard as I can. It hits the granite countertop and cracks, but doesn't shatter the way my heart is right now.

When I catch my breath from my little tantrum, half embarrassed even though I'm home alone, I go to pick up the bottle and examine the crack along the side. The thick glass is a fitting metaphor for how I'm feeling— holding something dangerous and volatile inside, but slowly cracking, my weakness starting to show. Because however thick and strong I am, I'm still just made of glass.

I look again at the note Jack left on the counter and the bag of his things still sitting on the floor near my office door. I should go apologize. It's late, but if I don't get all this off my chest, I know I won't be brave enough later. The last thing I need is Jack getting pissed off and doing something foolish. He needs to understand where I'm coming from, why this can't happen between us. He also needs to understand that fighting back or outing me could undermine all the work he's done. I'll follow through on my part of the deal and make sure the scouts come to see him, and I'll give him every leg up I can to get him on that draft board, but it's his talent and effort that will lead the way.

I'm shocked at how many people are still awake and

milling around when I get to his dorm. There seems to be a party of some sort happening in the room across from Jack's, even though it's a fucking Monday, for fuck's sake. Maybe I should see about securing a room for him at a different dorm or even one of the frat houses. The music and groups of people hovering in front of his door, having loud conversations over the thumping bass, can't be helping him get any rest. Not to mention how distracting that would be for studying. Some asshole wearing fake fangs and a cape bumps into me and keeps moving without saying a word. What the fuck is wrong with these people? Kids these days... Wait. *Is it Halloween?*

Knocking tentatively on Jack's door, I feel eyes on me, but when I turn around, it's just my imagination. None of the students pay me any attention, unconcerned that a staff member has walked in on their party.

He doesn't answer, so I bang my fist on the door louder, trying not to draw attention to myself. I'm just about to walk away, wondering where the fuck Jack is, when he walks up behind me.

"Coach? What are you doing here?"

His eyes are guarded, and I can't read his expression. It might be angry, and rightfully so, but he's also clearly exhausted. He's wearing only a towel, drops of water falling from his wet hair and rolling down his chiseled torso. In one hand, he holds a small basket of toiletries and he's wearing flip-flops. This dorm must have a communal shower. I hold up the bag of his stuff, momentarily tongue-tied and feeling like an idiot.

Jack watches the way my eyes rake over his bare body

before he looks at the people around us. While no one noticed me, there are more than a few girls blatantly appreciating his body. It rankles my nerves, as if I have the right to be jealous or angry about the way he's being openly ogled.

A blonde girl in a tight tube dress and bumble bee wings walks over to him and whispers in his ear, trailing her finger across his abs. I have to bite my tongue, trying to arrange my face into an expression of annoyance over the interruption, rather than upset about some random girl touching something that I perceive as being mine. Or is her presence here not random at all? Did he call her? Does he know her well? She looks vaguely familiar, but this isn't that large of a campus.

Jack steps away from her, pushing her back gently. "Sorry, babe, I'm contagious. Got the flu."

She recoils a little, but pouts. "I heard you got hurt. Aniyah and I have been coming by to check up on you, but you haven't been here."

"I'm alright. Takes more than a bitch hit like that one to take me down. I'll be back on the field for the next game. Won't I, Coach?" Jack says, turning their attention to me, standing there like an idiot. When she looks over at me in confusion, Jack actually has the nerve to wink at me. "Coach came to check up on me, yeah? Let me grab some pants and you can do whatever inspection you need to do."

Jack enters his room and closes the door, effectively dismissing both of us. The blonde sighs and flounces off down the hallway. I'm starting to wonder if I should leave too, but Jack opens the door, peeks around at the people still milling about in the hallway, and pulls me inside before anyone notices. After pulling me into the room, he closes the door and leans against it casually. He has not, in fact, put on any pants. He's still only in a towel, wrapped low around his waist.

Not helpful.

I force my eyes away from him, taking in his small dorm room. I've only been in here once, before he'd really moved in, so a lot has changed. It smells like him—his spicy body wash and the faint underlying scent of sweat. It smells like sex.

His room is fairly tidy for a college age guy, but it's clear he doesn't spend much time here. There are very few personal effects in his room, and I wonder what happened to the trophy I saw in his box of things on that first day. For whatever reason, he decided not to display it. The only thing hanging on the wall is a large calendar where he has his classes, training, and game schedule, each written in different colors. There are textbooks and notebooks on the small desk, and a school issued laptop that is open to a social media page. Apparently, his accident and absence have made him a trending subject around the school.

I open my mouth to speak, but the words to start the conversation we need to have won't come out. My mouth closes, and once again I feel like an idiot. I shouldn't have come here, and I really shouldn't be standing in Jack Perry's dorm room gaping at his half naked body while students are milling around directly outside his door. The walls are thin enough that I realize the music is coming from the room next to him, not across the hall like I thought.

My eyes meet Jack's. He's been watching me quietly since he pulled me in here.

He's probably pissed. I'm still pissed. But not at him.

Closing my eyes to block myself from the intensity of his gaze, I take a deep breath to steel myself. "I'm so—"

My apology gets cut off by a hard kiss. In the span of time it takes for me to force myself to start the words, Jack crosses the space between us and presses his lips against mine, stealing the breath it would take to finish my sentence. My weak resolve crumbles, and I kiss him back, our tongues wrestling, teeth clashing against each other. Jack puts his hands on my shoulders, pressing my arms to close around him, fitting his body against mine.

The embrace, however awkward it is, breaks through the last of my defenses. Holding him against me, I walk forward until his back hits the door. His hands push under my shirt, and my skin sears where our stomachs press against each other, skin to skin. He pushes my shirt up my chest, breaking the kiss to pull it over my head, then lowers his mouth to flick over one of my nipples. A shiver runs through my body when he starts to push the waistband of my pants and boxer briefs down, bending to lower himself in front of me. I let my pants fall, but hold Jack up against the door, pulling his hands above his head and pressing my chest against him to pin him upright.

"You didn't let me apologize," I grumble against his neck. Pinning his arms above his head with one arm, my other hand trails down his chest, tracing over his cut abs before pushing under the edge of the towel. I pull against the material, loosening it so it falls to the floor. My hand wraps around his thick erection, stroking precum down his shaft before cupping his heavy balls.

Releasing his hands, I do something I've never done before.

I lower myself to my knees.

With the flat of my tongue, I lick from the underside of his sac to the base of his cock before taking each heavy, round testicle into my mouth. I roll my tongue over each of them, reveling in the short gasps and moans Jack makes. When I lick up the underside of his shaft, looking up at him to see his reaction, his eyes are glazed. His mouth is parted, his hands held out at his sides like he isn't sure what to do with them.

When Jack is sucking my cock, my hands are in his hair, controlling the way his mouth moves up and down my shaft. But this is unfamiliar territory for both of us, and he's not sure what to make of the new development. Honestly, neither am I, but I'm even more surprised by how much I like my mouth on him. His spicy soap smell is stronger in my nostrils, the curls of his pubic hair tickling against my nose. His skin is smooth under my tongue, the slippery pre-cum he's leaking is salty and sweet in equal measure. I suck on the head of his cock like a lollipop, pressing my tongue into the weeping slit. Jack cries out, his hands flying up to steady against the top of my head.

I chuckle, pulling off his dick. "Don't come yet, Jack. I'm not done with you."

Standing, I grip his hips and turn his body around. My hands grasp his and press them against the door on either side of his head. My body crowds and presses into his, my cock nudging between his thighs. He trembles in anticipation.

Pressing once against his hands to let him know to keep them where I've placed them, I release his hands and trail my fingers down the sides of his body until I reach his hips. Teasing, perhaps frighteningly, I pull his hips out and use a foot to widen his stance. Bending my body to fit against his, I lick and whisper against the space between his shoulder blades. "I'm not going to fuck you, Jack." He relaxes against me, drooping almost as if he's disappointed. I wrap my hand around his cock again, pumping as my hips roll into him from behind.

"Why not?" he asks breathlessly.

I can't answer him, knowing that whatever he says in reply will change my mind. I'm weak, fucking putty in his hands just as he is in mine, and I don't know how to deny him when it's something I want more than air to breathe. Instead, I distract him by dropping to my knees again, taking his firm ass in my hands, kneading and spreading his cheeks apart. Leaning my head forward, I lick between his legs, tonguing the sensitive space between his balls and ass. Jack startles at the sensation, then leans his head against the door and lets out a low moan. The music is still loud on the other side of the door, so I don't worry too much about what anyone might hear.

His skin is still damp, and I itch to put my mouth on every inch of Jack's body. My tongue moves up through his cheeks, licking up any remaining moisture from his shower. He gasps and groans when my tongue teases over his hole, and I flick it over the puckered flesh the way I would a clit.

I didn't come here intending to do anything other than have a conversation with Jack about how we can't continue the relationship we've somehow forged out of the fucked-up situation I put us in. I know what I've done is wrong. I used my position of power to manipulate a student into pushing themselves harder than they should. So hard, in fact, that he could have been seriously injured, or worse. And as if that wasn't bad enough, I've been using him as a sexual outlet. It started as a power play, albeit a fucked up one, but it's turned into something far more dangerous.

I burn for him. *Crave him.* So much so that I'm willingly and enthusiastically pushing my tongue into another man's asshole.

"Fuuuck," Jack moans against the door, pushing his ass back against my face as I lick and probe him, eating his ass like a starving man until my mouth is sore. "Coach!" He pleads my name, panting and digging his fingers against the door. Jack's cock is visibly throbbing, the angry purple head hitting the door so that drops of cum are dripping down the wood.

I replace my tongue with a finger, and then two, slowly thrusting inside the tight hole. My eyes are locked on the way his ass swallows them greedily, and I feel the tight ring contract when I wrap my other hand around Jack's cock. His hips buck into my hand, shouting as I add a third finger to his ass. My mouth salivates, watching the way my fingers pump into his ass, spreading him out. He groans when I remove my fingers, looking down at me with wide eyes, silently asking me why I dared to stop. I try to reposition myself around his front to take his cock in my mouth and end up pressed between his body and the door. Jack's cock eagerly pushes into my mouth, and I relax my jaw, giving in and letting him take charge. He thrusts into my mouth, hard but still more gentle than I've ever been. I blink out a stream of tears, and focus on the way his abs contract when I lift one of my hands to squeeze and tug on his balls. They're firm and tightened against his body, and I realize that he's waiting for permission. His cock is lodged down my throat, but his hands are right where I told them to stay and he's slowing his thrusts to keep himself from coming.

Fuck, that does something to me.

My fingers push back into his ass to massage his prostate, and I push my head forward to take him deeper into my throat. The effect is instant. Jack chokes out a cry, and he fills my mouth. I keep pumping my fingers inside him, milking and swallowing as his cum keeps spurting into my mouth. When he's finally spent, I hold some of it in my mouth, savoring it for a moment before spitting it into my hand and using it to rub my cock. I didn't come here to get off, hell I didn't come here to get him off, but there's no way I could walk out of here like this. I'm harder than I've ever been in my life, painfully so.

Jack is still braced against the doorway, eyes closed and breathing heavily. "That was... Fuck," he groans, interrupting himself when he opens his eyes and looks down at me. He watches me with heavy, lust filled eyes. "I'm going to take my hands off the door now," he says. "And then you're going to put your fat cock in my ass and fuck me like I know you want to."

"Jack..." I warn him, but my warning is weak at best.

He lets go of the wall and drops to the floor in front of me. He puts his hand over mine and stops me from stroking myself, leaning forward to kiss me. It starts slowly, but he bites my lip and pulls, and I fall forward in a frenzy. I take his mouth savagely, recklessly, until I'm covering his body with mine.

"Fuck me," Jack says, and I pull back.

I've come this far, broken through all these boundaries, but I'm holding back on fully taking what I want. I know, beyond any doubt, that once I do this, there's no going back. Once I let up on this last barrier between us, I'll fall.

And that's it, right there.

I'll fall.

I'm a forty-eight-year-old man, falling for a twenty-year-old fucking college student. A male student, at that. My student. Someone I'm supposed to be molding into a better football player, not my personal fuckboy. But along the way, he's become more than that. He's an obsession. The dangerous next step on this slippery slope is a four letter word that I barely ever even uttered to my wife when I was married.

"I should go." I'll take something to hold in front of me when I leave this room. Maybe none of the students in the hallways will notice the massive erection I have.

I can't even stand up straight.

"No," Jack says defiantly, following me when I stand up and blocking the door. "I know you want to fuck me. Do it. Fuck me, Coach."

He turns around, putting his hands back on the door where they were before. His ass, his perfect fucking ass—muscular and round and wanting—pushes against my groin and I groan. I swallow, fighting back the heat that pricks at the back of my eyelids. I want him so badly I'm almost in tears over it, but this can't happen.

I step away from him, anger rising at the want burning inside of me. "Jack, I–"

"Please, Bryant. I want you. I need you."

Fucking hell. For all that is fucking holy, he had to say my name like that. Pleading. *My* name. I'm not even sure that I've ever heard him say it before, but it's my undoing. I stagger forward like a drunkard, curling my body around his and trying to gain some control.

"You want me to fuck this perfect, round ass, Perry?"

"Yes, Coach."

Fuck. Fuck. *Fuck.*

"Don't you move those hands."

My cock is still wet with his cum that I was rubbing into myself, but I spread his cheeks and spit directly on his crack, watching it trickle down. I rub the wetness into his hole, pushing my fingers inside and spreading him, spitting inside before I replace my fingers with the head of my cock. After spreading large beads of my pre-cum over his hole, I push just the head inside before retracting. I'm hypnotized, fascinated by the view of my cock breaching his ass and pulling back out. But Jack gets impatient and pushes back, forcing a few inches of me in all the way. He gasps and we both still for a moment.

He's so fucking tight, his body tensed up like a piano wire. "Relax," I tell him, forcing myself to slow down when what I really want to do is drive myself home. I reach around and fist his hardening cock, squeezing the head and getting him worked up again before I start to move.

I pull almost all the way out, and then thrust back in, giving him another couple of inches. Then I do it again. And again, until I'm fully seated. He's panting. I'm sweating. I stroke his cock and roll my hips until he seems accommodated to my size.

"I thought you were going to fuck me?" He challenges, biting back a moan.

"You're a fucking brat, Perry."

Still, I give him what he so clearly wants. Letting go of his cock, I push his shoulder blades down so his face is pressed against the door and his ass is stuck out as far as it can be in his standing position. I straighten my body behind his and grip his hips, pulling all the way out before thrusting all the way back in. The breath whooshes out of him and he grunts, the sound somewhere between pleasure and pain.

Fuck, I like that.

I pull out and plunge into him again, harder this time, picking up speed until he's all but bouncing off my dick and hitting the door with each thrust. He's moaning and grunting and crying out as my cock hits against his prostate, and I can feel the way his asshole clenches, telling me how close he is to coming again.

"Fuck, yes," I growl, driving into him relentlessly, spurred on by the sound of my skin slapping against his.

Shit. The music has stopped. I don't know how long the only sounds in the room have been my pelvis slapping against his ass, his face rocking against the door, or his rhythmic grunts. But I can't fucking stop, my hips moving of their own accord as I chase a release that will damn me for eternity.

Jack jerks against me and I wrap my hand around his mouth, muffling his screams as his cum paints the door.

"Fuck," I grunt into his shoulder, biting down into his skin to muffle the sounds of my own pleasure, emptying myself into Jack as his tight ass milks me for every stream of cum.

I'm so fucked.

CHAPTER 21–JACK

It's been five days since I've seen him.

After fucking me senseless the other night, I pointed out that he shouldn't leave until we knew that everyone in the dorm had gone to bed. If anyone caught him leaving, especially after the sounds that had come from my room in the silence that followed the music being shut off, we'd be fucked. And not in the good way that I'd just been fucked.

And *holy shit,* what a fuck it had been.

I can now say, unequivocally, that I'm probably gay.

It's never been something I've questioned or considered, and I'm pretty sure I'm attracted to women in general, but I have never had my world rocked like that before.

It hurt, at first. A burning stretch that was both delicious and excruciating, but then once my body relaxed around him, I relished in the fullness and the way his cock was hitting against that crazy pleasure spot inside of me. I think I might have lost consciousness. Wave after wave of nothing but pure, unadulterated pleasure rocked through my body, with each thrust of Bryant Nicks' long, thick cock. As I came down from the stars, the pulsing of his cock, shooting his hot cum inside my ass, was heady enough to make me keep orgasming until I was nothing but a trembling mass.

I fell asleep with him wrapped around my back, overthinking what the heavy, satiated feeling in my chest might mean.

He didn't kiss me when he left, and I felt like a fucking pussy for being disappointed by it. He only slipped out of bed, pulled on his clothes, and looked back at me with a terrifying expression, like he regretted every second. It hurt, and that pissed me off. I moped around for the first two days of not hearing from him, acting like a fucking girl that got jilted by a bad date.

After a couple more days, I've finally come to my senses again. This is nothing more than sex, and that's all I ever wanted it to be about. I was just exhausted, still sick. Now I've mostly recovered from my flu and the soreness from the hit I took—*all* the hits I took—has worn off. I'd be lying if I didn't admit to myself that I wouldn't mind my ass being sore again. There's something about sitting gingerly that sends a little jolt of pleasure through me, like a reminder of how fucking good it felt.

"Perry! Welcome back!"

A few of the guys hold out their hands for high fives and fist bumps as I walk through the locker room. There's no game today, but we're scrimmaging to work out some new plays. I haven't been in to work out or practice all week while I was recovering. I'm technically not supposed to come back until cleared by Coach Nicks, but he's not answering my calls or texts and I'm tired of waiting by the phone like a teenage girl waiting for an invitation to prom.

He sucked my dick and fucked me against my dorm room door—I don't think there's too much he can say or do to me that could prevent me from doing whatever the fuck I want at this point.

Coach Sanders comes in and gives us a five-minute warning to get our asses out on the field to start warm-ups. When we get out there, I don't see Nicks anywhere. Throughout the whole practice, I'm running about a beat behind. No one says anything, because I still don't miss a pass, and my slowness can easily be blamed on my illness and injury. Mostly, I'm just distracted. *Where is he?*

When Coach Sanders finally calls for us to hit the showers, I decide to just ask.

"He's been out most of the week," he explains. "Has the flu, apparently."

My cheeks heat, and I'm thankful for the helmet covering most of my face.

"You looked good out there, Perry. Does this mean we'll have you back for next week's game?"

"Yes, sir."

He nods approvingly and makes some small talk about gaps in the opposing team's defensive line on the way back to the locker room.

I stay late, deciding to spend some time in the gym before I head out. Even after only being out a week, I feel like a limp noodle, but I suppose that could be from the flu and not just the forced break. I'm feeling much better, but I know it'll take me more than a week to be back to my old self. I mix a packet of the Vitamin C powder that Coach left in my bag into my water and start towards the cafeteria. The soup tastes nothing like what he made for me. It's overly salty and has a distinct canned taste, but I still fill a to-go bowl full of it, and another with crisp veggies from the salad bar.

After knocking three times, I figure he's ignoring me. I try texting, and calling, and video calling. Finally, I make a last-ditch attempt with a text.

> JP: Open the door or I'll make sure the neighbors know I'm here.

To prove a point, I beat on the door and yell, "Hey Coach, you in there!?" just loud enough to make sure he knows I'm serious, but not loud enough to wake the neighborhood.

He opens the door and glares at me. His nose is red, and his usually close-cropped hair is disheveled. He was clearly in bed. I should feel bad about that, but I don't.

"What are you doing here, Jack?"

I hold up my offerings. "I heard you were sick. You look like shit, by the way. And this cafeteria soup tastes like shit, but I put some hot sauce in it, which helped a little. And I got you some salad to wash it down." I'm rambling as I push myself past him and into his house, heading towards the kitchen to make him a bowl of crappy soup.

"What are you doing here?" he repeats, and he even sounds tired.

"Why didn't you tell me you were sick? I thought you were just ignoring me." I cringe as the words come out of my mouth. I sound exactly like a needy girlfriend. "You took care of me. I owe you," I say, trying to cover.

He watches me with a bored expression. "I can take care of myself."

"So could I, but that didn't stop you. Just returning the favor."

"Okay, well. Thanks. Bye."

Seriously?

I give him a cocky grin and sit down next to the seat where I've placed his soup and gesture to it. I'm not going anywhere.

He rolls his eyes and sits down, wincing when he takes a sip of the soup.

"Yeah, I know. But it's better than dry protein bars."

"Is it?" He takes a few bites of the soup before turning to the salad, which he mostly finishes. I pretend to play with my phone, but I watch him eat every bite, focusing

181

on the way his Adam's apple bobs when he swallows. He notices me watching him and shakes his head, pushing away the food. "Alright, thanks for dinner, I guess. I'm going back to bed now."

I shake my head. "Not done returning my favors," I say, getting to my knees.

He doesn't push his seat back or turn towards me when I reach for his lap. Instead, he runs his hand over his face before leaning forward and resting his forehead in his hands.

"Go home, Jack."

"I distinctly remember feeling much better after getting my dick sucked. It's worth a try."

"Go. Home."

I stand and cross my arms, fully aware that I probably look like a petulant child, but I don't care. I'm annoyed at the way he's been ignoring me. "Why?"

He looks up at me with cold eyes, his expression hard and blank. "What happened Monday..."

"You're going to say that it can't or won't happen again, but that's bullshit. You keep going back and forth, but this will you, won't you shit is getting old. You want me, and I want you. It's as simple as that."

"If we got caught..."

"We won't. We'll be careful."

"I don't want you getting the wrong idea, either."

"Wrong idea about what?"

"I'm too old for you."

"This isn't a relationship, this is an exchange. A diversion until the season ends."

I'm not sure why my stomach clenches when I notice the look of relief on his face. He nods, almost begrudgingly, and I roll my eyes. He narrows his, and I laugh.

"Alright, old man. Pull your cock out so you can get back to your nap."

Coach Nicks comes back to practice a few days later, just in time to run us through our new plays and to push us through torturous workouts every night. He says Sanders was too easy on us. He's probably right.

The burn in my muscles makes my dick hard, and as usual, I stay behind to work out until everyone has showered and left. Coach's office door is ajar and his light is still on when I enter the locker room. I drop my clothes on the floor, a trail of breadcrumbs leading to the sauna. It takes about ten minutes before he comes in, just long enough for me to think he might not show.

He drops his towel the moment he walks in, standing there in all of his muscled glory. His whole body is thick with muscle. A thin layer of dark hair covers his chest and leads down to the very large, very proud, appendage jutting out between his legs. He palms it, running his hand up the length and pressing it against his hard stomach so I can see that bulging vein that makes my mouth water. Opening my towel, I let my erection free, stroking it as I watch his hand move over his cock.

"On your knees, Perry." It's clear by his tone that he hasn't come to play around, and it sends a delicious shiver over my heated skin.

The ground is hard and wet from the steam as I drop to my knees in front of him, waiting expectantly. I know exactly what he wants me to do, but I like to hear him tell me.

"Open," he says, running his fingers over my jaw. I comply, sucking in a breath of humid air as his thick cock pushes into my mouth. "Suck," he says, and I wrap my lips around the head, sucking and swirling my tongue around the tip until he starts to move deeper into my mouth.

He doesn't fuck my face the way he normally does, hard and fast and brutal. Instead, he grips my hair and guides me up and down his shaft, languidly, like he's savoring the feeling of my mouth on him. However gentle he's being, he's still large, stretching out my mouth so I can't suck in the spit that escapes and pools on the floor beneath us. I look up at him beneath my lashes, and he pumps farther into my throat. I've gotten more conditioned to having him all the way down my throat, so I don't gag, only work my throat to try and swallow around him, which makes him groan. Then he lifts his hands away from my head, leaning back against the wall with his hands behind his neck, my cue to take over and do it my way.

I bring my hands up, using one to cup and tug on his big, heavy balls. The other wraps around his base, stroking and squeezing while I hollow out my cheeks and bob on his big cock. I chance another glance upwards, watching him watch me with his mouth parted slightly.

"You love my fucking cock," he says, almost in awe. I hum around his cock in appreciation. Gay or not, I *do* love his fucking cock. I love the way it looks, the way it tastes, the way it feels.

The more I think about how much I love his cock, and all the things I love about it, like the thick vein that I'm currently caressing with my thumb, the more enthusiastically I suck and fondle him. "Fuck," he hisses, and pulls back. I look up, wiping drool from my mouth, unsure why he made me stop.

"Go bend over the bench, put your hands on the top platform," he says, bending over to pick something up near his discarded towel.

My heart beats with two kinds of anticipation, relishing the promise of both pain and pleasure. It took days for my ass to not be sore the first time he took me, and I've missed the soreness ever since it subsided. I place my knees on the bench and bend over the back, bracing my hands against the top.

Nicks moves behind me, trailing a hand down my right

side. He bends forward and licks up my spine, licking the sweat and moisture from the steam. A splash of liquid falls down my crack before he places a small bottle of lube on the top platform next to me. Whether he put it there for my benefit, I'm not sure, but knowing that he thought ahead to bring lube makes my chest flutter. The thought of him standing in line at a store to buy the lube gives me an entirely different thrill, one that goes straight to my straining cock.

He massages and squeezes my ass, spreading the cheeks and teasing his fingers down my crack, spreading the warm, slippery liquid. He pushes one, then two thick fingers inside me and I groan.

"This ass is so fucking needy," he murmurs, so quietly that I'm not sure I'm meant to hear it. My face flushes, and once again, I war with myself over the indignity of being his plaything, but the persistent ache and desire overpower any embarrassment I feel. He's right, I am fucking needy. Needy for his fingers, his hands on me, his cock filling me up.

My moment of hesitation has me wanting to skip the playfulness and get down to business. I push back against his fingers, demanding more, but he stops me with a loud smack across my ass.

"I'm in charge here, fuckboy."

"You learn some hip new slang, old man?" I say sarcastically, my abs clenching as the sting of the hit dissipates into warmth. My cock twitches and leaks with need and anticipation.

"Brat," he mutters.

"Yeah, what are you going to do about it?" I challenge, pushing back on him again.

There's very little warning before he's thrusting into me, filling me to the hilt in one hard push.

"Fuck!"

It hurts. The slickness of the lube helps him slide in, but the stretch is too much, the intensity of being so full is overwhelming. The ring of muscle that holds my ass shut burns, and I'm not sure it'll ever recover. I hiss out a breath as he begins to move, not giving me more than a second to adjust, complain, or get away. He grips my hips and plows into me in long, hard strokes that shoot sharp pains through my lower body.

"Baby bulldog wants to fight? Then fight me, Jack. Try it," he grunts. I cry out, but don't protest or tell him to stop. Instead of fighting, I push myself back on him, thrust for thrust, relishing the pain. Daring him to do his worst.

It doesn't take long before the pain mingles with spine tingling pleasure as his cock hits against my prostate. My asshole relaxes and adjusts to the onslaught, and then all I know is pleasure. My skin, near feverish with the heat of the sauna, breaks out into goosebumps and my chest seizes, the humidity making it even harder to draw breath.

My short breaths are coming out in pants and moans and pathetic little cries. For a moment, I remind myself of Millie and the sounds she made as I bent her over her father's desk.

I push back the thoughts of being the girl in this scenario and focus on the sounds of his balls slapping against my ass. My hands are gripping the top of the bench, knuckles white, trying to hold off my climax. But it's coming.

"Bryant..." I use his first name, and it comes out like a prayer. But I refuse to beg.

"You want to come, baby bulldog?"

"Fuck. Yes!"

He thrusts into me faster, still not telling me when. The sounds of him fucking me echo through the hot, hazy room, my moans getting louder as I get closer to not being able to hold back. It's coming. I'm coming, whether he tells me to or not.

Bryant reaches around and squeezes the base of my dick, hard, as his thrusts get jerky and he lets out a shaky breath. He slows, and I can feel the heat of his cum inside my ass. It leaks out a little when he pulls out. He's still holding onto the base of my dick, preventing the orgasm that was just about to wash over me. It's painful, an all over body fullness that concentrates in my balls.

"Stand up," he demands gruffly. He's standing too close for me to step down to the floor, and he pushes against the back of my thighs, letting me know he wants me to stand on the bench. "Bend all the way over," he says, and I flatten my chest against the top of the bench. I'm too far gone to think about what he's doing, only thinking about my impending orgasm and how I can please him so he'll let me come.

He lets go of my cock, my climax effectively controlled for now, and puts both hands on my ass. He spreads my cheeks and whistles before he lets go and steps back.

"Stay."

He doesn't say another word, picking up his towel and leaving the sauna. I wait, warring between patience and indignant exasperation. I like when he tells me what to do, but I also hate it in equal measure. *How does that work?*

It's only a couple of minutes before he comes back in, but it feels longer. I don't move, but the longer I stand here like this, exposed and waiting, humiliation starts to creep in.

Then I hear the click of a camera.

"The fuck?" I move to stand, but Bryant steps up on the bench next to me. He places a hand on my back, holding me down, as he curls over my body and shows me his phone. On the screen is a closeup of my ass. My hole is stretched and gaping, red from the assault, and there is a thick trickle of white leaking out, dripping onto my swollen looking balls.

His breath tickles against the shell of my ear, sending a fresh rush of blood straight to my aching balls. "Look at that," he says, his voice a low rasp. "Look at my cum pouring out of your perfect little fuckboy asshole." A full body shiver wrenches over me. He lays the phone just under my face and reaches down. "I was going to make you wait, but you followed instructions like such a good boy, and this picture pleases me." His hand, big and slick with steam, sweat, and cum, wraps around my cock. He pumps me with slow strokes, murmuring dirty, humiliating words that drive me wild with need. My hips buck into his grip, and I cry out when his other hand cradles my aching balls, gently tugging and massaging them.

"I'm going to save this picture, and whenever you try to pull your baby bulldog bullshit, I'm going to pull it out and remind you that you're nothing more than my toy to play with. You catch the ball when I tell you to, you run as fast as I tell you to, and you take my big cock when and how I tell you to. Isn't that right, Jack?" I'm assuming this is all rhetorical, because I'm past the point of being capable of speech.

Wrong. He squeezes me again and I almost sob like a fucking baby. "Yes, Coach!"

"Good boy," he says, and then his gravelly voice murmurs the words I've been waiting to hear all fucking week. "Come for me, Jack."

CHAPTER 22–BRYANT

The bus is loaded and I'm reminded why I don't typically ride with the players when we travel. Their rowdy asses are loud, like the bus is full of a bunch of middle schoolers rather than grown ass men.

"Calm the fuck down, you Jackals!" I yell. As usual, they laugh at the way I use our mascot as a pun, but they do calm down. Some, at least.

"Surprised you're riding with the team," Tuck Sanders observes, sitting across from me and stretching out his legs. He and I are taking advantage of the extra room our bus has, since only the first-string players are riding with us. We have four charter buses just for the team, and another three buses for the band and cheerleaders, plus a big box truck for equipment. It's a big production.

"I have some work I need to do, thought I'd make use of the downtime." It's a ten-hour drive to Manhattan, Kansas. Plenty of time to catch up on some emails and letters I've been sending out to the NFL scouts I know.

Riding on the bus will give me plenty of time to work on all of it, leaving me more time to rest when we make it to our hotel.

I've sent out a few videos of game footage, and people are starting to show a lot of interest in Jack. Some of them found out about his antics at his last school, so I've had to assure them and show proof of his complete change in attitude since coming to Groveton. I have leaned heavily on letting them know that, while Jack's behavior was inexcusable, it wasn't without reason; citing the lack of charges brought against him and his old coach's propensity for being an asshole with an ego bigger than the state of Texas.

I might have also sent a few emails back and forth with Tim Worth, not-so-casually letting him know that his threats to ruin Jack are not only baseless, but that if he tried anything, I'd ruin him after finding out the truth of what happened with his nephew and daughter. I might have given him the impression that I had proof that his nephew tried to drug his daughter, so if he tried to turn around and press charges against Jack, he'd be publicly shamed for his abysmal parenting choices. The promise of scandal and the might of the Groveton legal team have him pretty well in hand, and I'm confident he'll have nothing but good things to say when interviewed about his former player.

I haven't told Jack about any of my exchanges with his former coach. For some reason, it feels awkward admitting how much I've gone overboard in securing his future.

My eyes cut to Jack, stretched out in the very back

corner of the bus. He picked the short straw and has to sit across from the small bathroom, but gets the benefit of not having to share a seat, so he has more room to stretch out. The seat in front of him is just an open space, made to fit a wheelchair, so he's a bit cut off from the bustle and conversation with the rest of the team.

He catches my eye and winks. I frown, because what if someone saw him, but no one is paying attention. They're all laughing and discussing some party they went to the other night. A party Jack apparently missed because he was still recovering, but I happen to know that it's because he was at my house. That was the night he brought me soup and a blow job, which, consequently, did make me feel better. That was the night that I decided not to fight this thing.

It's just like he said, a diversion. *We'll be discreet.*

I'm starting to nod off when my phone buzzes with a text from Jack. He's sent me a link to download something, but with no explanation of what it is. I look up. Jack meets my eyes with a mischievous glint in his own. The bus is dark and quiet, and most everyone is asleep or watching a movie. Tuck is snoring across from me. My phone buzzes again.

> JP: Download it.
>
> BN: What is it?
>
> JP: The reason I decided sitting next to the shitter was worth picking the short straw.

He sat there on purpose? Now I'm intrigued.

The app turns out to be some kind of remote control. I download without reading what it's for, so it takes me a minute to figure out what it is. There's a control for intensity and different pulses. What...

I chance a glance back at Jack, who licks his lips before putting something in his mouth. He wets it and holds it up, without an ounce of fear that someone other than me might look back. It's too dark for me to see exactly what he has. My phone buzzes, a video call coming through. I put earbuds in before accepting it. Jack's face is illuminated for a moment, but then the screen is dark. I look across the bus to see him fumbling under a blanket. What the fuck is he up to?

The screen illuminates again. Jack has the flashlight on under the blanket, and he's pulling his shorts down. His big cock is hard, and I think for a moment that he's going to jerk off into the camera like we've done before. Instead, he holds the phone at an odd angle, pulling one of his knees up so I'm looking at his balls and asshole. My cock jumps, and I scramble to pull my jacket over my lap to hide my erection.

Then Jack holds an object up to the camera. It's only a few inches long and tapered. It takes far too long for my brain to catch up with what I'm seeing, only realizing what it is when he angles the camera so I can watch him slowly push the plug into his asshole.

Fucking hell.

Once it's all the way in, the bottom of it flush with his ass, I notice that there's a blinking light just before the call disconnects and I'm looking down at the remote control again.

Oh, holy fuck.

> JP: It's nowhere near as big as you, but it vibrates ;)
>
> BN: No.
>
> JP: Come on. Live a little.
>
> JP: I'll be quiet, I promise.
>
> JP: Make me cum, Coach.

I stare at the phone, frozen, for I don't know how long. My cock is throbbing with the possibilities of what I can do to him without even touching him.

He coughs audibly when I turn the plug on.

> BN: …
>
> JP: My bad, you caught me off guard.
>
> JP: Fuck, it feels good, Coach.
>
> JP: More, please.

I turn up the intensity just a tad and set it to a slow, intermittent pulse. My eyes glance over the seats at him. He's sitting sideways in the seat with his head resting back against the window, covertly biting his fist in a way that looks casual, but I know better.

> BN: What does it feel like?
>
> JP: Good. Pressure. I'm fucking hard as a rock.

BN: Show me.

A moment later, a picture appears on my screen. The lighting of the flash under the darkness of the blanket makes his cock look pale, but even bigger than usual. He sends me another picture of his hand wrapped around the head of his cock, liquid seeping from the slit. My mouth waters. I change the pattern of the pulse, three short bursts and then a longer burst.

JP: Fuck.

BN: You like that?

JP: Not as much as I like your fat cock inside me.

I nearly groan out loud, and reposition myself so I'm leaning back in the corner, with my knee up on the seat to hide my movements. I have to at least reposition my cock before I blow a load in my pants. I turn up the intensity on the plug.

JP: Fuck, I'm going to cum.

Shit, me too. Fuck. *What am I going to do with this?*

I glance back at him again, and aside from the pained look and sheen of sweat on his face, it looks like he could be sleeping. The bus is quiet. The few that are still awake are focused on the screens in front of them, or their phones. The bathroom door opens, and Grant Gipson walks out. He doesn't look around at all, heading right back to his seat, leaning back, and pulling his hat down over his eyes.

I'm so stupid.

Pulling my impossibly hard cock against my stomach, I hike my waistband up higher to keep it contained and yank my hoodie down to cover the unmistakable bulge.

With a crushing grip on my phone, I stand and make my way, slowly and cautiously, to the back of the bus.

Not one person so much as looks up to acknowledge me on my way back towards the bathroom, nor does anyone notice that I bypass the bathroom and stop in front of Jack's seat. Standing casually with my back to the rest of the bus, I lean on the seat and pull out my dick at the same time that Jack pulls the blanket away, showing me his trembling, leaking cock. With one hand, I turn up the intensity of the butt plug to high, while my other hand aims my cock, directing the spray of my cum onto Jack's lap. With a choked gasp, his cock erupts at the same time, splashing against his stomach and lap.

I watch him while I play with the control, moving the intensity up and down while he jerks his cock and pants. I'm certain that if anyone looked back here, they'd either think Jack was hurt or they would definitely guess what's really happening. But I can't take my eyes off him, fascinated by the way he keeps going, spasming even after he's run out of cum.

"God. Please. Stop," he chokes out. I take pity on him, but only because of the likelihood of him drawing attention.

"You should know better than to play with me," I say, tucking my cock back in my pants before closing myself into the tiny bathroom. My head is spinning, like I might have an anxiety attack. *What the fuck am I doing?*

I don't look back at Jack when I leave the restroom to walk back to my seat. Sleep comes easily after the intense release, and I nap the rest of the drive.

CHAPTER 23–JACK

By the time we reach the hotel, I'm bouncing out of my seat. I need to stretch my legs and run around to get some of this energy out. Most of all, I need to shower.

It's pretty late already, and our game is at 11:30 tomorrow morning. But most of us napped, and we're all starving. There's a chain restaurant across the parking lot from the hotel that is still open for another hour, so everyone plans to throw their stuff in their rooms and walk over to get food before calling it a night. I rush through a quick sponge bath and change of clothes, because I'm a mess. There's dried cum all over my torso and thighs, and my shirt got soaked. I wiped most of it away with the small blanket that the bus provided. I feel bad about shoving it in the trash before we cleared off the bus.

I wonder if the bus driver will know what those white stains on the back seat are, or figure out why he's completely out of the shitty, thin paper towels they stock the tiny bathroom with. My hoodie covered the damage to my shirt, but there are streaks on my shorts. Clearly, that got out of hand in a way I wasn't ready for. I hadn't anticipated coming that hard, or that I wouldn't be able to stop, since Bryant had the control and he's a sadistic bastard. I also didn't think that he would get out of his seat, march purposefully down to the back of the bus, and fucking cum on me before walking away like nothing happened.

Fuck. That man.

The guys are rowdy as hell in the restaurant, which turns out to be a buffet style place called Sirloin Stockade. I'm pretty sure we clean them out of whatever food they had left, and no matter how neatly we stack the plates we use, there is still a mess when we leave. The waitresses seem to be entertained by us, though, and I'm not surprised when I overhear a couple of the guys inviting them to sneak into their hotel rooms tonight. We make it worth all their time, because not only do the coaches pay for our meals with a gratuity added, but most of the guys throw some money on the table, so they get a hefty extra tip.

I have a little too much fun enjoying an ice cream cone on the walk back to the hotel, because I know that he's watching. Turns out, he's not the only one.

"Damn, Jack. You lick that cone like I wish Grant's mom would lick my cock," Alex jokes.

I tense for a moment, a small amount of fear flashing through me, but everyone's laughing at Grant chasing Alex across the parking lot, not paying any attention to my small panic attack. I get myself together in time for a comeback, knowing that the one way to throw someone off your tracks is to not be afraid of it. If I call him names or get upset, it'll only stand out. This is just how guys play.

So when Alex looks back at me, I jokingly wink at him and shove the whole cone in my mouth. Alex groans dramatically, setting off another fit of laughter from the guys around us. By the time we're back at the hotel, everyone is laughing about something that one of the rookies did on their bus, but I'm not listening. I'm busy planning.

At the front desk, I make a point to flirt with the hostess, and she gives us access to the indoor pool, which is normally closed after ten, if we promise to behave. The way she's winking when she says it tells me she's expecting me to come see her while my buddies are swimming, but she's not likely to see me again.

I'm sharing a room with one of the defensive ends, a quiet guy named Mike. He seems cool enough, but doesn't talk much. That suits me just fine. I'm busy thinking about how I'm going to sneak out and make it down the hall to the room I saw Bryant has to himself. When Mike grabs some swim trunks and asks why I'm not getting ready, I brush him off.

"Nah, man. I'm tired as fuck, and I didn't bring swim trunks. I might pop down later to talk to the redhead, though," I say with a wink.

After he leaves, I take a quick shower and mess up my blankets before looking to see if the coast is clear. If Mike comes back while I'm gone, I'll just say I got restless and went for a walk. I don't plan to be gone long, though.

I walk quickly and quietly down the hall in nothing but a pair of black sleep pants. My cock is already half hard and pressing against the thin fabric. I find myself flexing as I knock on the door, and I stop before I embarrass myself. *What the fuck is wrong with me?*

When the door opens, his eyes widen. Not with excitement, but with fear.

"What the fuck are you doing, Jack?"

"I dunno. What the fuck are you doing?" I sarcastically parrot back, grabbing my bulge for good measure.

His phone rings, and he backs into the room to answer it. I take the opportunity to come in and close the door behind me, even though he's shaking his head furiously and waving me out, mouthing, "No, get out!" I ignore him and drop my pants, because I know he can't resist this dick, and he fucking owes me after the cum bath he gave me on the bus.

"Yeah, alright. See you in a minute," he says into the phone, looking at me pointedly.

He hangs up and slams his phone down. "You have to get out of here, right fucking now."

"Why—" There's a knock at the door.

Fuck. It's too fucking late now.

Bryant looks panicked. "One sec," he calls as we scramble for a place to hide. I open the closet door, but it's too small and already has a large suitcase in there.. He waves me away from the bathroom, because what if they need to use it? There isn't enough space under the bed. The only place left for me to go is out on the balcony, which is where he pushes me before closing and locking the fucking door.

There's only one problem: I'm butt fucking naked, and it's fucking freezing outside. I scrunch down and hug my knees, listening closely to whoever's visiting him at this time of night. Don't they know he's old and needs his beauty sleep?

My humor isn't enough to keep me warm, and it doesn't take long before I'm shivering. I peek through a small gap in the glass door and see Bryant let Coach Sanders in.

"Come on in, Tuck," he says, holding the door open and looking calm, like nothing out of sorts is happening. Why the fuck is he letting him in? *Tell him to fuck off!*

I watch as Bryant kicks my pants under the bed before Sanders sees them, walking in and sitting down at the small table. They're having some kind of fucking meeting? *Now?*

"It's cold as hell in here, man," Sanders says as he takes a seat.

"Yeah, sorry. The heat was hiked up too high while we were at dinner. I opened the door to air it out a bit," he explains smoothly. Impressive cover, I'll give him that.

"I guess that's why you're so sweaty then," Sanders says, gesturing to the sheen of sweat coating his forehead.

"I guess."

"You alright?"

"Eh, bit of a headache, if I'm being honest. Let's make this quick and get some rest before tomorrow."

They go over what sounds like last-minute defense strategies while my balls shrivel in the cold. I miss a lot of what they're saying, the chattering of my teeth and the increasingly biting wind drowning out most of their conversation. I overhear something about a press conference, and then Sanders is finally standing up to leave.

"You sure you want to let him go after this season?" I hear Sanders ask, and my ears perk up. "He's damn good. If we talk him into staying through senior year, we could have two winning seasons in a row."

Bryant makes a non-committal noise. "You picked a good one, I'll give you that. But I made promises to get him here, and I don't know that I could keep him interested long enough to keep his shit together through another season."

Wrong.

My eyes widen at the realization that as much as I've been looking forward to my big break, I probably would stay—if he asked me to. The sudden epiphany makes me worry for myself. It's proof that this is more than just a diversion, more than just getting my rocks off.

I've got a big, gay crush on my football coach.

"You've done well with him, though. He's doing better than I ever expected, that's for sure. Not one incident, not one complaint. Whatever you're doing is working."

I wish I could see Bryant's face right now. A grin

stretches across my frozen cheeks as I chuckle at the thoughts that must be running through his mind.

Finally, Sanders leaves, but Bryant doesn't come and get me right away. By the time he opens the door and pulls me in, closing the curtains behind me, he's livid, and so am I.

We speak at the same time.

"Are you crazy? What the fuck do you think you're doing?"

"Why the fuck would you leave me out there so long?!"

I pull a blanket off his bed and wrap it around me, still shivering, while we stare each other down and fume.

"You said you could be discreet," he says, too calmly.

"Says the guy that frosted me on a bus full of people," I counter.

He narrows his eyes. "You asked for it."

"You're goddamn right I did," I retort, trying to force a smirk.

A moment passes before Bryant sighs loudly and walks over to me. "Are you alright?"

"I'm afraid you might have to work harder to edge me now that my balls have taken up permanent residence inside my body."

He rolls his eyes. "Come on." He pulls me to the bathroom and starts the shower, dropping the blanket to the floor. He rubs my shoulders while the water heats up, trying to warm my skin with the friction. "Fuck, you're freezing."

"I was outside. Naked. In November. In fucking Kansas," I say through my chattering teeth.

"Get in before it gets too hot. We'll work up to it." I want to question his use of 'we', but he pulls his hoodie and shirt over his body before stepping out of his pants, underwear, and socks. He shuffles me into the standing shower, bracing me against him beneath the spray. It's hot against my skin, despite there being no steam. As the water heats and the room starts to fog, my skin thaws, and I relax against his chest.

"Better?" He asks, his lips against my neck. I nod, unable to find words, and silently thankful that my dick still works, seeing as it's finally noticed Bryant's proximity. "I should punish you for being so reckless," he says, and his teeth rake against the tendon between my neck and shoulder. I moan, low and throaty. There's nothing cold about me anymore. I'm *thoroughly* heated through.

Despite being one hundred percent on board with his brand of punishment, I point out, "I got left outside in the freezing cold for an hour."

"It was ten minutes, fifteen tops."

"Felt like an hour."

He hums noncommittally. It's a sound he makes often around me, and it makes my dick harden in anticipation of what he might do next.

Although it's happened once before, I don't think I'll ever get used to the sight of Bryant Nicks getting down on his knees for me. He swallows my cock in one move, and I let out a string of curses, slapping my hand against the tile to steady myself.

With the water hitting my chest and rolling down my body, Bryant sputters, gags, and takes loud breaths as he works my cock. The sounds only make it better, sloppier, nastier. The fingers he pushes into my ass have me crying out.

"I'm close," I say, expecting him to edge me like he normally does. Instead, he doubles his efforts, adding a third finger, fondling my balls, and hollowing out his cheeks to suck me harder. "Ahh, fuck!" I cry out as I spasm and spurt, pumping cum into Bryant's willing mouth.

He pops off my cock with his mouth full of cum, but distracts me by spinning me around and pressing my hands to the wall. Fuck yeah, I know what he's telling me. But he says it anyway.

"Hold on, baby," he says after he spits the load of my cum down my ass crack. He rubs his length into the mess, lubing up his cock before slamming into me.

This time I'm ready for him, stretched and pliant from his fingers. My back arches as I bend as low as I can, trying to give him that perfect angle. His thrusts are fast and hard, and the way he pounds against my prostate has me ready to blow again. I'm going to need to hydrate at the rate I'm going today. He growls and I think he's coming, but he doesn't stop, he just slows. He keeps himself inside me, pulling my back against his chest and pressing me against the shower wall. He rolls his hips, still thrusting into me with slow, rolling movements that make my eyes roll back in my head.

"One more. Come for me, Jack," he demands, and I fucking whimper like a baby when he wraps his hand around my cock and pumps another orgasm out of me.

When he pulls out of me, it's all I can do to hold myself upright. We get washed up and Bryant hands me a towel. Outside the bathroom, he hands me a bottle of water, which I gulp down gratefully. The silence is awkward, and I know I need to leave, even though everything in me desperately wants to stay. I want to lie next to him and watch tv or talk, to fall asleep with his warmth wrapped around me, and then wake him up by choking on his morning wood. I know I can't, though. That's what *a boyfriend* would do. It would not only undermine what this is about, it would also put us at risk of getting caught. This is not a relationship, and I'm not his boyfriend.

Apparently, the guys are all coming back from their swim, because it's loud in the hallway.

"I'll have to stay until they settle in," I say awkwardly.

He gestures to the bed and turns the television on. We lay against the pillows in just our towels, watching ESPN. He gives me a proud look when I'm mentioned during a college football recap, and the announcer says I'm the number one player to watch, and they even launch into some of my future prospects. My chest swells with both pride and sadness, because although my future will be starting soon, something else will be ending at the same time.

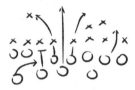

CHAPTER 24–BRYANT

I wake up to a warm body pressed against mine and groan. He smells different. The hotel shampoo washes out the spicy scent of his normal body wash, but underneath the generic floral smell, it's still Jack, and he still smells like sex to me.

My blood rushes, and my cock stirs. We must have fallen asleep watching TV, which isn't good, but it's still dark outside, which means we aren't in trouble. Yet.

It also means I can wake him up however I want before I send him on his way.

My mouth trails over his shoulder blade, across his strong bicep, and up his neck, enjoying the opportunity to explore him while he's asleep. He starts to stir, and I bite his ear.

"Time to wake up, baby," I grumble in his ear, my voice raspy from sleep.

That's the second time I've unintentionally called him

that, but he doesn't react, so maybe he doesn't notice? What he does notice is my cock pressing against his bare ass cheek, and he rolls his hips back into it. I press my cock between his cheeks and he groans.

I abandon his warmth for only a moment, reaching over to my bag that I left on the bedside table. Either I'm stupid or I'm just prepared, because at the last minute, I threw a bottle of lube into my small duffel. I'll examine the repercussions of that later. For now, I fill my palm with the slippery liquid and coat my cock in it before teasing Jack's puckered hole and pushing in with two fingers. I take my time stretching and fingering him until he's definitely awake and edging towards release.

He looks over his shoulder with sleepy eyes, barely visible in the beam of light from a nearby streetlamp, and kisses me. It's slow, and tender, and deep, tugging on my heartstrings as fiercely as it does my cock. In the bare hours of the morning, I can still pretend to be half asleep, and for a short time, I can allow myself to relax and just enjoy whatever this is between us. He said it— this is a diversion, something to keep things interesting. Only right now, it feels like more.

Instead of bending him over and dominating him the way I normally do, I want to look at him and kiss him. Rolling him on his back and settling myself between his legs, I angle his hips with a pillow and press my cock inside, entering him slowly. He moans as his body stretches to accommodate me. When I'm buried to the hilt, I roll my hips, luxuriating in the feel of the tight ring of muscle squeezing me.

I move in slow, languid thrusts, and Jack pulls me

against his body. Our kiss starts deep and gentle, but it grows hungrier and more fevered as we move against each other. My abs contract with the ache in my chest, and then my balls as his little moans and breathy pants turn me on, but I hold off, wanting him to come first.

With a quick bite and lick of his bottom lip, I set myself up on my knees and grip the hard muscle of his thighs, pressing his knees up against his chest.

"Fuck," he pants, as I roll my hips into him again, building to a quicker pace as I begin to lose control. My hands tighten on his thighs, digging into his skin, marking him the way I want to mark his entire body. I watch, in the growing light of early morning, as my cock slides in and out of him.

"Fuck," I agree, echoing him as my eyes threaten to roll back in my head. The sight of my cock disappearing inside of him is making it hard to hold myself together. I grit my teeth. "Touch yourself, Jack. I want to watch you cum."

With a breathy moan, he reaches down and grabs his cock, pumping in time with my thrusts.

"That's right baby, come for me. Come all over me."

I'm not able to hold off until he's done. The squeeze of his ass around my cock, and the way his eyes lock on mine, glazed over with pleasure as his orgasm overtakes him—it's all too much. My orgasm hits me out of nowhere, and I come with a shout, thrusting deep. He spasms around me, my name on his lips almost setting me off a second time.

"Yes, Bryant, Fuuuuck," he cries, and his cum splashes

against my abs and his.

I close the distance between our bodies, pressing our torsos together and smearing the cum between us as I take his mouth. I keep moving inside him until my dick softens, smiling at the way Jack whimpers when I pull out of him.

We lay there for a few minutes, staring at each other, touching, kissing. Until it's too light outside to ignore. I send Jack to the shower without me in case it gets one or both of us started again. I'm like a fucking teenager around him, insatiable.

The team plays their best game ever, and we dominate the Wildcats in their own territory. Jack is on fire, and I can't wait to watch the recaps of this game later. While Jack was simply on the radar before he came to Groveton, he's now at the top of everyone's list for the most talked about player this season. He's a fucking star, and even though he's only a junior, there is no doubt in anyone's mind that he is destined for greatness. There's a lot of talk about whether he'll announce his draft intentions or stay to finish his degree. I should talk to him about making an official statement, and maybe we can hold a small press conference after our next home game.

I think about what Tuck said, and spend a little too much time imagining how I could persuade him to stay here longer. For the team.

For me.

The players are pumped after the game, and they're still jazzed up by the time they get on the bus. Coach Sanders decides to ride with the cheer bus, probably because he's been chatting up their coach for the last six months, which leaves his seat open. The team decides Jack should get the honor of sitting up front instead of near the bathroom, so he ends up across from me in Tuck's seat. I try not to stare at him the whole time while he shoots the shit with Alex and Francisco, who are sitting behind him. We stop for barbeque in Oklahoma, and after lunch, everyone's pretty tired and docile. One of the guys hooks up another movie, and they all zone out on some action flick I haven't seen.

I pull out my phone, hiding it behind the screen of my laptop.

> BN: You played well today.
>
> JP: Thanks. Started with a good morning ;)
>
> BN: That it did.
>
> JP: What are you doing tonight?

I don't answer, but my eyes flick up to his in confusion.

> BN: Sitting on a bus, mostly.
>
> JP: I mean after.
>
> BN: It'll be after 3AM by the time we get back to campus.

> JP: And everyone will be too tired to notice
> if I follow you home.

My lips quirk.

> BN: Aren't you tired?
>
> JP: Are you? Do I need to give you a break,
> old man?

I look up at him with a raised eyebrow.

> BN: Is there any part of the last 48 hours
> that makes you think I can't keep up?

Jack lets out a throaty laugh, which gets the attention of the guys behind him.

"Yo, lover-boy, who you texting?" Alex says, reaching to grab his phone.

I nearly have a heart attack, but Jack thankfully swats his hand away and tucks it into his back pocket. "Dude, mind your business!" He laughs it off, but I can see the tension in his shoulders.

"That's what he said to Mike this morning, when he walked in after five, freshly showered and a love-struck grin on his face. Won't tell anyone where he was."

Jack's eyes cut over to where I'm sitting, and I know he knows I'm listening, but I am still their coach, so technically I should be picking up on the conversation and punishing him for being out of his room after hours. Instead, I'm pretending to be engrossed in some footage of the game, turning up the volume slightly so they don't think I'm listening.

"Apparently, you've never gotten your dick sucked in the shower. You should try it."

Alex leans forward excitedly, lowering his voice, but not enough to actually keep his conversation private. "Dude... Was it that receptionist? She came looking for you at the pool."

"She was fucking hot," Francisco says. "Unbuttoned the top few buttons of her blouse and had her lipstick right and everything, looking for you."

"I guess she found you, then?" Alex says, nudging Jack's shoulder.

He shrugs, like he isn't the type to kiss and tell. Which, if I hadn't seen video proof otherwise, I might even believe him. I look up, because it's not as if I could ignore that much noise, but they're not paying me any mind. A satisfied grin crosses over his face and the guys around him cheer.

Alex goads him more. "How was it?"

"Best fucking blow job I've ever gotten," he says, and I can feel his eyes on me when the other guys start to talk amongst themselves.

My lips quirk and I surreptitiously lick my lips.

My phone buzzes.

> JP: Don't do that.
> BN: Don't do what?
> JP: You fucking know.
> BN: Clear your messages. And pictures.

I put my phone away and try not to stare at Jack the entire way home.

CHAPTER 25–JACK

"Can I come over tonight?" I ask quietly, wiping my mouth.

We're eating lunch in Bryant's office, with the door open, and we're supposed to be going over footage from the last two games. I kicked ass in those games, though, so I'm less interested in watching the players run around, and more interested in getting in the coach's pants.

"We have a job to do," he admonishes. "We're getting too distracted."

Next, he's going to tell me we need to pull back. Or that I need to start making the rounds at parties again, even though I think he hates the idea of me even pretending to be with someone else as much as I do. I've never been in a relationship serious enough to consider monogamy, and while I know this isn't a relationship, I legitimately don't *want* to be with anyone else.

No one else gets my dick up the way he does. No one else hurts and heals me at the same time. No one else can bring me to the fucking brink every time he touches me.

He won't deny me. I wait for the nod, and the look that says, *you know the drill*. On the days he lets me come over, I make sure to wait until late enough that the neighbors aren't likely to be outside. Considering they're all teachers or staff members that live on campus during the school year, the last thing we need is someone noticing how often I come and go. Once or twice can be brushed off as a friendly meeting, but lately I've been over there more often than not.

I just don't want to be in my cramped, empty dorm. I'd prefer to be sleeping with his warm, hard body pressed against mine, but as much as I like waking up in the morning with my dick in his mouth, or his fingers in my ass in the middle of the night, the last thing we need is the school counselor next door noticing how frequently his favorite player comes to visit him. So I dress in dark clothes and quietly slip in through the back door that he leaves unlocked for me.

"Can we focus now?" He asks, and I grin, because annoying him is high up on my list of favorite pastimes.

"Jackson needs to bend his knees," I say, pointing to the paused footage. "He needs to be ready before he needs to be ready, if you know what I mean. The rest of it is just being tired. Defensive line doesn't have enough stamina."

"Tuck!" Bryant calls out to the defensive coach as he's walking by.

Coach Sanders sticks his head in the office. "What's up?"

"We're going over game footage. Perry says you need to beef up their workout routine."

I narrow my eyes at him for throwing me under the bus, but we're all here for the same thing. To get better. To win. Hopefully, Coach Sanders doesn't mind hearing a constructive criticism about his defensive line from a student.

"Specifically running, sprints, that sort of thing. And agility drills. They lift enough. Jackson's a fucking tank, but if he could run and move with any flexibility, he'd be unstoppable."

To his credit, Sanders doesn't balk at the recommendation at all. "I agree," he says. "I've been letting them focus on lifting when it comes to workouts, but we could definitely mix it up. I'll push it. Thanks," he says jovially, shooting a grin at Bryant before making his way back to his office.

"What was that look about?" I ask.

"He likes being right."

"Didn't seem to mind the suggestion, although it would have sounded better coming from you."

"I knew he wouldn't mind."

My nose scrunches. I'm confused.

"He was right about you. Tuck was the one that found you and suggested I bring you on the team. We're having our best season yet, you're getting along great in class, and now you're in here helping me try to improve the team as a whole."

I squirm under the praise. "Yeah, well, you have a good incentive plan."

He knows what I'm talking about, but he enjoys pretending to be a hardass. "Two hours of workouts every day, even after practice?"

I smirk and look him in right in the eye. "A good workout never hurt anyone."

Bryant actually bites his lip and rakes his hand over his face. I know he's thinking about my new favorite game. The one where I wear the remote-control butt plug during workouts, and he torments me while I see how many reps I can get in before I'm trembling putty in his hands. The last time ended with him bending me over the bench press and fucking me hard and fast, right there where anyone could find us.

"Go somewhere else for a while."

"Why?"

"Because I want to bend you over this desk and fuck you until you cry."

"Do it." I'm not embarrassed about the sounds I make when he's lighting my body up, because I know how much he likes it.

"Jack..."

"Bryant," I say, mimicking his tone.

"You can't call me that at work."

"Yes, Coach," I say, winking, because I know that's almost worse for him.

"Don't you have a tutoring session or something?"

Fuck, I almost forgot.

"Yeah, that's what I thought," he says, getting up to usher me out. My eyes flash down to the half-chub he's sporting. "Stop looking," he says, exasperated.

"It misses me," I say, making an exaggerated sad face.

"It'll see you later, and it'll make you wish you didn't fucking test me."

"Yeah, yeah." There's no one in the hall, so I get bold. Pushing him back against the open door and pressing my lips against his in a short, passionate kiss, nipping his lip as I rush out of his office. He all but growls, which makes me giddy.

Movement behind me has me turning around to see Aniyah, stepping out of the gym just as I'm stepping out of the coach's office. My first thought is whether she saw us, but she keeps her head down and runs off the other way. She is definitely not supposed to be in the football gym or near the locker room. I wonder what she was up to, but she seemed too preoccupied to see anything on her rush out the door. I'll try to follow up with her later.

I race all the way to the library, arriving three minutes late. The pretty librarian waves at me, but I notice she looks troubled. I don't know her well enough to ask her how she's doing or what's going on with her, so I give her a wave back and keep walking to the study table we have reserved.

"Sorry, Luke, I got caught up. But," I say, before he can chastise me for wasting his time, "I have this to show you." I pass him my most recent American Lit exam, that I got an eighty-nine on.

"No shit?"

"No shit. I didn't cheat or anything," I add, because I know he wants to ask. I'm not offended by it, it's a fair question.

"You're doing really well, Jack. I wasn't sure about you the first couple of times we met, but you're doing the damn thing. I honestly don't even know what to work on, since Thanksgiving break is coming up."

I nod, knowing we didn't really need this session, but I also know he gets paid for the time spent tutoring, and I wanted to show him the test. I've also been trying to get comfortable around him because I have questions, but I'm too much of a fucking pussy to come right out and ask them. Maybe this will be my opportunity.

"Are you going home for the break?" He nods. "You live far?"

"I'm from Austin, so it's just like three and a half hours."

"Oh, easy drive then," I say dumbly.

He nods again, and the silence is awkward.

"What about you?" He asks, throwing me a proverbial bone.

"Nah, too far, and my mom's going to be working, anyway. I'm going to stay around here, I think."

"I heard the big cafeteria in the Student Union does a Thanksgiving dinner; with a turkey and everything, whole shebang."

"Good to know," I say, looking at my feet.

"Whatever it is, just ask," Luke says, perceptive as ever.

His new darker rimmed glasses make him look like even more of a nerd than his vintage Nintendo t-shirt, but it works for him. He's a decent-looking dude. My eyes roam over his body, wondering if he's as skinny as he looks. Even when I was on the thinner side, I still had definition. I bet he does, too. But nothing about him interests me, or calls to me the way Bryant does.

I've been... experimenting. Not trying anything with anyone, just looking at other men, their bodies, trying to gauge if they were attractive to me. There's a lot of free-swinging dicks in the locker room, but not once have I caught sight of one and had my mouth water the way it does when I see *him*. I tried to watch gay porn, and while it did get me hard, I think it's only because it was giving me ideas for things to try with Bryant, not because it was two dudes going at each other. It was the same when I watched straight porn and lesbian porn.

"Did you have a question, or are you trying to read my mind?" Luke asks pointedly.

I huff out a breath, shaking my head. I don't even know how to start, and it's too awkward.

"Uh... Is your boyfriend going home with you?"

"What?"

"You know, for Thanksgiving? Is your boyfriend going?"

"Oh. No, he's going back home to see his own family. We're going to meet up after, though."

"Oh. Cool."

The silence is agony. I shuffle in my seat.

"Listen, we can just tell them we stayed the whole time —"

"Jack," Luke levels me with a glare. "Just fucking ask. You've had something to say to me for months. Just come out with it. I promise I won't get offended, and if it crosses a line, I'll say so. Just get it off your chest already."

I swallow, suddenly feeling sweaty. My voice shakes, and I stutter, barely getting out, "I, uh, I—"

"Fuck, Jack." He leans forward. "Are you trying to come out right now?" he whispers, kind concern etched on his features.

"What? No! Of course not. Why would you—" I stop myself. Protesting this much is way too fucking obvious, and I don't want him to think I'm a homophobe. "Not that there's anything wrong with being gay—"

"You're just not."

"Right."

"Right."

"But..." I hesitate again, unsure how to ask what I want. "Can you, you know, be gay for just one person? But not anyone else?"

Luke's eyebrow raises, and he looks at me pensively. "Yeah, I guess."

"What do you mean, you guess?"

"I just mean that, well, sexuality is a spectrum, a wide array, really. There's no one way to be. It's not as black and white as that. Some people are only attracted to one gender, or people who present as one gender. Others are maybe attracted to everyone under the sun. And for some it's not about the parts they carry, it's more about who the person is."

"What's that called?"

"You mean like a label?"

"Yeah—what do you call it when you like the person, despite the parts?"

"Despite the parts is a funny way to put it," he says, scrunching his brow. "And I'm not one hundred percent sure, because there are a lot of nuances. It could be pansexual, where gender or identity isn't a factor. Or maybe demisexual, which is where you only feel sexual attraction to someone that you form a close emotional relationship with."

I shake my head. "That's not it."

I definitely felt some attraction, some magnetic pull, towards Bryant Nicks that first night I saw him standing in the shadows of the warehouse I was working at. Then, that first day I arrived at the sports complex, I didn't even know it was him I was looking at, but I couldn't help but admire the body of the man I was watching. If I'm being honest, it's only been in the last month or so that I've really felt an emotional connection. Before that, it was easier to deny that I might be some form of gay, because it was only physical. I can't deny how happy I feel in his presence, and I find myself wanting to do even the most mundane activities with him. Like sitting at the table in the morning, eating fucking cardboard for breakfast, watching him read the paper with his goddamned reading glasses perched on his nose. It's something more now.

"What about... *heteroflexible*?"

Luke laughs, which annoys me. I'm being perfectly fucking serious right now. "What the hell is that?"

"I don't know. I found it on Google," I say defensively.

"You've thought a lot about this, yeah?" He frames it as a question, but it's more of a statement, so I don't reply. I only sit there, frozen. Wishing I hadn't said anything because he's not being very fucking helpful and I feel like I've exposed myself, like everything could come crashing down because I opened my fat mouth in a moment of insecurity. "Look, I'm gay. I like dudes. Not all of them necessarily, but I don't think of women that way at all. But that doesn't make me an expert. And honestly, if you ask me, all these labels do nothing but separate us from what we all are—human. It doesn't really matter if you're gay or maybe just not entirely straight. What matters is that you find someone that makes you happy."

I want to tell him that I wasn't talking about me, that this was all rhetorical, or that I was asking for a friend. But I know he'll know the truth, whether he calls me on it or just smiles and nods.

"Jack," he says, and I pull my eyes away from the lines in

the wood grain of the table. "I'm here if you ever want to talk it out, and I promise I'd never say anything to anyone. Your secret is safe with me."

"Thanks," I mutter, but I don't look at him or try to talk anymore. Instead, I grab my books and make a hasty exit.

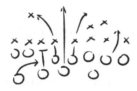

CHAPTER 26–BRYANT

He looks peaceful when he sleeps, and it makes me wonder what troubles him during the day. Whenever he's not in the throes of a play, running down the field at top speed, or getting the breath fucked out of him, Jack's brow is creased in concentration.

Maybe that's why this arrangement has worked so well for him.

Maybe what he needed was someone or something to get him out of his head, to refocus his energy. For all the talent and brains he obviously has, he was getting in far too much trouble not to ruin his chances. Talent like his isn't easy to come by, but it seems effortless for him. Knowing what I do about his record, not just the official stuff, but his sealed juvenile records, I can't help but feel like he was purposefully trying to stall his future. He really seems to want it, so why would he do that to himself?

I'm afraid that if I let him go, if I release him into the

wilds of the NFL, that he'll end up back in that same situation. How will he fare without the guidance? I can't keep him on the hook, texting me all day every day, for the rest of his life, and it's not like an arrangement like this could last long distance.

The dean called me again yesterday. Both he and Tuck think I should convince him to stay for another year. Why would he, though, if greatness is within reach? Everyone wants him; I've made sure that all the right eyes are on him. I've patched up what I can about the public relations nightmare that the incident with his last school was, and thankfully the coach never leaked the footage, because of course it was his daughter in the video and everyone knows it. Having read through the report of how thoroughly Jack fucked up that other player, putting him in the hospital for over a week, and physical therapy for years, ruining his chances to play football ever again, I know it could have not only ruined all of his prospects, but landed him in prison. He'd told me that he'd beat the kid up, and why he did it. At the time, I'd found it admirable, and maybe a part of me still does. But he'd downplayed how brutal the attack was.

It's hard to imagine the peaceful man lying next to me could have done that to someone.

Jack shifts in his sleep, and the sheet slips lower down his back, exposing more of his ass. That fucking ass could make me forget a lot of things. Kind of like how I forget how to sleep for more than a couple of hours straight when he's in my bed, because I'm acutely aware of that perfect ass lying next to me. It's become a new hobby of mine to see how far I can go before he wakes up, and he hasn't complained about waking up to his cock getting sucked.

I groan and turn my body towards him, lightly brushing my fingers down his spine. His deep breaths don't change, but the little hairs on his skin stand up. I brush my fingertips around his round ass cheeks, palming and lightly squeezing, feeling the muscle. He still doesn't wake up, even when my fingers find their way between his cheeks, rubbing along the crack of his ass. I shift down the bed, laying at the bottom between his legs, and pulling the sheet fully off him. I palm both of his cheeks, spreading him open to me. I look my fill and lean forward to lick along his crack, pressing my tongue against the puckered hole that takes my cock so well. He tastes like cum–my cum–and that fills me with an unnerving level of contentment. I push my index finger inside, just to the first joint, and his breath hitches before evening out again. I push farther in, slowly, until I reach my knuckle, and then pull out again. I toy with his ass like this for a while, edging him until he's close to waking, until my cock is so hard it hurts. I remove my finger from his ass and grab the bottle of lube that now lives on my bedside table. Laying down next to him, curled over his back, I coat my fingers in the slippery liquid, then push two fingers inside. He groans as I pump my fingers, spreading the lube inside and stretching the tight ring. He's getting better at taking me with less prep, but I think he also likes it when it hurts a little. Deviant that I am, I enjoy hurting him.

He gives a sleepy whimper when I pull my fingers out so I can spread lube over my cock. I've never tried fucking him when he's asleep, but I like how pliant his body is right now, how responsive he is to me, even in his dreams. I want him to wake up, though. I want him to wake up to my big cock spearing his ass, making him mine, taking him whenever and however I want.

I brace my arm next to his shoulder and wrap my hand around his wrist, dragging it above his head. Using my free hand, I line myself up, then hold his hip and press slowly into him, holding my breath. He lets out a throaty moan when I'm fully seated, and I stay still like this for a while, cuddled up against his back with his ass swallowing my cock. My lips press against the back of his neck, and I inhale his scent before I start to move.

Slowly, gently, I rock my hips into him. My mouth pressed against the back of his shoulder. He moans and pushes back against me.

"Good, you're awake," I murmur against his neck.

I thrust harder, and he cries out. Fuck, I love the noises he makes. I wouldn't say this to him, because I think he worries about his manliness being the bottom in this twisted relationship of ours, but the sounds he makes are far sexier than any I've heard from any woman. They're throaty and raspy—animalistic—when I can get him to whimper or make a higher sound than a low moan, I know I've hit a good spot. I live for those moments that he's crying out my name and trembling, begging me to let him cum.

Wrapping one leg around his hips, I turn our bodies so I'm fully on top of him, his face pressed into the mattress. His ass cheeks are pressed together, adding extra pressure to my cock as I slide it in and out of him. He tries to push up, but I hold him down. He might be younger and faster, but I'm a hell of a lot bigger and stronger.

I brace one hand against the back of his neck, the other on his hip, and I pound him into the mattress until he's screaming my name, muffled into the mattress. I pull out quickly before I come, and flip him over before straddling him again. He's breathing heavily and trembling, and his cock is starting to spurt. I press our cocks together and stroke us both to completion, both of us erupting in my hand and splashing down on his abs.

"Fuck," he breathes, as I collapse against his side and pull him against my chest.

"Shhh," I whisper. "Sleep."

"I was sleeping," he whispers, laughing drowsily.

"Stay with me for Thanksgiving break," I say, digging myself a little deeper into this hole. It's just a couple of days. We have our last regular season game a few days after Thanksgiving, and then we'll be in playoffs mode.

"Okay."

"Great game tonight, Coach." The dean reaches down from his seat to shake my hand.

"Thank you, sir. They played well."

"Exceptionally well, especially that Jack Perry fellow. You talk him into sticking around yet?"

"Not just yet, sir. We've been in full training mode. We've got a bowl game coming up, and then the playoffs."

"Hmmm. Well, you've got most of the month off before the bowl game. I expect you'll find time." The dean gives me a leering grin that turns my stomach. I know that grin. It means he'll find a way to get what he wants, whatever it takes. What he doesn't understand is that, while I don't have enough self-preservation instincts not to fight back, I won't let him try to ruin Jack's future to benefit himself.

With an understanding nod in his direction, I jog off the field behind the team. The dean can threaten me all he wants. It won't change a thing. I can placate him for now and we'll win this championship. And then after, with the way I've turned this team around, I'm sure I won't have a problem finding another coaching position.

Jack is waiting just outside the tunnel entrance to the locker rooms.

"What was that about?"

"Nothing important," I say, because that's the truth of it. I won't be asking him to stay. I've already started the process of doing exactly what I promised Jack I would. Neither Jack or the dean know it , but there were some rather important scouts in the crowd tonight. "Before you head into the locker room, I have a surprise for you," I say, steering him down the hall instead of following the rest of the team.

"Oh, really?" He says suggestively, but I nip that shit in the bud.

"Down, boy," I mutter under my breath. "Not that kind of surprise."

He has the nerve to bark a little, and I smile despite myself. "Would you fucking behave?" I scold him, but it's not convincing to either of us. I love playful Jack.

I love *Jack*.

Fuck.

I lead him to one of the conference rooms on the opposite side of the sports complex, where three of the most important contacts he will meet are waiting to shake his hand and fawn over him.

I lead him to his future... away from me.

CHAPTER 27–JACK

I leave the sports complex feeling dazed, but also excited. I'm fucking pumped.

This is really happening. I just shook hands with scouts that represent some big teams, including my first hopeful—The Carolina Panthers. They've got the first-round draft pick this year, and they're fucking interested in me. *Really* interested. As in six-point-nine million dollars a year and a thirty fucking million dollar signing bonus interested.

Thirty. Fucking. Million.

I know I come off cocky, but something about actually achieving my dreams, and having the finish line so fucking close, has made me realize I didn't think I'd ever *actually* get here.

I'm a bastard child from the boonies, the off-shoot of a drunken one-night stand with a rando my mother never even got the name of. I'd have been aborted if she'd realized she was pregnant before she was too far along. Considering she drank well into her sixth month, and I was born prematurely, I'm probably lucky to be alive and as healthy as I am.

I'm a nobody from nowhere. Who really would have expected me to amount to anything? My anger at the world and chronic boredom have always gotten me in trouble, and I've always been too stupid to get out of my own way. For all my big dreams about playing in the Superdome someday, I never honestly believed I'd make it. I assumed I'd end up working at the power plant, or moving stolen electronics from warehouse to warehouse. That's just what the future held for me. It was predetermined.

Until Groveton. Until Bryant.

I might have had some talent when I walked through the gates of the Groveton campus, and I certainly had just enough bravado to make things interesting. But he was the one that stripped me bare and rebuilt me into a fucking machine. And now I feel like I can take on the world.

I dial Bryant and listen to it ring. His voicemail picks up.

"Hey, it's me. Are you home right now? You skipped out too fast for me to tell you how it went, and right now, I'm desperate to swallow your cock. Unlock the back door. I'm coming over."

I'm halfway to his house when I get a text.

> BN: Not home. You need to be at the party, anyway.
>
> BN: Glad it went well, though.

JP: I'd rather celebrate with you.

JP: *eyebrow waggle GIF*

BN: Go to the party. You'll be missed.

I sigh audibly and throw my head back. I really don't want to go to the party. My teammates are great and all, and we're getting along well, but I don't feel like I can be myself around them. Whenever I'm around my so-called friends, all I'm thinking is that I wish Bryant were there. There's really only one person I want to celebrate with, but he's not in the mood. I do know one thing he's always in the mood for, though...

JP: What the fuck am I supposed to do with this thing?

Looking around me to make sure I'm alone, I turn on the flash and snap a quick picture of my junk and send it to him.

BN: I'm sure you can find plenty of willing orifices. Wear a condom.

Are you fucking kidding me? I can't tell if he's joking. I know we keep saying this isn't a relationship, and we specifically set boundaries for me to mess around with girls just to keep the heat off us, but I haven't actually been able to follow through. I simply have no interest.

I can't help but feel a little hurt and angry.

JP: So it's like that, is it?

BN: It's what it needs to be. Have fun, party safely, sleep in tomorrow. I'll see you Monday at practice and you can tell me all about the meeting.

God fucking damnit.

I turn around and head the other way, feeling like my bubble has burst. I don't want to go to the party, but I also don't want to go home alone and stare at the walls while trying to block out the sounds of my entire dorm throwing an all-night rager. Now that everyone knows where my dorm room is, I get far too many unexpected visitors knocking on my door at all hours of the night. Bryant is right that I can find plenty of willing orifices for my cock, feels like everywhere I turn girls are all but bending over and presenting themselves to me. I literally had a girl—a complete fucking stranger —follow me into the men's showers and aggressively try to suck my dick. I've been showering at the sports complex or Bryant's house exclusively since then.

Getting my dick sucked, or more, is no problem. Which reminds me of the one thing I know will get under Bryant's skin. He wants to pretend like he's okay with me getting with anyone and everyone I want? I'll show him just how bothered he can be. He wants to tell me to wear a condom like it's no big deal? I'll show him.

The party is in full swing by the time I arrive. Beer and liquor are flowing, and there is the heavy scent of weed in the air. The music is loud and thumping, but the cheer that goes up when I walk in is even louder. As I pass through the house, people shake my hand, hug me, or thump me on the shoulders. Most of these people I don't even know. I wave and greet my teammates, most of whom are blitzed already.

Lane is in the kitchen when I pass through and he comes over to pull me into a one-handed bro hug and thumps me on the back.

"Dude, is it true you met with some big scouts tonight?!"

Despite my reckless mood, my grin is real. "Yeah, man. It's nuts."

"Not as nuts as it's gonna get tonight! Alex! Pour my man a shot!"

He doesn't pour me just any shot. When I turn around, I see three half-naked girls laying on the table. Alex pours tequila into all three of their belly buttons, hands me a salt shaker, and sticks a lime in the last girl's mouth. I pull my phone out to record the action, and Aniyah appears at my side.

"Here, let me," she says, taking my phone from me so I can get a better camera angle.

"I'll make sure to thank you later," I say, giving her a kiss on the cheek and a purposely suggestive grin. I won't, but she'll be too drunk to remember if I did or not.

The light for the camera comes on, and I survey my options, deciding to go all in. I shake the salt on the first girl's cleavage and lick before slurping the booze out of her belly button, then move to the second, doing the same. On the third girl, I reach for the salt shaker and sprinkle it on her thigh. With a wink at the girl, who I'm pretty sure is a freshman but who cares, I lick a long line up her thigh, all the way up to her panty line, before suggestively licking and sucking the booze from her navel, then bending over her to bite and suck the lime from her mouth. She makes it even more of a show by pulling me down for a sloppy kiss once I've put the lime down.

The room erupts in leering whoops and cheers, and I spend a few minutes flirting with all three of the girls, talking about all the other things I can do with my tongue. I realize that Aniyah is no longer recording and wonder where she went with my phone. When I look around the room, I find her near the entrance to a hallway, dangling the phone and crooking her finger at me. My mouth quirks into a smirk and I excuse myself from the table, much to the loud dismay of the girls there. I mentally high five myself for my performance, knowing no one would ever suspect me of bending over for the head football coach after that.

I follow Aniyah down the hallway into a small half bath, and realize the hard part of my performance is about to begin. She doesn't seem drunk at all, so I'm not sure how I'll manage to distract her from my flaccid dick.

She pulls me into the bathroom and locks the door, and I do what's expected of me, pretending to be excited by her, pressing her against the door and kissing her. Her tongue is like a dead fish in her mouth, and I'm honestly not sure how she got my dick up before I fell for Bryant Nicks. I move my mouth down to her neck so I don't have to taste her mouth anymore. When her hand reaches for my pants, where I'm barely sporting a half-chub from the friction, I distract her by lifting her up and setting her on the sink. She opens her legs for me, and I rub her pussy through the lace of her panties. She moans and lifts my shirt.

"God, your abs are insane," she says, and her fingertips start to move lower. My brain scrambles for anything I can use.

"I don't have a condom," I say, putting a little whine into my voice like I'm suffering for it.

Her hand doesn't stop its downward descent, moving to fumble with the button on my jeans. "That's okay, I'm on the pill."

"I don't fuck without a condom," I say against her mouth, moving her hand away.

It's true, or at least it was before I started letting Bryant fuck me, but that's different. The last thing that I want is a baby mama, or an STD.

"Don't worry, baby, I'll still make you feel good." My fingers move under the edge of her panties, rubbing through the folds of her wet pussy. I don't waste time teasing her, pushing two thick fingers inside her and moving my thumb over her clit. The quicker I can get her off, the quicker I can get this over with.

Her breath comes in pants as I begin to work her over. To avoid kissing her mouth, I pull one of her breasts over her skimpy top and pull the nipple into my mouth. I suck hard and she cries out, her pussy clamping down on my fingers.

"Oh, God, Jack!" she screams, overly loud, making sure anyone in a five-foot radius of the bathroom knows what's happening in here. Luckily for her, I want them to know, too. I keep my thumb moving while she rides my hand through her orgasm. "That was so good," she purrs. "But I really want to have you in my mouth again."

I'm trying to think of a reason to protest when she says,

"You can take a video of it to watch later. I know that's what you like to do, right?"

She has no idea. The idea of catching her mouth around my cock on video has my dick perking right up, but not for the reason she thinks. It's because I know what kind of reaction I'll get out of Bryant when he sees me feeding my cock to someone else.

I start to unbutton my pants and pull out my growing erection.

"Damn," she says, eyes wide. "It's bigger than I remember. If I take a picture of it, will you text it to me?"

"Sure, whatever," I say, stroking my length to keep myself hard. "You gonna suck this?"

She doesn't seem to mind my rudeness, only grins and hands me my phone back, so I can point it at her while she ties her hair back and gets on her knees. She licks my cock like an ice cream cone, looking up at the camera through her lashes. She's acting for the camera, for me. It's all fake. Her performance is annoying me more than my own, and I can feel my dick starting to wilt. Before it does, I grab her by the ponytail and push my cock into her mouth. Her lips stretch around me, and she gags and struggles for a moment.

"Relax your throat," I tell her, repeating the exact words that Bryant once said to me, knowing it'll drive him crazy. "That's it. Just open up and let me in."

Using those words makes my cock jerk in her mouth. The memory of sucking him off in his office, of what it feels like to have his big cock hitting the back of my throat, is enough to have my balls tightening. Aniyah's amber eyes aren't close enough to his hazel ones for me to keep looking at her, though, and I close my eyes and imagine it's him sucking me instead. It's enough, and in a few more harsh pumps, I'm unloading into her mouth.

"Don't swallow," I tell her. "Let me see."

She opens her mouth, and I zoom the camera in on my cum, coating her tongue and pooling in the back of her throat.

"That's it," I say.

Once the camera is off, I'm done and ready to escape this bathroom. After she fixes her clothes and I tuck my dick back into my pants, Aniyah tries to kiss me again, but I shirk her away, pushing past her to wash my hands. I'm getting ready to open the door and make a run for it, but Aniyah sulks, clearly upset about me blowing her off now that she's blown me. I'm sure I'm coming off like a complete prick, but as long as I'm not coming off as a gay prick, I don't really care. Girls like her love that shit anyway. Why else would she keep coming back for more?

"What about my picture?" she pouts.

"What?" Oh, the dick pic. I suppose it couldn't hurt to have that floating around campus. "Fine," I mutter, rolling my eyes to the ceiling to try to keep my composure. I'm growing more impatient by the moment.

"Here, I'll do it," she says, snatching my phone. Her eyes go wide. "What is this?" she says, looking up at me, and then back at the phone with a confused look on her face.

"What?" I'm bored with this. I want to send the video so I can get punished, and then I can really get off.

"That's not your dick," she says, turning the phone to show me the picture of Bryant Nicks' erect cock. It's definitely not my dick, but it is my hand wrapped around it, which she'll be able to tell by the scar on my left thumb if I let her look long enough to notice.

"Give me that," I say, reaching for the phone back, but she holds it out of my reach.

"Why do you have a picture of some other dude's dick on your phone!" she shrieks, too loudly, and I wince. *Fuck. Fuck. Fuck.*

I scramble for an excuse, trying to remain calm. Make a joke out of it. "Ha. you'd be surprised how many weirdos send me pictures of their junk. I saved that one to show the guys. I mean, look at that fucking monster. It's bigger than mine!" I exclaim, laughing like this is nothing. Like my heart isn't beating frantically in my chest, or that my mind isn't spinning out of control with fear.

Calm down, Jack. Worst-case scenario, she tells people you have a picture of another man's dick on your phone. Make excuses, or hell, who even cares if they think it's there for a reason. As long as they don't know whose dick it is.

Then the other foot falls.

Aniyah hits play on a video. Whether she's done it by mistake or on purpose, a recording of one of the many video calls we've made over the past couple of months begins to play on the screen. One where Bryant, in all his glory, is stroking his cock and telling me how to play with myself. You can clearly see his face, watch him say my name, and hear my voice saying, "Yes, Coach," every time he gives me an instruction.

Fuck.

Aniyah's eyes are wide, watching the video with her mouth wide open, a look of shock on her face that melts into something else. Her brow furrows like she's putting puzzle pieces together.

Fuck. Fuck. Fuck.

"That day at the sports complex, you were so close together you could have been kissing. I thought I was seeing things. And at the donor brunch, he was watching you so closely. I thought it was weird, but... you're fucking each other?" Her face screws up, like she's disgusted, and she looks up at me with unbridled judgment. Suddenly, I feel small, despite being well over a foot taller and at least fifty pounds heavier.

"It's not what you think!" I blurt out, but I'm too frozen to come up with anything clever to say.

Fuck. Fuck. Fuck. Fuck. Fuck.

I've ruined both our lives because I'm a fucking idiot.

What do I do?

What the fuck do I do?

CHAPTER 28–BRYANT

Jack barges into my office, interrupting a meeting with Tuck and one of the freshman coaches.

"I need to talk to you. Now."

I sit up straighter in my seat, appalled by his tone. I know he's mad at me for putting him off last night, but disrespecting me in front of my colleagues is a step too far.

"Excuse you? This isn't a good time, Jack."

He looks straight at me. The fear and panic in his eyes cut me to my core. "We have a problem."

I hesitate, looking over to the two coaches that are watching our exchange with concern. Jack's head gives a curt shake, letting me know that this is definitely a private matter. His face is too pale, his body language too agitated to ignore.

Fuck.

I assess him from head to toe. It's clear that he hasn't slept, and I'm pretty sure those are the clothes he left in last night. I didn't lie to him when I said I wasn't home, but I also wasn't exactly busy. I was sitting in the parking lot, I watched him leave, and then followed him. I was far back enough that when he looked around before snapping a picture of his dick, he didn't even notice me. I followed him all the way to the party, and finally left when I saw him kissing a girl through the kitchen window. What could have happened between then and now to make him this upset?

My anxiety goes immediately to the worst-case scenario. He got too drunk and caused major damage to campus property. He had sex with a staff member's daughter. Or *son*, and got caught. Or maybe he beat someone senseless and put them in the hospital.

The two coaches in my office stand up. "We'll leave you to it," Tuck says. "Let me know if I can help," he tells me, his concern obvious.

Jack slams the door behind him and locks it. Then he starts pacing, rubbing his hands over his face and pulling his hair.

"I fucked up, I fucked up, I fucked up," he repeats with every stride.

"Perry!" I bark. "Sit down and tell me what the fuck happened. Whatever it is, I'll try to help you out of it. But you need to calm the fuck down."

"We're in trouble," he says. It takes me a moment to process it. We. *We're* in trouble. It's not the words, but the way he looks at me, tears welling in his eyes, that

245

breaks my heart.

"What happened?" I ask, keeping my voice controlled, forcing my words to come out low and slow.

"Aniyah got my phone at the party last night."

"And?"

I think I know what he's going to say before he says it, but I need to hear it from his mouth. What I thought could be the worst-case scenario doesn't even touch this. Because all of those things are fixable, but this...

"I think I have it handled, but you should know..."

"Fucking spit it out, Jack."

"Aniyah saw a picture and a video that were saved on my phone. Of us. One of the video chats."

"You recorded it? Fuck! Jack, what were you thinking?!"

"I wasn't! Obviously. Or I was letting my dick think for me. I'm—"

I stand up forcefully, sending my chair crashing into the wall behind me, and tipping over. Now I'm the one pacing.

Fuck!

"How could you do this?"

"I'm sorry, I–"

"Sorry doesn't cut it, Jack. I'm out of a job if this gets out, and you can kiss your draft prospects goodbye."

"It might not come to that. I think I've got a handle on it, but—"

"But *what*, Jack!?"

"I don't know. I don't exactly trust her."

The pulse in my temple throbs so violently I feel like it could burst at any moment. My heartbeat is pushing nausea up my throat, and it burns like bad reflux. I'm so dizzy that I need to sit down, but I knocked my chair over. I walk around and sit in one of the chairs in front of the desk instead, putting my head in my hands, trying to steady the spinning room.

"Exactly how are you handling this?" I ask, my voice as calm as I can make it.

"Bribery," he says. "I told her about the signing bonus that the scouts all but promised me."

"And that was enough?" I ask, skeptically.

He makes an uncomfortable face, and I know that isn't the end of this. "There's a bit more to it, but I'm handling it."

I want to ask, but I also don't want to know. I need to know, though. Jack's phone pings and his face blanches. He swipes a hand through his hair.

"I, uh, I have to go, do a little damage control. But I've got it under control, okay? I just needed you to know. And..." he takes a shuttered breath. "I'm so sorry."

I can't even look at him.

"Bryant—" I give him a warning look, because he doesn't get to call me that. Not here. Not now. Maybe not ever again.

He drops to his knees in front of me, looking up at me

with pleading eyes. "Please don't—"

His phone pings again, twice in quick succession.

"You should go," I say flatly, not looking him in the eye.

As he's leaving my office, he stops and turns around one last time.

"I'm sorry."

For a while after he leaves, I'm completely rooted to my seat. My mind is racing, but none of my thoughts are clear or useful.

The most overwhelming of all my thoughts is that I'll never have Jack again, not in the way I want him. If we somehow escape this unscathed, it will be even more unsafe to continue the way we have. We'll be walking on eggshells for the rest of the year, or perhaps even longer. Who's to say if she'll keep her end of whatever bargain Jack made with her? And what kind of deal could he have made, anyway?

Whatever the case, I'm fucked.

Possibly fucked out of a job. Fucked out of a reputation that could keep me from getting another job. And worst of all, fucked out of a relationship that was beginning to mean something to me. To mean everything to me.

"Hey, Bryant. Is everything okay?"

I blink up at Tuck, who stares down at me with concern. How long has he been there?

"Are you alright?"

My nod is unconvincing at best, but I can't put enough words or thoughts together to make any excuses.

"I, uh... I need to go," I say. Without any further explanation, I stand up and grab my keys and walk out.

I don't remember the drive back to my house, or coming inside. I don't remember opening the bottle of Macallan and pouring a glass. I don't remember what the first sip tastes like, or when I started drinking directly out of the bottle.

The only thing my brain can process is Jack's face when he shows up on my doorstep and sees me holding a half empty bottle of scotch.

CHAPTER 29–JACK

Jesus.

He looks terrible. Swaying on his feet, with a depressed, glazed look in his eyes. Somehow, the past eight hours have aged him. He looks older, and broken.

His strong shoulders are sloped forward, arms drooping at his sides. His head hangs, and his posture is slouched. A half empty bottle of booze hangs loosely from his right hand.

I did this to him.

"Bryant," I whisper, my chest aching to see him this way.

He stumbles, and I lunge forward to catch him under one arm, walking him back into the house and into the small sitting room. The leather creaks when he sits down, evidence of how little this furniture has ever been used.

"I'm so sorry," I tell him, keeping my distance because I

know he's upset with me. I'm upset with myself, and I wouldn't want anything to do with me if I were him.

I've undermined everything we've accomplished, both of our entire futures so close to getting flushed down the drain. All over a stupid, boneheaded decision made with the wrong head.

What's that expression—*young, dumb, and full of cum?*

I'm not sure dumb cuts it.

"I'm so sorry," I repeat.

"It's my fault," Bryant says, slurring a little. "I shouldn't have started this. It was inappropriate, and I pushed you into–"

"You didn't push me into anything," I say quickly, crouching down in front of him. I want to reach out to him, to touch him, console him, hold him and tell him everything is going to be okay. But I can't. "If anything, I pushed you."

"Pushed me to the edge of sanity," he says, laughing humorously as he takes a swig from the bottle.

"Right back at ya, big guy." I take the bottle from him, raise it to my mouth, and take a hefty gulp. It burns all the way down my throat and chest, warmth settling heavily in my stomach. One more swallow, and then I put the bottle on the coffee table, out of his reach.

We're silent for a long time. I snuck over here to explain what I've done to protect us—to protect him—to let him know how it has to be from now on. But he's in no condition to hear it, and he won't remember it if I tried.

I'm worried about him in this state. He's so unlike himself. So out of control. So defeated.

He notices me looking at him. "It's been almost seven years since I've had a drink. I thought it would help me feel less—care less. But it seems to be doing the opposite." His hazel eyes are dark, bloodshot. Full of pain. "It never was a reliable crutch."

"Why did you open it?" It's a stupid question.

"Might as well go for gold." He takes a deep breath, his head hanging low with the exhale. " I'd rather not be sober when they come to escort me off campus, anyway. Maybe they'll think I was drunk the whole time instead of...of..."

I bristle. "Instead of what?"

He shrugs and hangs his head.

"Better to be a drunk loser than a faggot?" He winces at my harsh words, brushing his hand over his face and shaking his head. "What then?" My voice raises.

I feel bad for the state he's in, but I can't help but feel something about the way he's trying to use his drunkenness to explain away what's happened between us this year. It makes my chest ache more than it already does. I don't want every sacrifice I'm about to make to be for nothing.

"Better to be a drunk loser than let everyone see how broken I am. I'm broken, Jack. So broken that I tried to break you." Once he starts talking, he doesn't stop. It's like he's picked a scab and now the wound won't stop bleeding. "That first night I saw you, I knew that something was off... with me. I looked at you like I'd never looked at a player before. Like I'd never looked at anyone before. I told myself it was just excitement over the team's prospects. But it was more. It was darker than that. Deeper. In the time between that night and you showing up here, I dove into everything I could find about you. Where you came from, what your hobbies were, your social interactions, your record, everything. I rationalized that I was helping you, making sure to keep Worth off your back and give you a fighting chance at a better future."

He stops and looks at me with pleading eyes. "If this goes public, he'll realize that some of my threats were baseless. I want you to carry on like you have video proof of that twat spiking the girl's drink. It should keep him off your back, even if he comes after me for extortion."

"Extortion?"

He shrugs again. "I did everything I said I would do, and I did my best to give you everything you wanted. But I also took something from you. I used a part of you that I had no right—"

"Bryant—"

"That's what my statement says. Officially. I wrote it up tonight when I got home. You might have to deal with the embarrassment of being violated, but if they know that I used my position of power to coerce you—"

"No!" I'm standing now, raking my hands through my hair. "Bryant, no. What the actual fuck!? You didn't coerce me. For fuck's sake, if anyone coerced anyone, it was the other way around."

"I knew better. I knew it was wrong, what I was getting you to do. You were an obsession, Jack. You are my obsession. I can't think of anything else, and the level of," he sighs heavily, "...the level of pleasure I get from hurting you, dominating you... It's not natural, Jack. I'm fucked up, and I fucked you up, and now I'm trying to do anything I can to prevent this from fucking up your future."

It's then he finally breaks. In one fluid movement, he's up, crossing over to where I sat the bottle, and grabs it. He turns the bottle up and chugs, and I watch him guzzle his poison with wide, terrified eyes, blurry with unshed tears. One swallow. Two. Three.

"Stop," I say, and pull the bottle down. "Are you trying to kill yourself?"

His eyes look away from me and another piece of my heart crumbles.

"You didn't force me to do anything I didn't want to do. After all of these months, I'm surprised you don't know better." He scoffs, because he knows I'm right. "Ain't nobody can make me do shit and you know it."

We both know that there's next to nothing and no one in the world that can get me to do anything I don't want to do. Almost. Truth is, he's the only one that could be the exception to that rule.

I take the bottle from his trembling hands and put it down, placing my hands on his shoulders, his neck, and cupping his jaw. I run my hands across his stubble and steel myself to be more vulnerable than I've ever been.

"I wanted everything, Bryant. I wanted you. I wanted this. These past months I've felt more capable, stronger, freer, than I've ever been in my life. You give me something that takes away all the heaviness and lets me see the finish line. I've loved every minute of my time with you." I can only hope he's drunk enough to overlook or at least not remember the tears slipping out of my eyes. Tears slip out of his eyes, too, but at least he has the booze to blame for his outburst.

I lean forward and capture his lips, tasting the sweet whiskey on his tongue. I don't know how to say how I'm feeling, because I'm not really sure I know what it is. I only know that something is being taken away from me that I don't want to lose. I pull back and look at him again, wanting to try to tell him...

His knees buckle, and he wraps his arms around my waist. My arms hold his head against my stomach, and I comb my fingers through his hair while he sobs.

Bryant Nicks is larger than life, and not just in the physical sense. His personality, his presence. His strength.

The sobbing man on his knees before me seems so much more human than I've ever given him credit for. He's always seemed so infallible to me, and the sight breaks me, wrenching hot tears from my own eyes. And while I know he probably thinks that breaking down and showing this part of him is a bad thing—I know I've always thought that about myself—it only endears me to him more.

When our tears are spent, and he's caught his breath, he

tries to stand but stumbles. I help him up, but when he stands up straight, he looks pale, his eyes unfocused.

"I'm going to be sick," he says.

"It's okay, it's okay. Come on, I've got you."

I escort him to the bathroom and rub his back while he vomits, all bile and rancid amber liquid. After helping him out of his clothes, I turn on the shower for him and he sits on the edge of the tub with his head in the stream of cool water for a while. I hand him his toothbrush while he's in there and then lead him to bed, tucking him in with a glass of water and some painkillers for the headache I know he's going to have when he wakes up.

"Don't leave." He says, his voice low like he didn't want to say it out loud, but couldn't help himself. It makes me grin.

"I'm not going anywhere until morning," I say, stepping out of my jeans and pulling my shirt over my head. I slip into bed behind him in just my boxer briefs, and marvel at the satiated feeling in my chest over embracing him like this. He's so large that I'm not the most effective big spoon, but pressing my ear to his back and listening to his breaths grow heavy as he falls asleep brings me a joy I can't describe.

I listen to him sleep and think about my next steps for a long time. Hours even, before I finally start to doze off.

I startle awake as Bryant shifts, rolling himself on his back and pulling me onto his chest. The bedside alarm clock says it's just after two in the morning. When I lower my head back down, Bryant is looking at me, bleary-eyed, but coherent.

"How are you feeling?" I ask, pulling back.

"Still drunk enough that I don't have a massive headache yet, but clear minded enough not to bawl like a little girl and puke again." His face twists into a sarcastic grimace.

"It wasn't that bad," I say, resting my head on his bicep so I can see his face better. The blinds are open, and the moon is bright, casting a dreamy haze over his bedroom and giving just enough light for us to see each other clearly.

"Liar," he says, and his wry grin helps take some of the pressure off my chest.

"I hear it gets harder to hold your liquor when you reach old age."

His chest shakes with silent laughter, and then he lifts his arm, causing my body to tip and roll onto him. He grabs my face and looks into my eyes before kissing me deeply. Electric flames of desire lick up my spine and buzz through my veins, and my cock grows hard against his hip. He shifts and grinds into me, letting me feel his reaction to me.

"We shouldn't..."

"Shhh," I whisper. "Don't think about it. Not tonight."

I crawl down his body, trailing my tongue and lips down his broad chest. I stop to pull his nipples into my mouth, giving them each a hard suck and a little nip before continuing down his body. My nose skims the ridges of his hard abs as I kiss each and every muscle, clenched and flexing. I silently say a prayer of thanks that I put him to bed naked, and rake my teeth over his hip bone as I grasp his hard length in my hand. His hips buck, his cock expanding and hardening before my eyes. He's fucking magnificent.

Dragging the flat of my tongue from base to tip, I wrap my mouth around him and twirl my tongue around the ridge of his cock head. He moans and presses his head into the pillow before propping himself up on the elbows to watch me. I keep eye contact as I release his cock with audible suction, and move down to lick and suck each of his heavy balls. His eyes roll back when I run my tongue over the flat spot behind his sack, so I double down there. I lift his balls with one hand, while pushing his legs out and up so I can better reach the tender flesh.

"Fuck," he says on a breath, as I lick and suck at his taint.

I tease my fingers along his ass, and he twitches in response, but doesn't protest. I don't want to take advantage of his drunkenness, but there is something I haven't gotten to try yet, and I wonder if he's relaxed enough. It seems appropriate that tonight, likely our last night together, whether either of us wants to say it out loud, that we take everything each other has to offer. That we give each other everything.

Bryant stretches, and then a bottle of lube lands beside

me.

"I can never say no to you," he says roughly, in answer to my questioning look. "And if tonight is..."

Launching myself on top of him, I cut him off with a kiss. "Don't say it."

We wrestle around on the bed, kissing passionately, fiercely, pulling at each other's limbs. We can't get close enough, can't get enough of each other. It's both desperate and tender, and intensely emotional.

I pull back to pull my boxer briefs off, and Bryant lays back against the pillows. He's propped up, spreading his legs on either side of me, giving me permission to explore and take charge.

His cock looks huge at this angle. It always looks huge, but it looks even more massive, and I'm impressed with myself that I can take him on a regular basis without it tearing me apart. I remember how sore I'd been in the beginning, and the idea of giving Bryant the same pleasure and pain makes my breath catch in my chest. I reach out and touch him, dragging my fingers up and down his cock before gathering the drops of pre-cum on the tips of my index and middle fingers. Shuffling closer, I force him to spread his legs wider for me, and then I reach between us to rub his wetness over his hole. I keep my eyes on him the entire time, watching his eyes dilate with the pressure of me pushing my fingers inside him. His ass is tight.

"Take a deep breath," I tell him, and I push my two fingers all the way inside on his exhale. He groans and his cock twitches, several more drops of fluid leaking from the tip. With my fingers deep in his ass, I lean down and stretch my lips around his big cock, taking him all the way into the back of my throat. I start to bob my head, sucking him hard but slowly, as I start to move my fingers inside him.

It takes him a few minutes to loosen up, and once he does, he's rocking his hips against me, pushing down on my fingers harder.

"Are you ready for more?" I ask him, my cock straining.

His eyes lock on mine. "I'm ready for *you*," he says, his voice low and serious.

Keeping my fingers inside him, I use my other hand to squeeze the lube on my dick, careful not to stroke myself too much, because I'm close to the edge already. I'm not sure how I'm going to do this without blowing my load the moment my dick so much as touches him.

With a deep breath, I look up at him to make sure he's sure. My gaze is locked on his, and as much as I want to see my cock push inside his ass, I can't look away from him. His expression is unlike anything I've ever seen. It's reverent, and vulnerable, and also completely sure of himself at the same time. When I press my cock into his tight hole, those feelings become my own and I can only hope he sees them reflected back in his eyes.

His ass grips my cock like a fucking vice, and it feels like it's sucking me inside his body, until I am settled flush against his body. I don't move right away, letting him accommodate to the intrusion. He wraps his arms around me, and we're kissing again. I move my hips in slow strokes, in time with the movement of our lips. I roll against him, shuddering and laying my head against his shoulder.

Something other than an orgasm is welling up inside me, and while it's just as imminent, it's a different feeling altogether. Like a taut string, or a radiant heat, ready to burst. This other thing, settled deep in my chest, is like a balloon. Except instead of popping, it swells bigger and bigger. Threatening to engulf me, cutting me off from the air around me. Suffocating me.

When I come, it hits me with a different kind of intensity. One that sends waves of euphoria over my body and inflates the balloon beneath my rib cage. My last breath catches, and I cry out Bryant's name, along with something I didn't mean to say out loud, but the balloon forced out of me in order to make room for more air.

"I love you."

I gasp, as if I can choke the words back into my body, but I can't take them back and I can't stop my hips, rutting into Bryant like some kind of animal. It feels like I come forever; my cock just keeps pulsing inside him, spurting like a fountain, filling him up with my cum. I'd stay inside him forever if I could, but Bryant moves, pushing me away and out of him.

For a moment I think he's truly pushing me away, offended or disgusted with my confession, and I wilt on the bed. But the next moment I realize, I'm on my knees and Brant is behind me, pouring cool lube down my crack and over himself. He presses himself inside me, and I pant. I just got off, but my cock still hasn't gone all the way down, and it's getting harder all over again with the pressure of him pushing himself inside me.

Being inside Bryant was fucking amazing, but this is where I belong. Taking him. I'm his outlet and he's my escape. I can't think of anything else but him when his cock is stretching me open and filling me so entirely, that I don't know where I end and he begins. And when he starts to thrust inside me, hitting that unbelievable, overwhelming spot inside me, I come undone in so many ways.

My body and my mind both feel like they're unraveling. I lose control of everything and become his entirely.

Except... I've been his since the moment he tracked me down in some shithole warehouse in South Alabama. Since the first time I saw him on that bench press. Since well before I signed a contract giving him ownership of my body.

I am his, and he is mine.

These are just the only moments that I can admit it to myself. It hurts knowing I won't feel this again, with any other person, ever.

Once I've done what needs to be done, to protect us both—but especially him—will he ever want me again? Is a long-distance relationship between two people that can't admit they're in a relationship even possible?

"Say it again," Bryant grunts, and it takes my brain too long to catch up. Say what again? He thrusts his hips into me harder, making stars dance behind my eyelids.

His arm wraps around my chest, pulling me up against his body.

"Say it again," he grumbles into my ear.

Every hair on my body stands on end.

"I love you," I gasp.

Thrusting into me at a punishing pace, Bryant reaches around and strokes my cock, hard and fast.

"Fuck! I love you! Fuuuuck—" I cry out, the heaviness inside me breaking like a dam, and cum sprays everywhere. The pillows, the wall, even the mattress, since the sheets have been pulled off the corner of it in our tussle.

My body shakes with the force of everything crashing down around me, and Bryant lowers me down onto my stomach, still inside me. He rolls his hips, his thrusts firm but slower. I feel his cock pulse inside me, the warmth of his cum filling me.

"I fucking love you, Jack," he says as he collapses on top of me.

The words are both a balm and a punch to my gut. Because this is it. Tonight is all we have.

CHAPTER 30–BRYANT

Walking out of the church basement, I check my phone for messages. None. I keep walking down the path, waving but not stopping to chat with anyone. I'm starting to recognize faces, even just in the past week. The meetings have given me something to focus on other than the lack of communication with Jack, but I don't feel like dawdling or talking to anyone else.

I didn't realize how used to his presence I'd gotten. It's not just the sex. It's sitting in my office over lunch, going over game footage; having someone to challenge me through workouts. Watching ESPN in bed.

His absence is a gaping hole, and even just after a week, I feel like I'm going crazy. The only time I see him is on the field, and other than the occasional long eye contact across the field, he barely acknowledges me.

Jack has, unsurprisingly, been nominated for the Heisman Trophy this year. We haven't been able to celebrate further than a quick clap on his shoulder when I made the announcement after practice last night. I'm not sure if I'll get a chance to talk to him on the flight to New York City for the awards banquet and announcement of the winner. I know, without a doubt, that he's going to win. I want to tell him how proud I am of him, without making it weird. I said too much the night he found me drunk. I gave away too much.

He said he loved me too, but he seems to be having an easier time moving past it.

He's been spending a lot of time with her—Aniyah. I don't know what happened between them or how he's keeping her quiet, but nothing has happened yet other than the two of them have apparently become Groveton's hottest new power couple. It has me on edge. Every moment, I'm waiting for someone to walk through my door and escort me from campus. I have nightmares about it, about press conferences and hitting rock bottom. The worst part is worrying how it will affect Jack.

I still have my statement typed up and signed. I carry it with me everywhere I go, in case today is the day.

Six feet away. That's how far he's sitting from me right now. One row up and across the aisle. *She* is closer, sitting on the aisle seat like some kind of sentry, knowing that I'd have to reach over her to get to him. Knowing how badly I just want to reach out and feel his body heat.

I'm fucking pathetic. I'm a grown ass, almost fifty-year-old man, simpering over someone less than half my age. He turns twenty-one next month. I wonder how he'll celebrate.

My neck stretches to look over the seats. All I can see from this vantage point is the top of his head. He's buzzed his hair short again. I feel like it's more proof that we're over, because I know he kept it long on top for me. So I could rake my hands through it, grip it tightly in my fist while I used his mouth for my pleasure.

"Would you like another bourbon, sir?" The flight attendant moves into the aisle next to me, blocking what little view I have and thankfully breaking me out of my inappropriate thoughts before anyone notices.

I reposition the suit jacket I have laying over my lap and nod. "One more, and then I'm cutting myself off. Thank you."

She smiles down at me, pouring a little airplane bottle of Maker's Mark over ice. Her hair and makeup are so pristine she could be a walking Barbie doll. She looks a little like my ex wife, actually. Except maybe nicer.

I've been thinking a lot about Penny. I read an article yesterday that she gave birth to her third child with my former friend and teammate, Vance Mitchells. They seem happy together, and it made me glad for her. Through all of this, I've made some big realizations. Whereas before I was filled with bitterness over her leaving me to chase the lifestyle she wanted, I would have been more miserable with her than I was alone. I now know I never actually loved her, and she obviously didn't love me.

The reason I know I didn't really love her is because I didn't know what that feeling was until now.

That terrible, painful, overwhelming gnawing inside my chest whenever I see Aniyah lean over to whisper in his ear? As mad as I was about Penny leaving me for Vance, I didn't feel this way about it.

And the way my chest fills like a hot-air balloon whenever I see him walk into a room, or out on the field, and I get to share space with him. I never felt that way about her. About anyone.

The flight attendant hands me my glass and moves up the aisle, checking on the needs of the other first-class passengers. As she clears out of the space between us, I notice Jack looking at me. His gaze drops to the glass in my hands, and then back up at my eyes. I see his concern. I'm fine, though. I haven't had more than one or two drinks here and there while out celebrating with the rest of the coaching staff, and I haven't been drinking at home at all. But he doesn't know that. Doesn't need to know.

He whispers something in Aniyah's ear and kisses her on the cheek. My stomach twists, but his eyes hold my gaze as he gets up from his seat and walks past me, presumably to the restroom. Following him would be too obvious, and despite the fact that he was just making eye contact with me for the first time in days, I didn't get the feeling he was asking me to. *Don't be pathetic, Bryant.*

The plane hits a spot of turbulence, and my hand bumps against the armrest. Bourbon splashes out of the glass and all over my hand. It isn't much, but I should probably wash my hands. I hand the glass to the flight attendant, who hurries over with napkins, and walk to the back of the plane. Not following him. Just not wanting to smell like booze when we land and meet the journalists and other bigwigs that will be waiting for us when we land.

As I'm opening the curtained area where the restrooms are, Jack is starting to make his way out. He steps back out of my way, and I go to close the curtain behind me, but he holds it open.

"She's watching," he says, but then quickly pulls back and kisses the side of my mouth. It happens so fast I could almost think I imagined it, and then he's gone, walking back down the aisle like nothing happened.

My eyes are glued to his back, confusion pulling my brows together. Then I notice the young brunette watching me watch him, a smug look on her face at the way Jack seems to be ignoring me, and I close the curtain.

Loud applause fills the room after Jack Perry is

announced as the winner of this year's Heisman Trophy Award. I watch as he stands and shakes hands with the other contenders, graciously accepting congratulations from his would-be competitors. No one is surprised, except for maybe Jack. As cocky as the bastard is, he still doesn't seem to believe the track to stardom he's on.

Before he walks up to the stage to accept the award and make his speech, he turns around and heads to where I'm sitting.

Correction. To where she is sitting. He lifts Aniyah up in a big hug and whispers something in her ear, while she stares up at him with stars in her eyes. He shakes hands with everyone sitting around us, the other coaches and random strangers. When he gets to me, he grips my hand tightly and pulls me in for a one-armed hug.

"Thank you for everything, Coach," he says loudly enough for everyone to hear. But then he lowers his voice and whispers, "I'm sorry."

After giving Aniyah one last kiss on her cheek, he runs up to the stage, where everyone starts applauding again.

"Thank you so much for this great honor. I know I already wasted some of your time by going back to kiss my girl and thank my coach, but I have to give credit where it's due. Coach Bryant Nicks is the one that gave me the chance that changed everything for me. I'm a nobody from the backwoods of Alabama, and he and the coaches at Groveton saw something in me. I'll never forget that," he says, and looks me in the eye with what looks like sadness. Or pain. "This month is about to be the biggest month of my life so far. Thanks to all of you, I was chosen to win this prestigious award, I'm playing in the Texas Bowl in Houston a few weeks from now, the Groveton Jackals are on our way to a national championship... and I'll be spending the holidays with the most beautiful girl on my arm, who's told me she'll follow me wherever I go next."

He winks at Aniyah, who yells out, "I love you, baby!"

The crowd erupts in awws and applause, and Jack stays up there for another few minutes to finish his speech. I don't hear another word. Everything spins around me and I feel like there's cotton in my ears. How anyone else could hear that as anything but a threat feels insane to me. Instead, he looks so genuine, especially when he jumps off the stage, trophy in hand, and Aniyah meets him halfway. She throws her arms around him, looking for all the world like the happiest girl on earth.

"You're mad." His voice comes from behind me, following me into the restroom.

"Shouldn't you be posing for pictures?" I realize how it sounds when it comes out of my mouth and take a breath. "I don't mean that as a jab. I'm serious. You'll be taking photos and doing interviews for hours."

"I did a bunch and asked for a quick break, gave them the idea that my stomach hurts, so the staff directed me to this bathroom. They said it's less busy. I didn't even know you were back here," he says defensively. I was kind of enjoying the idea that he'd followed me back here, despite my protests. "I'm not great with crowds," he huffs.

"Me either," I chuckle. An awkward silence hangs over us, and I shove my hands in my pockets. I didn't even need to use the restroom. I just wanted to get away. Because he's right, I am upset. And I couldn't watch her hanging all over him like she was the trophy he should be so proud of.

"I'm sorry."

"It's fine. I'm happy for you."

"It's not like that, Brya—"

"Coach," I correct him quickly. Lowering my voice, I add, "anyone could walk in here."

"If it wouldn't get you in trouble, I wouldn't give a fuck."

"You don't know what you're saying."

He's too young to understand the full weight of the consequences of what he's suggesting. I'm too old to let him throw his life away for me.

"I—"

"Shut the fuck up, Jack," I growl, cutting him off.

He grits his teeth and gives me a defiant look that spells trouble. The very one that makes my blood rush hot through my veins. *My baby bulldog.* He steps towards me, and I take a step back.

"Don't," I warn him. My cock is throbbing, tenting my

slacks so much that my suit jacket can't do anything to cover it up.

A glint of malice shines in his eye as he smirks and crosses the space between us in two long strides. He grabs my face and presses our mouths together, and I fold so quickly, I barely even put up a fight. The moment his tongue touches mine, I'm a fucking goner. It's been too long, I've been so alone, I've been wanting him too much.

I have the wherewithal to move us into a stall before Jack is unbuttoning my pants to pull out my cock. He gets down on his knees and I have a brief moment of conscience where I realize that I'm letting a student blow me in the bathroom, but then his mouth is on me and I hiss.

"Fuck, your mouth feels so good."

Nothing should feel this good. There's only one thing that would feel better.

"Spit all over my dick, baby. Get me good and lubed up."

Jack moans around my cock before slobbering all over it. His shoulders move with the effort of unbuckling his own pants, and they drop when he stands to kiss me. He slips off his jacket and throws it over the edge of the stall door. I ravage his mouth before spinning him around and pushing him roughly against the wall. The stall is too small for our large bodies in here together, so I have to position him towards the corner of the stall door and hope I don't fall in the goddamn toilet. Jack's hands automatically place themselves up on either side of the wall, and I know I don't have to tell him to keep them there. He fucking knows.

"This is going to be quick and rough, Jack. You know better than to test me."

"Make it hurt, Coach."

Fuck. Me. You're goddamn right I will.

I line myself up and bury myself to the hilt in one hard thrust. Jack lets out a choked burst of air with the impact.

Pulling almost all the way out, I ask him, "You get off on dangling your little girlfriend in front of me, baby bulldog?" He doesn't get a chance to answer before I'm thrusting back in. A grunt of pain and pleasure escapes him, and the sound sets me off. I start rutting into him like an animal, not caring how loudly our skin is smacking together, echoing off the bathroom walls, or how we're shaking the sides of the stall. I fuck him so hard he doesn't have a choice but to whimper and grunt and gasp for air. I fuck him so hard I know he'll be feeling it for days.

"Every fucking time you sit down, I want you to remember who fucking owns this ass, Jack."

Our bodies are bouncing off each other, the force of my thrusts turning his perfect fucking round ass red.

"Jerk yourself, Jack. Stroke that perfect fucking cock and tell me who fucking owns you."

"Ahhh fuuck. Yessss," is all that comes out of his mouth. So I smack the side of his ass, hard.

"Tell me, Jack."

"You do. You own me, Coach."

You're fucking right, I do. This ass is mine.

"Come for me, Jack. Fucking milk my cock so you can go out there and put on your little show and pretend you didn't just get the shit fucked out of you by my fat cock."

"Fuuuck!" Jack shouts, far too loudly, but I'm too overcome by the feeling of him pulsing around me to focus on anything else.

When I pull out, I keep a hand on his ass, waiting for the first signs of my cum to start trickling out of him. It's my favorite sight, and also the reason I can't blame him for having those pictures on his phone. Because even after everything that's happened, I still have the picture of Jack's asshole on my phone, my cum dripping out.

"There it is," I say appreciatively, and use my fingers to swipe the first trickle out and push it back inside. "Clean yourself up, but leave your ass sloppy. I want my cum dripping out of you while you shmooze all these assholes and try to get hard for your little girlfriend after remembering how good I fuck you."

I bite the back of his neck, enough to leave it red, but not enough to be too obvious. Then I pull up my pants and squeeze out of the stall, leaving him messy and panting. I wash my hands and leave just as someone walks down the hall to check on him.

CHAPTER 31–JACK

"My parents are going to love you," Aniyah says. "Actually, they already do. They watched the Heisman presentation on ESPN. My mom cried. She thought what you said was sooo sweet."

I give her a tight-lipped smile and pretend to be paying attention to the GPS display, even though we're on a highway and our exit isn't for another twenty minutes. The three-hour drive to Highland Park is both not long enough, and too long. Not long enough for me to calm the panic that is clawing at my chest, and too long to sit next to Aniyah and play pretend.

We both know why we're here. Why she's in the passenger seat of her own car, while I drive us to her parent's house to spend Christmas. We both know, but she's either an excellent actress, or she's delusional enough to believe her own lies.

She unbuckles her seatbelt and gets up on her knees. "I could get you off, help settle some of those nerves, if you like," she says, unbuttoning the top three buttons of her cardigan and exposing her lacy red bra.

I take a moment to marvel that she's doing nothing for me. This time last year, I would have been pulling out my cock enthusiastically. She's gorgeous and has a killer body. Her hair, clothes, and makeup are all perfect— it's clear she comes from money. And underneath it all, there's a naughty little freak that likes to act innocent. Until you've made her cum all over your hand, with her face stuffed in her best friend's pussy. On camera. She was definitely a better actor than her friend. Still is.

She's had me traipsing around campus with her on my arm, accompanying her on shopping trips and putting on a show when we get together with her friends. She even gave me a credit card to use to buy her gifts and offer to pay for things when we're around other people, making a huge deal out of how much I spoil her. Which is ridiculous, because everyone knows I'm one of the few scholarship students on campus. I'm the underdog charity case that everyone looked down on until they saw what my future holds. I don't think she's actually fooling anyone into thinking that I'm paying for shit, although she has spent a lot of time talking up my big NFL signing bonus. That six-million-dollar salary, which was enough to make my head spin, is nothing to these people. Getting handed a thirty-million-dollar check is nothing to scoff at, though, even for the Richie Riches of the world. Especially because they know it's just the beginning.

And that's exactly why she's sticking to me like glue, showing off our fake relationship. Because at least half of whatever they give me will be hers, if not more. But she seems to be forgetting that the whole thing is a sham, and that makes it ten times more uncomfortable. It's bad enough I have to kiss and grope her in public, but she keeps trying to do things in private, too. When we got home from the Heisman awards, there was a huge party, and she all but humped me on the dance floor. I had to lift her up, wrap her legs around me, and carry her off to a private room before I could get any space. But she was riding high, rubbing herself on my leg like a cat in heat. She believed me when I carried her into the room, thought I was really going to fuck her. She started crying and told me that I was being a bad boyfriend.

Bitch. Is. *Nuts.*

"I'm, uh. I'm good. Thanks."

She huffs and returns to her seat, fixing her clothes. Aniyah sulks the entire rest of the drive until we're pulling into her neighborhood, and then once again it's like she's forgotten everything.

"Turn left up here, bae." I wince. Every time she calls me bae, I want to lobotomize myself with a screwdriver. "My house is the big one on the left."

I can't help but whistle as we pull into a circular driveway. She wasn't kidding when she said it was a big house. It looks like it might be the same size as my entire dorm building, or bigger if you count the detached five-car garage and two other smaller houses in the backyard. Those buildings–which turn out to be the pool house and guesthouse–are each two to three times bigger than the trailer I grew up in. This place is ridiculous.

When we walk in, I'm overwhelmed by the three-story tall foyer with a massive chandelier that I'm pretty sure wouldn't fit in my dorm room by itself. Just the entryway to her house looks like what I imagine an opera house would look like. It's huge–cavernous–and I'm afraid to so much as walk on the polished floors, even though my shoes are clean and new. Thanks to *him*.

Aniyah shrieks as a girl that looks almost identical to her, but clearly younger, comes bounding down one side of the grand staircase.

"Bae, this is my little sister, Brenleigh, but you can call her Bre."

"Nice to meet you," I say, putting on my most charming smile and shaking her delicate hand. The younger girl blinks up at me like she's meeting a celebrity, and it makes me uncomfortable.

"Come on," Aniyah says, pulling me along. "Let's go find mom and dad."

"They're in the dining room, planning out the seating chart," Bre says, hooking her arm with Aniyah.

They walk ahead of me, whispering and giggling, while I try not to panic about what a seating chart is needed for. How big is her family? How many people are going to be here to witness this travesty?

"Mommy! Daddy!"

Aniyah runs over to her parents like she hasn't seen them in years, when I know they visit her regularly since they're close enough and her mother is on the

Board of Trustees. I narrowly avoided meeting her two weeks ago.

I stand back awkwardly for a few minutes until Aniyah gives me a look that clearly is meant to spur me into action. Right. Clearing my throat, I step up beside her.

"Hi, Mr. And Mrs. Wilcox, I'm–"

"Jack Perry," her father answers, unimpressed. He gives my hand an overly firm grip, but it's nothing I wasn't expecting. Aniyah had mentioned that she's a bit of a daddy's girl and that he's super protective of his daughters.

"Yes, sir. It's nice to meet you." I turn to Aniyah's mother and turn on the charm as best I can. "Ma'am, it's nice to finally meet you. I almost got the chance a couple weeks ago, but I had to get in some extra practice time."

"Gotta get ready for that bowl game coming up!" Mr. Wilcox says, slapping me on the back. It's like the reminder that I'm Groveton's football star opens him up, and then we're talking about football while the women retire to look at the dresses Mrs. Wilcox picked them all out to wear to Christmas dinner. There's also apparently matching Christmas pajamas for us all to wear tonight, which is apparently a family tradition. They all wear matching jammies and drink hot cocoa while they watch 'It's A Wonderful Life' in the screening room. *A fucking screening room.*

Before that, we head out to Aniyah's favorite French restaurant and then drive around looking at Christmas lights. We are spending tomorrow with the entire extended family, followed by a formal Christmas Eve dinner, and then a "traditional Christmas morning" which is the moment my life will basically end. I don't bother telling them that I have no idea what a "traditional Christmas morning" means, because we didn't really do Christmas growing up. My mother was usually working, or drunk. We didn't do presents or celebrations for any holidays. That might seem sad if I told anyone, but it just wasn't a thing that we did. Maybe it bothered me some when I was little, because I thought I wasn't good enough for Santa to come, and never got a cake with candles on my birthday. But I grew out of that pretty quickly, and it didn't bother me.

Aniyah did make sure that "I" got her family gifts, though. I told her that giving people jerseys with my name and number on them was gross, but she bought one for every member of her family.

"Why don't I go get the presents from the car and put them under the tree," I say, desperate for some fresh air and space. As huge as this house is, I feel it closing in on me.

"I'll help you, son," Mr. Wilcox says, and I wince, remembering the joke I'd once made to Bryant about calling me that. I suppose it's a generational thing. Mr. Wilcox is probably about the same age, although he seems much older, with his stuffy looking Ralph Lauren sweater, pressed khaki pants, and suede loafers. He's at least six inches shorter than Bryant and has a paunch. They're such different people inside and out that it's impossible to compare or even think of them in the same light.

I smile awkwardly when we open the back of Aniyah's

SUV and start unloading the ridiculous amount of luggage and gifts.

"These girls," Mr. Wilcox chuckles, rolling his eyes indulgently. "All this luggage for a few days, and there's a closet full of clothes upstairs. She'll probably bring more back with her than she left with."

"For the record," I tell him, dropping my voice. "I didn't pick out the gifts." I hope I don't come across as too rude, but I really don't want anyone thinking that I'm that conceited.

"I suppose you wouldn't have," he assesses, and I don't miss the undertone. He knows his daughter bought all of this. And he probably knows she bought the obnoxious diamond ring that I'll be "surprising her" with on Christmas morning.

Fuck my life.

"Fuck yeah," I groan, as wet heat envelops my cock. "Goddamn, I missed waking up to your..."

Wait.

"What the fuck?!" I screech. Startled, I buck my hips, effectively jabbing Aniyah hard enough in the throat to make one of her teeth graze my dick as I scramble away from her. She chokes and bounces off me, and I can't help the pained shout that comes from me. "Fuck!"

I jump off the bed, still cursing, and turn on the light. Aniyah lifts herself onto her knees, wearing nothing but a completely see through nightgown. "Keep it down, Jack! Someone will hear you!"

"What the fuck did you expect?!" I hiss back at her. "What are you doing in here?"

"We didn't have any alone time to celebrate today. I wanted to fuck my new fiancé." The loathsome rock on her finger sparkles obnoxiously, reflecting the lamp's light. I do not look forward to seeing what that thing looks like in the sunlight. Or at all, really.

I feel sick.

"Aniyah, we've talked about this."

"We're getting married in a month, Jack. You're going to be my husband. I'm going to be your wife, and that entitles me to certain things, and one of those things is your dick."

"Are you fucking serious?"

"I know you like my body, Jack. Come see how wet my pussy is for you–"

"No, Aniyah. For the last time, this isn't a real marriage. I agreed to do this and you'll be entitled to whatever I get in the first year of my career. My paycheck, my signing bonus, endorsements—everything. We're doing it this way because you wanted collateral, and this is all I have to offer. I've played your game, I've put on the show. Beyond that, I want nothing to do with you. Do you understand?"

"And do you understand that I don't need your fucking money? Look around you, Jack. I get whatever I want. And right now, I want you to put that big dick to use and fuck me. For real this time."

"I agreed to one year of marriage so you can take me for all I've got, but that's it. That's the deal."

"A marriage doesn't count if it's not consummated."

"And who the fuck is going to know?"

"I will."

"Well, I hate to break it to you, Aniyah, but my dick isn't going to do tricks for you. I'm not interested."

"You were pretty hard a minute ago."

"Yeah, well, that's when I thought you were—"

"Say it. Say his name. I fucking dare you. Because here are my new terms, asshole: either you act like you're in this thing, or I won't just take that video to the dean. I'll take it to the press and leak it all over the internet."

My whole body flushes with anger. I'm seething, my arms trembling with the effort not to pick her up and shake her until her head pops loose. "We had a deal."

"Yeah, well. I changed my mind. I don't just want the name, I want the perks, too. I want to know what's so good about your dick that it turned a man like Bryant Nicks."

"I don't ever want to hear his name come out of your mouth. And if that video ever leaks, I'll fucking kill you with my bare hands."

"You wouldn't."

"Fucking try me, Aniyah. You can't blackmail your way into the only good thing that's ever happened to me and expect me to treat you like anything other than the conniving bitch you are."

"Why don't you want me?!" she cries.

"Other than you're a crazy fucking bitch that's blackmailing me?"

I try to keep my voice down, but I'm close to blowing my top.

"You're not him."

CHAPTER 32–BRYANT

"I hope you had a Merry Christmas?" Susan, one of the regular AA members, asks as I help her stack the chairs. As much as I don't feel like being social, I really don't want to go home right now. There's too much of him there to remind me how fucking angry I am.

"It was alright. Quiet. How was yours?" I ask, deflecting the conversation away from me. She talks a little about getting to see her kids. They were taken from her after she got caught drunk driving with her kids in the car when they were three and five years old. That was four years ago, and they've been with her parents ever since. She's been sober since the night it happened, but only recently started getting unsupervised visits with her kids again. She's hoping she can get them back next year.

"You seem lost in thought," she says, and I realize I wasn't listening.

"I'm sorry, that was rude. I'm a little off. Holidays, you

know."

"Wanna go grab a cup of coffee and talk about it?"

"Thanks, Susan. I'm good. I have your card, though." She offered me her contact information after I started coming to meetings and admitted I'd relapsed. Of course, I haven't mentioned that I've been drinking somewhat regularly, although not to excess like I did that first night.

She gives me a polite hug, and I head out to my car. I don't go home, I just drive around, looking at Christmas lights. It's peaceful. I don't even turn on music, I just keep driving, letting my thoughts overwhelm the silence.

Honestly, I wish I could talk to someone about it. The student I fell in love with got engaged yesterday. I know he's not in love with her. At least, I think he's not. But they look pretty convincing in the engagement photos I saw on social media.

Why would he have sex with me in a bathroom, with a high risk of getting caught, if he was about to pop the question? Maybe it's just something physical for him? It seems a little far to be just a cover.

I remember he said he loved me. He said it first. But I was drunk enough to let him top me, so maybe I'm remembering wrong?

Maybe he's not gay at all, and the novelty, the experimentation, gives him something that a pretty girl with perky tits can't give him?

I love him. I guess that makes me gay. Maybe I've

always been gay, and didn't realize it, and that's why I never really had a meaningful relationship? I thought it was because I didn't have the best example of healthy relationships growing up, since my parents hated each other and fought all the time. But now that I've met Jack, I'm wondering if maybe I was just looking in the wrong places.

My tires take me three towns over, and I pull up at a place that Google informed me is a gay bar. It doesn't look gay from the outside. Although, honestly, how would I know what a gay bar in the middle of Texas looks like? I'm not trying to stereotype anything or anybody here.

I sit in the parking lot for so long that I expect the place to close soon, but when I look down at the clock on my dash, it's only just after eleven, which I suppose is still early for a bar. A couple of very normal-looking guys wearing jeans and cowboy hats walk in. It must be some kind of cowboy bar.

With nothing else to do and nowhere else to go, I decide I may as well go in and see what it's about. Can't hurt anything. I grab my jacket and put a ball cap on, pulling it down low over my eyes. My job is already on the line. I don't need to be recognized right now.

It's dark inside, but clean for a dive bar. I have a seat at the bar and order their best scotch on the rocks. Then I sit with the bar to my back and look around.

It's really just like any other dive cowboy bar, aside from the fact that there aren't many women. There are a couple over by an electronic jukebox, and one or two at various tables. There's an upbeat country song playing, and a few people are doing a line dance. It's so... normal.

Honestly, the only thing that could out this place as a gay bar is the banner of tiny flags at the very top of the shelf behind the bar. That, and the shirtless guy in tight jeans slowly riding a mechanical bull. I can't see much of his face because his black cowboy hat is pulled low over his eyes. He's got one arm up, holding the hat to his head, the other holding onto the rope handle on the mechanical bull. The bull rolls and bucks, smooth and slow, and the cowboy rolls his body with the movement. His hips undulate, abs contracting and rolling. His skin is covered in a sheen of sweat that makes the light catch on each defined muscle. It's definitely erotic. And I can see the appeal, but I don't feel that spark of heat until I imagine it's Jack up there. I imagine how his abs would contract, how his hips would roll forward and snap, and my cock starts to press against the front of my jeans.

My eyes glaze over, and I'm lost in my own imagination. Until I become aware of someone standing right in front of me.

It's the guy from the mechanical bull. He's close enough that I can tell the glossy sheen to his skin is some kind of oil, not sweat. He's young. Probably not as young as Jack, maybe in his late twenties. The hair that peeks out from under his hat is sandy blonde, and his eyes look to be a dark green color, but other than that, I could pretend that he looks somewhat similar to Jack. If Jack had a slimmer build. This guy has full lips like he does, but a thinner nose, a more pointed jaw.

"Like what you see, Daddy?" The cowboy says, looking at me appreciatively. My brain tries to morph his Texas accent into Jack's Alabama twang.

"Daddy?" I say, lifting an eyebrow.

"Yeah, you've got that Daddy vibe. Like you might want to spank me and send me to your room."

"Is that so?" Am I really flirting with this guy?

"I haven't seen you here before."

"I haven't been here before," I answer, taking a deep swig of my drink.

"What's your name?" He asks, leaning up against the bar and gesturing for a beer.

I hesitate. "Nick," I lie.

"Well, Nick," he says my name like he knows it's not real. "Were you looking for something in particular?"

I'm not sure I understand his question, but I shake my head. "No, just stopped in for a drink. You... reminded me a little of someone I know."

"Oh yeah? This person have a name?"

"Jack," I answer honestly, because it would be a reach for this guy to put two and two together.

He leans in close enough that I can smell coconuts. Must be whatever oil he used to gloss his skin up.

"Well, isn't that a coincidence," he says huskily. "That happens to be exactly my name."

I swallow, and he catches the movement. His hand comes up to touch my Adam's apple, and I swallow again, letting him feel the movement. He makes a low humming sound, like he's thinking of something, before leaning forward and whispering in my ear.

"Follow me, Daddy."

He walks away, towards the back of the room, and through a hallway. At first I just stare after him. Then I drain my drink and stand to leave the bar.

At some point, my feet curve around and follow Cowboy Jack down the dark hallway.

I don't know why I follow him. And I don't know what I'm expecting. I'm not drunk, and obviously I know he isn't my Jack. But I'm... curious. Can I find the same connection, the same release, somewhere else?

I hear a little whistle, and look up to see Cowboy Jack darkening the entrance to a strange room. The music here is different, more intense, thumping, like dance music but slower. It's dark, except for a dim disco ball type projection.

Cowboy Jack pulls me into the room. His hand in mine feels strange, but I let him lead me to the back of the room. From here I have a vantage point of the door, so I can see if anyone walks in, but I have a feeling no one really cares what happens back here. Cowboy Jack presses himself against me, and my back hits the wall. He ghosts his lips over mine, but doesn't try to kiss me, which I'm thankful for, because I don't want him to. He presses his lips to my neck instead, and I close my eyes.

"That's right, Daddy, close your eyes."

"Coach," I correct him.

"What?"

"He calls me Coach."

"Alright, Coach," he agrees, and licks my neck. His hand trails down my stomach and cups my crotch.

I'm not hard, but my thoughts of Jack earlier still have me at maybe half mast.

"Well damn, Coach. I knew you'd be packing, but shit."

He doesn't sound like Jack. He doesn't smell like Jack.

But his hand, when he reaches inside my pants and pulls out my half-hard cock, is warm enough. And when I close my eyes and focus on only his hand stroking me, I can almost pretend it's Jack.

It's even easier to pretend when he stops kissing my neck and gets to his knees in front of me. When his warm mouth sucks me in, my cock doesn't seem to realize that it's not Jack. It grows harder in his mouth, and he takes me all the way back in his throat. He's not doing that thing I like, that *he* always does, with his tongue around the ridge of my cock head. But he's enthusiastically sucking, and it does feel good...

"Fuck, Jack," I whisper, and my hand reaches to fist his hair, knocking off his hat in the process.

My eyes fly open, because the hair I'm fisting feels nothing like Jack's. And without his hat, this guy looks nothing like him, either. Which is also stupid, because I've never seen Jack wear a cowboy hat, or any other kind of hat aside from his football helmet.

What the fuck am I doing?

I pull the man off me, tuck my rapidly deflating dick

back in my jeans, and all but run out of that bar.

CHAPTER 33–JACK

"But why can't I stay with you?" Aniyah pouts.

"Ani, listen," I say, using the shortened version of her name as an endearment, because I can't stomach calling her anything else, even in front of people. "I told you, the team has to stay in the hotel."

"I thought that was just for before the game. I overheard that some of your teammates are going out clubbing downtown to celebrate the win." She puts her hands on her hips and looks at me expectantly.

I rub my hand over my face. "Well, you're welcome to join them, but I'm tired. I took a big hit, Ani." While I mostly just don't want to be forced out in public with Miss Spectacle herself, it is true that I got tackled pretty hard during the game. I actually had to sit out for a few plays before Coach would let me back on the field. "We've got our semifinals game in two days, on New Year's Eve. We can party after that. Okay?"

Aniyah glares at me and stomps her foot a little. We're standing on the sidelines, with a few of my teammates just behind us. We just finished up some interviews after we successfully trampled Ole Miss 42 to 25. I'm dirty, I'm sweaty, I'm sore, and I'm irritated because I didn't want her to come to the game at all. But of course, her parents have tickets to every game, so she got to follow me to the bowl game. More than once the cameras sought her out, showing her on the jumbotron screens, standing up in her seat and waving her "#53 ON THE FIELD, #1 IN MY HEART" sign and turning around so everyone can see her "FUTURE MRS. PERRY" Jackals football jersey.

She huffs and I notice her eyes cut to someone behind me and narrow. A quick glance behind me shows Coach Nicks talking to a few of the sports reporters. My eyes don't linger on him the way I'd like. We've had very little contact since the Heisman awards, and he hasn't spoken to me at all since we got back from Christmas. I'm sure he saw the announcements, not to mention Aniyah's embarrassing public display. I never got a chance to tell him what the plan was. I didn't make enough of an effort because I was afraid of his reaction. I'd be upset too.

I'm exhausted by it all, and to think that this is just the beginning makes my temples throb.

"Want me to come by later and give you a massage?" she asks, running her hands up my chest and around my neck.

I give her a pleading, don't fuck with me right now, look. Then I wrap one arm around her back and kiss the top of her head, just for show. Before I leave her pouting on the sidelines, I look up towards the box I know her parents are sitting in and wave. I have no idea if they saw me, and I don't really care. It's all for show, anyway.

The guys are rowdy in the locker room, excited about our big win tonight. When I walk in, they start chanting, "Magic Jack," and try to convince me to come out with them.

"Y'all, I don't want to be a downer. I'm not feeling great and just need to lie down. But have a drink for me, and I'll make it next time, alright?"

I hurry through my shower and head out before most of the guys are finished dressing, grabbing a rideshare back to the hotel. Before I go upstairs, I talk to the front desk and ask them not to share my room number or allow any visitors in case my crazy ass fiancée tries to come see me. The last thing I need is her showing up, especially when I plan to corner Bryant.

I have to get him to talk to me, so I can explain what I did and why I did it. I need to know if there's any chance of a future with this thing we have. Does all of this end when I leave Groveton? Either way, I want him to know his reputation is safe. I'm playing a long game here and he needs to know. After we're married and far away from her friends and family, I'm going to make Aniyah so fucking miserable she eventually decides she can't take it anymore, and hands all the evidence over in exchange for her freedom. She can keep the money and half of everything I have. I've lived on way less. Having any money at all feels like being rich when you've always had nothing.

Once I'm in my hotel room, I take a real shower. I put on a pair of dark grey lounge pants without underwear, and a tight, white t-shirt. I'd go shirtless, but I want to ease my way in by telling him I want to talk first. This shirt is just thin enough to see all the ridges of my muscles, without making it seem like I'm trying too hard. Between the shirt and the grey pants, with my cock so clearly, yet casually on display, one could think that I just wandered down the hallway to speak to him. Maybe if he's thinking about my body and sex while I'm explaining everything, he'll be a lot more amenable to the process.

Fuck. I don't know.

Bryant's room is on the floor above mine. I might have purposefully eavesdropped during check-in to get his room number. I was disappointed that his room was so far away, but at least the coaches' rooms are more spread out and the first string players don't have to share this time. Perks of having a whole hotel to ourselves for the bowl game.

I knock on the door, overthinking everything from the clothes I'm wearing to how hard I knock, just hoping he's in there. I've been trying to catch him alone since we checked in two days ago, but he's been in planning sessions and interviews down in the conference rooms. There's a chance he could be out celebrating with the other coaches, but that's never really been his style. Then again, I saw him drinking on the plane, so maybe he's venturing out more. I hope he's being safe.

Jesus, listen to me. I'm as clingy as my fake fiancée.

I hear a scratching sound behind the door, and I'm almost positive he's uncovering the cover of the peephole to see who's out in the hallway. Maybe I should have stepped off to the side so he couldn't see who it was.

"I'm going to have to make a scene to get you to open this door, huh?" I say, feigning more confidence than I feel.

There's a small thud against the door and a pause. Just as I'm about to bang on the door with my fist, the door opens. Bryant stands there, his hair wet from a shower, looking more delicious than ever. He's obviously tired. The dark circles under his eyes make the ring around his hazel irises more apparent. His scruff has grown out into a short beard that has a few streaks of grey, giving him a distinguished look. Manly. Sexy as fucking hell.

He gives me an expectant look, silently asking me what I'm here for, and my stomach knots. I need to be calm, casual. Though it's hard to play it cool when I'm imagining myself rubbing my face in his chest hair like a cat.

I clear my throat. "I just needed to talk to you. Alone."

"I was just getting out of the shower," he says. "Let me grab a shirt and we can walk to the ice machine?"

He's trying to avoid letting me in. It's like we never had a connection at all. Maybe it was all in my head? Our only moments together in the last month have been fleeting glances and one quick bathroom fuck, where it seemed like things were still good between us. He'd said I was still his.

Well... he said my ass was his. Is that really the same thing?

Either way, I still need to talk to him, though, but obviously not out in this hallway.

My shoulders droop. "I don't want to be overheard. It's about Aniyah." I lift an eyebrow, letting him know that I'm not just talking about my relationship with her, but about what she knows.

His whole body stiffens at the mention of her name, but he nods. After looking both ways down the hallway, he steps back and lets me in. His entire demeanor is cool and professional, the way he is with everyone else. The way he used to be before this thing became more than a game.

He gestures to the small sitting area in his suite and grabs me a bottle of water before opening a small bottle of whiskey from the minibar. I don't say anything, but he catches me watching him. My eyes cut to the other side of the room, landing on the sliding glass door to the balcony. When I look back at him again, his lips quirk.

"At least it's warmer here," I joke.

"At least you're not naked," he retorts.

"Not yet."

"Jack."

"*Bryant.*"

Like always, his eyes fly to my mouth when I use his first name. I used to think it was because he liked it, but now I'm wondering if he's just considering my audacity.

Now his gaze feels more like a warning, but predictably, the danger he projects sends a lick of excitement up my spine and my cock twitches. His eyes flick to the movement, but he quickly looks away.

"I hear congratulations are in order," he says in a low voice.

I release a heavy huff of air, my chest clenching at the tone in his voice. The judgment. The resignation.

"That's what I need to talk to you about. You need to know, it's not real."

"That rock looks pretty real to me."

"The marriage is real. It's happening. But the relationship isn't."

"Could have fooled me," he gruffs out, taking a large swig of his whiskey.

"It's the deal I made. For her silence. To keep our secret."

"What are you talking about, Jack?" He looks both angry and confused.

"I was grasping at straws, and tried offering her money I don't have yet. I told her about the numbers that the scouts discussed with me. She wanted more than just the money, though. She wants the status of being an NFL wife, and she needed collateral, which I obviously don't have."

"So you agreed to marry her?"

I nod, bending over to rest my elbows on my knees and raking my hands through my hair. "The deal was I marry her right after the championship game, so we're married before I sign anything. So that way she'll be entitled to whatever I earn for the whole first year, when I'll have the most income from the bonus and any rookie endorsements. After the year, we separate and divorce on good terms, and I won't fight her to take half of everything plus a year of alimony."

"Jesus Jack."

"I don't care about the money. It was an easy deal to make to cover up my stupid mistake, to keep us both safe." It *was* an easy deal... when I thought I'd get to keep *him.*

"Except she wants more now?"

I look at him, sitting across from me with a fierce expression. "How did you know?"

"Because I've spent a lot more time in the circles of these people. And enough is never enough for people who are used to getting everything."

My head drops into my hands, and I rub them over my face before leaning my head against the back of the chair and venting my frustration to the ceiling. "Arghhh!" I yell in frustration.

He's just confirmed what I already know, that she'll never let me go without a fight. She'll keep using that video as collateral, yanking me along, trying to force me into a real relationship with her. What happens when she wants kids?

"People like her, like her family—like the dean. And all the entitled assholes of the world that consider themselves elite and above the rest of us. They know how to make demands, and they know how to use our weaknesses against us, because they're born honing those skills."

"I know the dean is threatening your job if we don't win this season," I say in understanding. I've known it for a while, guessed by the interactions that I've witnessed.

"Among other things," he says, offhandedly. "People like us are pawns in their games, and we go along with it because it's better than living in the gutters where we come from. We tell ourselves we can play the game and win, pull ourselves up to their level. But really, you just get deeper into the game, and they'll keep using you to get ahead. And then when they're done with you, they'll throw you out with yesterday's trash. That's why you need to get out of this deal with Aniyah Wilcox, and you need to focus on building your future without strings attached. Use your signing bonus to save, invest. Be smart, because when you're not useful to them anymore, you'll be nothing again."

My heart aches for him, and a few more pieces of what makes Bryant Nicks the way he is fall into place.

"What else is the dean trying to get you to do?"

"Doesn't matter. It'll never end. Which is why this will be my last year at Groveton either way. Don't drown yourself to save me, Jack."

"Even if I was willing to throw you under the bus, which I'm not—under any circumstances—my face and voice are in that video, too. Clearly and enthusiastically enjoying your attention."

"I can make sure it doesn't see the light of day."

"I'm not letting you drown to save me, either!" I yell, jumping out of my seat.

"Jack. I'm a forty-eight-year-old drunk. A fuck up. I've lived my life and I've played my cards—poorly." He looks up at me with pleading eyes. "You have a chance for greatness. *True* greatness. To not only join the so-called elite, but to own them. Don't miss your chance."

"Don't act like your life is over. You're fucking amazing, Bryant. You inspired me to quit being a dipshit."

"I manipulated you into not being a dipshit. I took advantage of my position and I violated the contract—"

"Don't you dare say you're sorry for what happened between us."

"I'm not sorry," he snaps. I'm momentarily dumbstruck by his raised voice and sincere tone. "I should be sorry, but I'm not. I'm not a good enough person to regret this thing between us. I think we were good for each other, until we weren't."

His voice trails off. "My only regret is that I can't stop watching you, wanting you, *craving you.* If you want the truth, I don't just want you to cut off the deal with Aniyah because she'll just keep taking advantage of you. I want you to cut it off so I don't have to watch you be happy with her."

"It's all fake."

"You're too good an actor."

"I never had to fake it with you. Why can't we just—"

"What, Jack? Why can't we just say to hell with all of

them, come out as a gay couple with an almost thirty-year age gap and live happily ever after?"

I feel every cell in my body wilt in the defeat I hear in his voice. We live in a conservative town in Texas. Both our lives and careers revolve around football. There have been very, very few openly gay players in the NFL, and even fewer that have gone on to have decent careers. It could be career suicide. But it wouldn't be impossible.

One look at Bryant tells me he's not willing to go that far with me, to take that risk. And that hurts.

Am *I* willing? Is this something that I want?

It's overwhelming to even think about. After six months of obsessively lusting after one man, after pushing myself beyond my limits to prove myself to him, and then finally admitting to myself that I've fallen in love with him along the way... I can't really imagine my life without him.

"I suppose it was naïve of me to think I could marry Aniyah and still keep you. I didn't realize that being with you wasn't an option either way."

Bryant looks away from me and drains his cup. I feel like a fucking idiot.

Forget looking like a pussy, or being a pathetic simp, or any of this macho bullshit that I let hold me down this whole time. I'm an idiot that can't think past his dick to realize when someone doesn't want them. I'm really no better than Aniyah.

The heat of anger and humiliation rushes over me, and I stride for the door, turning around at the last moment, because I'm weak as fuck.

"If you don't want to be with me, then why the fuck do you care if I marry her?"

"I don't want to see you get taken advantage of. By anyone. Including me."

"With all due respect, *Coach*, that's bullshit."

CHAPTER 34–BRYANT

The offensive line sets up against TCU's defense. We're ahead by seven, but we need another touchdown to secure the win. It's the fourth down and we're just four yards from the red zone and a first down conversion. We either secure the win, or push through a first down so we can keep running down the clock. There's just enough time left that the other team could push through our defensive line and tie it up if we don't, sending us into overtime. After a full season of all but dominating every game, this game has been tough. The team is tired, pushing through blood, sweat, and tears to secure this win in the last minutes of the game.

Jack Perry is still the dominant force on our team, helping QB Lane Masters work out the best plays to get through the other team's defenses. He's run four of our six touchdowns through the end zone himself tonight. But he isn't himself, isn't pushing as hard as he usually does. I can see it in his eyes that he's all but given up, but he knows winning this championship is his best chance of making something good out of his life. So he's still there, still doing the legwork.

His heart isn't in it, though.

"Come on, baby! Bring it home!" I hear a shrill voice scream from the sidelines, sparking more cheers from the crowd of Jackals Football fans. Aniyah Wilcox has left the cushy private box her parents pay for, and is standing on the railing, as close to the players on the field that she can get, blocking the people in the seats behind her. They don't seem to mind. In fact, one of the men is very graciously holding his hands against her waist to secure her so she can use her hands to cup around her mouth and wave frantically.

Jack gives her a little wave, but I notice his eyes cut back to me. I keep my face impassive and direct the team to pay attention.

The whistle blows. Jack pushes through two defensive linemen, dodging the players that come at him from all angles. Lane should throw to Grant at this point, because the TCU defense has been up Jack's ass, but no, Grant is blocked. Switch gears, Lane, run the ball! We only need four yards for the first down.

I hear Jack yell Lane's name. Lane throws the ball, but he's sacked just as it launches, and the throw is off. Magic Jack contorts his body, seemingly midair, and plucks it from the air. He tucks the ball, and lands just inside the end zone.

The stadium erupts, wildly cheering. There's still time on the clock and game to play, but everyone in the stadium knows we've clinched it. We're going to the national championship!

Jack does a showy kick up from the ground, landing on his feet and pointing at the sidelines where Aniyah is screaming. The people around her are lifting her up on their shoulders, celebrating her man's game saving play.

He looks over at me, and I can't see his eyes from this far down the field, but I'm more or less positive he's fucking *barking* at me. It's confirmed when the rest of the team starts jumping around and barking. I fight not to grin, because I know, as much as he's pointing to his fiancé in the stands, he's putting on this show for me. He wants me to know he's invincible, that he can handle the repercussions of the conversation we had two days ago.

But he's wrong, full of his baby bulldog bravado. And I can't do that to him.

I tear my eyes off of them and motion for defense to get set up.

Behind me, Aniyah is screaming, "I love you baby!!!" and waving a flag that says, "SOON TO BE MRS. PERRY!"

Goddamn, I just want to go home. We have ten days to get ready for the championship game, minus the travel days to Charlotte, North Carolina. The Bank of America Stadium, home of the Carolina Panthers, and Jack's top pick for teams he wants to be drafted to, is where we'll be playing against the Alabama Crimson Tide for the championship.

I should be happier. And he should be more excited. But all I see on his face, as he hugs his teammates on the sideline, is exhaustion.

A thumping sound rouses me from a disturbing dream that I can't quite remember.

The door. Someone's knocking on the door?

I sit up in bed, looking over at the hotel's analog clock. It's fucking three a.m.

Not thinking clearly through my sleep muddled haze, I rush over and open the door. Jack stands there, leaning against the door frame in dark jeans and a black button-down shirt. His hair, which has grown a little again, looks mussed. He looks fucking edible. He smells like a bar and dried sweat, and the spicy body wash that I secretly keep in my shower at home just so I can rub him into my skin when it all gets to be too much.

"Happy New Year," he says casually, his eyes looking me up and down. I'm in nothing but a pair of boxer shorts, and the erection from my sleep is trying to push its way through the folded area at the front.

"What's wrong?" I ask, trying to pretend like I'm not standing in front of my biggest weakness, half naked with a hard on. Something about the way he's leaning into the doorframe reminds me of Cowboy Jack, and that actually helps clear my mind a bit.

"Nothing's wrong. I just wanted to wish you a Happy

New Year."

"Why aren't you out with the guys... with her?" I can't force myself to say her name, despite my attempt to pretend I'm above it all.

"I was. It got old. I wanted to be here."

"More like you got drunk and your fiancé doesn't do it for you, so you hoped you could come here and get off?"

His brow furrows, like he might take offense, but then the shithead shrugs. "Could have been a little of that, too, I suppose."

"Get out of here, Jack. I'm sure the future Mrs. Perry would be more than happy to suck your dick for you."

I move to push the door closed, but he steps forward and blocks it.

"Not interested," he says, invading my space and pushing his way into my room. Not that I put up a lot of fight, because I'm a fucking idiot. I can never say no to him.

"What are you doing here?" I say, covering up my dry swallow by running my hand over my face exasperatedly.

"I have a proposition for you," he says. "And yes, it's *that* kind of proposition."

His crooked smirk is fucking sinful. I need to tell him to leave, to go back to his future wife and turn his charm on her instead. But I can't. I'm rooted to the spot, thinking of that first night I laid eyes on him. Did I know then? Was there any inkling of what he would do to me?

How he would make me feel?

I don't say a word, counting on the shadows of the room to keep my thoughts from being obvious. I also don't kick him out, though.

"How about we pretend we're both drunk from celebrating the holiday? Then you can take out all that pent out aggression on the only person that's ever been able to handle you. Just for tonight."

My pulse picks up. I know I'm going to agree before I even consider it. "Just for tonight?"

"Just for tonight," he repeats, stepping out of his shoes and unbuttoning his shirt.

He's going too fucking slow, though, and I've been getting closer to the edge with every glance, every thought and memory. Every anguished daydream over what he might be doing with her.

Crossing the room in long strides, I rip Jack's shirt open. Buttons fly everywhere, pinging off the walls. The rest of his clothes come off in a fevered rush; each article of clothing drops as I push him backwards to the small bedroom at the back of my suite. My mouth luxuriates in the taste of him. His clothes smelled like a bar, but he doesn't taste like one at all. I know he hasn't been drinking, and I haven't either, for once. But it doesn't matter, we're pretending, so we can be free to indulge in each other for one last time. Never mind that this is the third last time, or that I know I'll never stop thinking about him for as long as I live. I have him now, and that's all that matters.

I push him back against the bed and crawl up his body,

dragging my tongue along his cock, his abs, his pecs, his neck, on the way up.

"Fuck," Jack moans into my mouth as our cocks press together.

Part of me wants to draw this out, make it last all night, for as long as I can. But a bigger part of me is so starved for him that I can't control myself.

"I have to be inside you. Now," I say, leaving the bed momentarily to track down some lube. There's still a bottle in the zipper case I keep my toiletries in. I grab it and run back to the room, like I'm afraid that he'll leave, or that I'll wake up and this will have been a dream. If it's a dream, it's going to be a wet one.

I stalk towards the bed, spreading lube over my cock before I kneel at the bottom of the bed and yank Jack down to me. I press his knees to his chest and gruffly order him to hold them. Then I use one hand to pump his cock while my other hand lubes his ass. I don't take much time to stretch him out. I want him to feel every inch.

My cock lines itself up, knowing where it belongs, and I push my hips forward. I push in slowly so I can revel in the feel of his tight ring of muscle rolling over every inch of my cock, until I'm fully seated, and he's writhing against me. I smack his ass.

"I'm in charge here, Jack."

There's a glint of challenge in his eyes before he wraps his legs around me and rolls his hips.

Fuck, he feels so good.

I meet his hips roll for roll, thrust for thrust, until we're both dripping sweat, panting against each other's mouths.

"Bryant! I'm gonna—"

I lean down to bite his ear, and my voice comes out strained. "Come for me, Jack."

"You first this time," he says, and locks his legs around me. Before I know it, he flips us over, seating himself on top of me.

His thick thigh muscles flex and his abs contract as he moves up and down on my cock.

"Fuck," I grunt, my balls growing tight against my body.

"Come for me, Coach," Jack says, his choked voice pitched a little higher than usual.

He fists his cock and strokes it while his ass slams down on me.

"Together," I choke out, and he nods. I thrust upward, driving my cock into him hard and fast.

"Fuuuuuuuck," Jack cries out, and jets of cum splash all over my stomach, chest, and neck. My cock pulses inside him with every spurt of his cum, filling him as he paints me.

I sit up, pressing our chests together and wrapping one arm around him for stability. We writhe against each other, leaching out every last moment of ecstasy as my release feels like it goes on and on.

"Fuck is right, " I say breathlessly, falling back against the pillows and pulling him against my chest.

We lay that way for I don't know how long, completely silent, as our breaths and heart rates come down.

Jack finally speaks, laying with his head on my shoulder. "The whole time I was out partying with my teammates and the stupid bitch that won't keep her hands off me—" I bristle at the thought of her hands on him. And then I remember the time he sent me a video of his hands on her. What a fucked-up journey this has been. "All I could think about is that I wanted to be here, with you. I wanted to just spread out on the bed and watch the recaps of the game on ESPN."

"That's all?" I ask, laughing huskily.

He grins but shakes his head. "That's how I know."

"That's how you know what?"

"That I'm fucked."

CHAPTER 35–JACK

Lights are flashing everywhere as our defensive line stops their offense at the forty-yard line. I stand on the sidelines, soaking it all in. The NFL scouts that I met with before are here. I saw them shaking Bryant's hand.

"Perry!" Bryant says, jogging over to me. "What are you doing? Get your tight ass out there!"

I blink back in shock, wondering if he realizes what he just said out loud or if anyone heard him. Up in the stands behind our bench, Aniyah sneers down at us. She must have noticed some kind of exchange. I roll my eyes at her and run out onto the field. She's still mad about New Years, that I'd left her to go back to the hotel. I think she can probably guess what I went back for, but I don't give a fuck. When I saw her the next day, she made sure that I knew she let half the defensive line run a train on her after I left. When I told her I didn't give even one fuck what she did with her worn out pussy, she got even angrier.

"I bet you've got more cum in your ass than I do," she spat, like that was some kind of insult.

"Maybe, but only because he's more of a man than all of those assholes put together," I responded. I never use his name in case she's recording me. She's always trying to get more leverage on me.

We've barely seen each other in the past week and a half while I was getting ready for the game and she planned our wedding. She called me a few times to ask me stuff about decorations and shit, and I keep telling her I don't fucking care about any of it. It's all about her, after all. The last time we spoke at all was a fight about not sending an invitation to my mom.

"I'm not inviting my mother to this fucking sham. Hell, I probably wouldn't invite her if it was real, so don't feel bad." The more I mentioned that it was all bullshit, that none of this means anything to me and never would, the angrier she got.

I'm almost surprised that she came at all, but she's surprisingly still putting on her little show for the public. After she showed up at the sports complex and slapped me across the face in front of everyone, I thought for sure we were done. But no one came for Bryant, and nothing's been leaked on the internet. Yet.

She's wearing her ridiculous "FUTURE MRS. PERRY" jersey again, and she has "5 days" written below each of her eyes. I can't believe I'm going to be tied to this woman for the rest of my life. Because Bryant's right, she'll never have enough. My only hope is that I can introduce her to a whole lot of single NFL players with the hopes they will keep her satisfied, and maybe entice her to give up on me.

I'm still going through with it, because even if his rejection hurts me, I love him. He's leaving Groveton College after this year, he said. His resignation letter is already typed up and ready to hand to the dean when we get home. The dean is here, of course, sitting in his private box up next to Aniyah's parents. I've noticed him badgering Bryant a lot lately, and I wonder what it's about. I have a sneaking suspicion that it's about me. Coach Sanders had mentioned they'd like me to stay on for my senior year, and I gave it serious consideration. The only thing that's keeping me from doing so is that I have to get drafted to fulfill my part of the deal with Aniyah, and also Bryant isn't staying, anyway. He'd be my only reason to stay.

"Perry!" Lane calls, and smacks me on the side of the helmet, knocking me out of my thoughts and getting my head back in the game. "We're going to run a pull and trap. Run up the middle, go long."

We're able to score, Grant making a great save and holding onto the ball, getting hit into the end zone. But then the Bama offense breaks through our defensive line and makes a hell of a long pass into our red zone. They score again two plays later.

Play after play, we make our way up and down the field. Bama's defense is easily the hardest we've played this year, and they've been able to hold us back on our last opportunity to score.

Lane calls a huddle before our final play. It's fourth down. This is it. We're three points behind with less than a minute on the clock. If we don't get the first down conversion, Bama has won. Not only do we need to get that first down, but we need to be quick, because we have forty-two yards to cover before we reach the end zone. We need a Hail Mary.

"Should we call in the kicker?" someone asks.

"No," I say. "He's not reliable enough at this distance." I know Lane is the captain and QB, but we're all faltering. We're exhausted and injured. Half the players out here are second string and are apparently too awestruck to not fumble the ball. I look at Lane. "Just get me the damn ball," I say. He gives me a curt nod and we break.

"I'm relying on those magic hands, Jack."

I clap my hands together in response, and we line up. I take a deep breath and look over at Bryant. He doesn't even look worried. He's clapping like he knows the outcome of the play. He believes in me, believes I can do anything that I set my mind to.

Everything slows, the sounds of the crowd are muffled. I hear my deep breaths, my rhythmic heartbeat, and Bryant's words in my head, my favorite four words that make my lips quirk with anticipation. "Come for me Jack."

Lane calls the play. There's the snap, and he takes three steps back. Bama's defense backs up, anticipating a throw. I feign right before turning around, taking the ball that Lane hands off to me. The defensive line starts to rush in towards me on all sides, a linebacker right on my ass. I dodge an oncoming player and hear a thud of impact behind me, but I don't look around. My eyes are set on that white line as I push through two players, determined to get every yard of distance I can. I plow through them, dance around another, and then take off. Ignoring my sore body, and the muscles protesting their exhaustion, I straighten my posture and tuck the ball securely against my side, lengthening my stride. I push myself harder and faster, harder and faster.

I run clean through the end zone, pausing as the sound of the crowd catches up to me. Securely in the middle of the safe zone, I drop the ball and turn around. My team is racing towards me, still twenty yards away. There wasn't a player even close to catching up to me.

My eyes roam the sidelines, looking for the only person I want to see right now. Finally, walking swiftly towards me, my eyes lock on the intensely proud gaze of my coach, and the man I fucking love. Bryant Nicks.

CHAPTER 36–BRYANT

He fucking did it.

I don't acknowledge a single other person–player, coach, or official. I'm making my way down the sidelines of the field before the whistle announcing the end of the game is even blown. My eyes haven't left his since he turned around in that end zone and those grey orbs locked on mine. He starts walking towards me, barely noticing his teammates as they reach him.

The whole crowd starts to rush the field, pouring over the walls, but we meet in the middle and I wrap my arms around him and pull him against my chest. It's a good thing he's wearing his helmet because I know without a doubt that I would go right in for the kiss right now. I don't want anything more at this moment.

I squeeze him tightly and murmur in his ear, although it's so loud he might not hear me. "I'm so fucking proud of you, baby. I fucking love you."

Freezing cold liquid gets poured over us both, which shocks me back to myself. I pull back, blinking orange sports drink out of my eyes and swiping my hair back with a laugh. I give Jack a proud nod and step back, letting his teammates and fans swarm him. I watch as they lift him up on their shoulders and parade him around the field before finally dropping him so the reporters can take turns talking to him. Unlike the cocky bulldog that I first met almost a year ago, Jack graciously attributes the win to the team as a whole and how they all worked together. When it's pointed out that he made a hell of an impossible game saving play, easily the highlight of the entire NCAA College Football year, he says he's thankful that he had a coach that rode his ass hard to make sure he was good enough to pull it off.

I have to look away when he says that, not only because he's cussing on live television, but because of the implications behind his words. They might not know, but I do.

And so does Aniyah, who is glaring at me from the sidelines, where she's been ignored by her supposed fiancée. I'd feel bad for her if she weren't blackmailing her way to ruining a stunning man's future. The dean is standing not too far behind her, chatting with her parents, accepting congratulations for his winning season. I don't even roll my eyes. Let him have it.

Aniyah glowers at me, cutting her eyes over to the dean and then back at me. Again, I can't even be bothered to care about her little threat. Tell him, I dare you. Because he's going to find out, anyway.

I've already decided what needs to be done. Because I love him, I'll give up everything I have to make sure he doesn't have to feel the boot of a shitty world holding him down more than ever before. I took care of Tim Worth and his shithead nephew, so that even if they see my name in the news, they can't threaten Jack ever again. Jack obviously hasn't been in contact with anyone back home very recently, or been on social media even, because Randall Worth, former quarterback and nephew of Coach Tim Worth, was arrested for multiple counts of rape and sexual abuse. It seems an anonymous private investigator provided the police with insurmountable proof that the reprobate had a long history of drugging girls that came to his parties. Tim Worth was likewise arrested after it was uncovered that he helped cover up his nephew's indiscretions, including the attempted assault of his own daughter. Millie Worth is now on her way to New York City to continue her education at Columbia Law School.

Now the only loose end to tie up is the other college football coach that underestimated and took advantage of him. And he'll be getting his due as soon as we arrive home in Texas. There will be no delay, because I'll be damned if that sham of a wedding is going to happen.

But that's tomorrow's problem. Today is about Jack's success.

After giving a few of my own interviews, I spend a few minutes talking to the NFL scouts that came to watch the game. They're all foaming at the mouth to get Jack on their teams, but I want to make sure they have his best interests in mind, as well as their own. One of the scouts, the one that I think will report back to the exact right team for Jack, seems to be very understanding of my concerns and is taking everything I've discussed regarding the type of contract that would be right for Jack, into consideration. There are things, like injury clauses, that many rookie players overlook. It's easy to only see dollar signs when you come from poverty. I know from experience.

Jack walks by me, cutting his eyes at me with a pointed gaze, before making a beeline to the stadium tunnel. After he's a good ten feet past me, I excuse myself to go change my sticky shirt.

The dean tries to get my attention, looking none too pleased to see me discussing Jack's future with the NFL scouts. I tell him we have much to talk about when we return to campus and jog off the field.

Jack walked through here a good three minutes before I could make it, since I kept getting interrupted on my way. I'm not exactly sure where he would have gone. I'm ninety-nine percent sure that he was giving me a signal to follow him, but maybe I was wrong. If he was, he wouldn't be in the locker room or the showers, because there are other players and staff in there. I walk down the blue carpeted hallways, past the locker room and gym facility, which is locked. There are a few conference rooms, but I can see through the clear glass walls that he isn't in there. Maybe he was just going to the showers.

There's a sound like a whistle behind me, and a door creaks open. I don't try to hide my grin when I walk into a random office and the door closes behind me.

We come together in a clash of tongues and lips.

"You were fucking amazing," I tell him between kisses. His lips and face are sticky sweet with the sports drink that was poured over our heads. I lick it from his lips and neck, pressing him against the wall.

"It's all because of you, Coach. It's all for you. I... I love you."

His vulnerability makes me ache from my jaw down to the erection pressing between us. I want so badly to tell him how I feel, but it would undermine everything I've set in motion to give him the future he deserves.

"I'm so fucking proud of you," I tell him, before deepening the kiss.

Less than a minute later, I've got Jack pinned to the wall with my tongue down his throat and my hand fumbling with the ties to his football pants. All I want to do right now is swallow him down.

The door opens with a crash, and in walks the dean, Tuck Sanders, and three other people whose faces I don't process. Behind them, I see Aniyah Wilcox standing out in the hallway with her arms folded.

CHAPTER 37–JACK

"Mr. Perry?" The woman, who happens to be the same school counselor that lives next to Bryant, gets my attention again.

"I'm sorry," I say, shaking myself to attention. I've barely slept in three days. "What was the question?"

"I was asking, one last time, if you're very sure that you don't want to press charges against Mr. Nicks. We have his signed statement that he used intimidation and coercion to force you into a sexual relationship with him, that he used your scholarship standing as a threat against you. He has assured us that under no circumstances will he fight due process or draw attention to you or the school." She shifts in her seat, obviously uncomfortable. "The dean is asking us to pursue this with the most discretion possible, as to not draw scandal to the school. However, with these documents left by Mr. Nicks, and a statement from you, we can involve the appropriate authorities and take whatever measures necessary to ensure your safety and well-being. The college will pay for any necessary medical exams or mental health treatment–"

I stand up, cutting her speech short. "Look... ma'am," I say, because I've already forgotten her name. Although funnily enough, I remember she has a yappy dog named Pepper that would sometimes try to announce my visits when the little furball was in the backyard. "I don't need any of this. I don't want to press charges, and between you and me, I didn't feel at all coerced." I give her a very pointed look.

She purses her lips and tries to interject again. "Sometimes victims take a while to come around to the realization that–"

"I'll take your card, if that makes you feel better. And I'll sign whatever the dean wants that promises I won't go public with this, although I think he knows as well as I do that it's also in my best interest to stay quiet."

With a sigh, and a thinly veiled look of relief, she pulls out some paperwork for me to sign. I look it over carefully, knowing that the dean is a slippery bastard, but it's more or less a standard non-disclosure agreement from what I can tell. I sign it and push it back across the desk.

"May I leave now?"

"Yes, you may go. Here's my card. If you need anything, the offer for treatment remains for the remainder of the year, in case you change your mind."

"Thank you," I say, and make a beeline for the door.

"Oh, Mr. Perry?"

I hold back my sigh of frustration. "Ma'am?"

"Good luck. You have a big future ahead of you."

I dip my head in thanks and escape through the door. The sports complex is all the way across campus, and I still have my tutoring session that I need to get to in an hour. I decided it was probably smarter to keep going to class until I know what's going to happen next. In the event the NFL gets wind of what happened and decides not to draft me, I might transfer to another school. The "incident," as they are referring to it, won't affect my public record. With my killer stats and the grades I've made this year, I should be able to transfer anywhere I want.

But before I make any decisions, I need to talk to Bryant. I haven't seen him since we were busted in on, right before Bryant was about to suck me. He didn't even care that I was sweaty; he wanted to taste every part of me.

I shiver a little at the memory, still frustrated that the firing squad couldn't wait for five more minutes. Although I'd rather they'd never found out at all.

"Jack! Wait up!" A shrill voice pierces my ears and my legs move faster. "Jackie, Bae..." she whines

Halting my steps to let her catch up, I spin on my heel and stare at her with every ounce of hatred I feel. "I'm not your fucking Bae, and I never was."

Her neck cocks back like she's been slapped. "How dare you talk to me like that! We're getting married this weekend!"

I laugh, loudly. And then I can't stop. I'm fucking full out cackling. "You are the craziest fucking bitch I have ever met in my life! I never wanted to marry you in the first place. You fucking blackmailed me. Which, by the way, is fucking illegal. Not only that, but you already fucking made your bed, Aniyah. I know you led the dean to us. I fucking saw you."

Her mouth gapes open and closed like a fish.

"I don't care how much money your daddy has, or how rich you marry—you are fucking scum. I hope you catch something incurable and rot, because you deserve to be as ugly on the outside as you are on the inside."

She gasps and stomps her foot indignantly and shouts, "The NFL only takes real men, you know. They won't want you when they find out you like to take it up the ass."

I laugh again, actually ashamed that I ever let her bully me into her little extortion deal in the first place. I really should have talked to Bryant first, but I let her loud mouth dramatic meltdown frighten me into making any deal she wanted, not only afraid that people would find out about me, but more than that, that Bryant would be punished. And it happened anyway. We could have made a better plan than him just disappearing. He moved out of his campus housing before my plane even touched down, and he's not answering his phone.

Before she can open her mouth to try to threaten me with anything else, I shut her down. "Go ahead and leak your little video. Tell anyone you want that I love Bryant Nicks and his big, hard cock. Not only will I sue you for everything you have, but Groveton College will too, because their top priority is keeping it quiet. More than that—I'm not fucking afraid of you, nor am I afraid of anyone else's opinion of me."

I step towards her menacingly, purposefully showing off my full height and bulk. I want her to feel intimidated. She might think that just because I have a gay lover that makes me less of a man, but she has no fucking idea what it takes to unlearn the bullshit and even begin to accept yourself for having feelings you don't understand. Honestly, it's something I've barely begun to process. It's only been since I realized that I was losing him that I understood what I had in the first place. Talk about a mind-fuck.

"I don't give a fuck about anything other than the fact that it's your fault he's gone. I fucking loved him, and you took that away from me. Cross me again and you'll regret it."

I leave her planted in the middle of the sidewalk, gaping like a blow up sex doll, which is all she's good for, anyway. It occurs to me that no one has probably ever called her on her bullshit before.

The door to Bryant's office is open when I come around the hallway. Coach Sanders is in there, looking through some files.

"Hey Coach Sanders." I greet him tersely, unsure if he's even going to talk to me. He didn't do much more than stare at us after Bryant and I were caught. He looked like he might try to speak to me once on the flight home the next day, but he never did get any words out of his mouth.

"Hey Perry," he says awkwardly. "What can I do you for?" He grimaces at his choice of words, and I can't help but bark out a laugh. Nothing in this situation is particularly funny, but his discomfort is making me feel better.

"Don't worry, I'm not interested," I assure him, mostly jokingly. "Are you taking over as head coach?" I ask, trying to make conversation.

"In the interim, yes. The dean is giving me a trial season to see how I do." He looks pretty uncomfortable with the prospect, and I suppose he knows better than most what kind of demands the dean made on Bryant Nicks. He sits back in his seat. Or rather, Bryant's seat. The very same one I gave him multiple blow jobs in. Sanders clears his throat. "Are you, uh, moving forward with the NFL draft?"

"It doesn't look like any of this is going to follow me outside of campus, at least not immediately. So, yeah, I think so. But if they find out anything and don't want me, I'm going to see about transferring to another school."

"You wouldn't want to stay?" He asks, and I raise an eyebrow, surprised it would even be an option. "You're a hell of a football player, Perry, and I don't think you're a bad kid. I'm sorry you got caught up in all this."

"I'm not a victim, Coach. Whatever that statement said, I was a willing participant in everything. I had... *have* feelings for him."

He seems a little taken aback by my admission and clears his throat again. Seems to be a nervous tick or something.

"I, uh. I didn't know he was–"

"He wasn't. Neither was I. Still don't know if that's what we are, honestly."

The look of confusion on his face is hilarious. He's trying so hard to be kind and accepting, in his own way.

I shrug and think about what Luke told me. "I struggled with it for a while, and I know he did too. But I think that sometimes the parts you have don't matter. What matters is what's in here," I say, awkwardly thumping my chest. However much I'm coming to terms with my own feelings, it's still awkward as fuck to talk about emotions and shit with other dudes, especially when you're only used to being around macho athletes. And in the South, of all places? Forget about it.

Sanders looks distinctly uncomfortable.

"Do you know where he is?" I ask him, finally getting to the point of my visit.

"All I know is he was fired on the spot, which you were there for. They sent him on the next flight home, where he had to make some statements to the school's lawyers and counseling staff. He left me a stack of instructions for how to take over." He starts looking through the pile of folders that I suppose are what Bryant left him. So fucking meticulous and organized. My head drops, and I find myself staring at a small white stain on the floor in front of the desk. It makes my eyes well up. "He left something for you, too."

My head snaps back up, and I reach for the blue folder

he holds out to me. "Whatever went on between y'all is none of my business. But I'll tell you this—he cared about your future."

I thumb through the folder. Some of it is notes on what to expect in a sports contract, including what should and should not be negotiated on. There's also copies of emails back and forth discussing some of the terms I might be looking at in a contract with my top picks. He started the whole process of getting me the best deal for my draft signing, the way an agent would, if I could afford one.

In the back, I find something even more surprising. A record of arrest for Randall and Tim Worth, plus information from a private investigator that found proof that little twerp was more of a creep than I thought he was. There's even a copy of Millie's early acceptance letter to Columbia, like he made sure she was safe.

Fuck.

A tear rolls down my cheek, and I'm too overcome to worry about anyone's reactions to a man twice their size crying. Sanders clears his throat one more time, which is honestly getting annoying, but I look up and meet his worried gaze.

"He was told not to leave the county until they cleared him of any charges, but I don't know where he is or where he'll go next. It's not that big a place. Only so many hotels."

I shoot up to my feet and reach over to grab Coach Sander's hand, shaking it firmly.

"Thank you, Coach. Really."

I bound from the office and sprint across campus. I need to drop off my backpack at my dorm and grab a different jacket. I'll probably be walking around a lot and will need something warmer. I'm looking at my phone, texting my tutor, not paying attention to where I'm going.

"Oof."

"Oh, shit—I'm sorry!" I look up, noticing that I've run right into the exact person I was texting. "Hey Luke! I'm sorry. I wasn't paying attention—I was actually texting you."

"Hey yourself, Jack. Ouch." I apologize again and help him off the ground.

Hurriedly picking his books off the ground, I explain I was texting him that I was going to miss our tutoring session today. "I'm sorry for the late notice. Bit of an emergency."

"Everything okay?" he asks, taking his disheveled books from me. I'm sure I look like a fucking maniac right now.

I pause, not sure how to answer that question. "Uh... Remember when I was asking all those weird questions about being gay for one person and all that?"

"Yeah," Luke says,

"Well, I was asking because I found a person. Someone that means something to me, despite their parts, like you said. Although, in all honesty, I kind of really like the parts, too." I shake my head, trying to clear my thoughts, which makes Luke laugh. I'm getting off track. "Anyway, he got into some trouble and got fired. He's around here somewhere, possibly in town, but I don't know where. And I need to find him."

"Alright," Luke says, straightening his bag on his shoulder. "How can I help?"

"What?"

"Do you need a ride or anything to help find him?"

"You'd do that for me?"

"That's what friends are for, man."

After three hours of searching every hotel in Groveton and the surrounding three towns, I'm losing hope.

"Hey man, don't worry. Let's take a break, get something to eat maybe, and we'll keep driving around until it gets dark. And then we can start again and look somewhere else if we need to."

"I was a dick to you. And then I was weird. Why are you being so nice to me?" I ask Luke, sitting across from him at a burger joint. Everything tastes like sand, even though I know the food here is good normally.

Luke makes a face and then begins to speak. I don't

know why he's telling me this story, but he usually has something smart to say, so I try to be patient and listen.

"I never came out. My mom, who raised me and my sister on her own, she just knew. She kind of knew before I did, actually. We were sitting at a restaurant. I must have been, I don't know, twelve or thirteen? Old enough that puberty had started, but not full force, you know?" I nod, because I do know. I think I hit puberty a little earlier than some of my friends. It was fucking awkward. "Well, there was this bus boy at the restaurant. I didn't even realize I was looking, but my mom said, 'Luke, close your mouth.' Just like that. No judgment, no conversation. It just *was*."

He puts his burger down on his plate and takes a sip of his soda. "It's not like that for most people. The first boy I ever kissed," he smiles awkwardly, but his eyes are welling up, so I hand him some napkins. He wipes his eyes and does this funny head shake, like he's trying to forget something he just remembered.

"You don't have to tell me anything," I say, feeling bad and uncomfortable.

He shakes his head again. "No, it's important. If we don't talk about shit, it can keep happening, you know? Anyway, this boy–Chris. He was an athlete, like you are. We were fifteen, playing soccer in his backyard, when it just happened. It was just a little kiss, so innocent." He looks down at the napkin he's shredded in his lap, puts the pieces on the table. "His mom saw us. They sent him to a 'pray away the gay' camp. Conversion therapy. He killed himself a year later."

I only have a vague idea of what conversion therapy

is, but I know enough to know that it's nothing good. Brainwashing and torture and shit.

"That's fucking awful."

We both stare at the glass tabletop for a long while. I'm tracing the pattern of an old vinyl record, thinking about what my mom would say if she knew. Thinking about whether I care. I imagine Luke is thinking about the friend that he lost.

"I'm sorry about your friend."

He nods, sniffs, and sits up straight again. "Anyway, the point is there are so many ways that we all learn about ourselves. Who we are, who we love, what we're capable of. However much of a dick you were when I first met you, you're clearly on a journey. And I'd like to see yours have a happier, healthier ending than what some people have to endure." Then he dusts his hands off like he wasn't just mangling a napkin. "So, let's go find you a motherfucking happy ending."

"Oh shit! There!" I point at Bryant's green Jeep Cherokee in the parking lot of a rundown building that might be a bar. Immediately, my mind prickles with worry. I don't know everything about his struggles with alcohol, but I know he went to rehab more than once before. I wonder if he's going to need to go back after all of this.

Whatever happens, I'll be there with him. I'm not going to let him turn me away again.

Jack and I step inside the doorway of the dimly lit room, and he chortles. "Oh, shit. I heard about this place, but I've never been."

"An old hole in the wall cowboy bar?" Seems like a pretty standard Texas kind of place. Jukebox, a few pool tables. Normal stuff.

"This isn't just any cowboy bar," Luke says, and he points across the room to where a topless guy in a cowboy hat is riding a mechanical bull. Slowly. Suggestively. "This is the only gay bar in like three counties. They keep it pretty well on the down-low."

"Huh," I said. "I wouldn't have guessed, honestly."

"You have a lot to learn, baby gay."

"What does that mean?"

"Nothing—let's find your man. What's he look like? But first, please tell me that it's *not* the guy climbing off that bull, because I'd really like to—" he sees the look on my face and steers the conversation in a different direction than he originally intended. "Um, I'd really like to introduce myself."

I chortle. "That's *definitely* not my guy," I tell him. "My guy is–"

"Is that the Groveton Football coach?" Luke says, eyes wide.

I follow his gaze to where the topless cowboy sits down, right across from Bryant. As confused as I am about him being here, and talking to some oiled up topless guy in a cowboy hat, I'm mostly just so fucking relieved to see him. It's like I've been carrying around extra weight this whole time, and finally put it down.

"No shit," Luke whispers to himself.

Then the topless cowboy puts his hand on Bryant's arm, and I stiffen, processing a lot of feelings at once.

"Keep your cool, man. Don't, like, start anything," Luke says, patting my shoulder.

I take a step into the bar to head over to him, and it's as though he senses me walking into the room. He looks up and his mouth moves. The cowboy, who still has his fucking hand on his arm, turns around and looks right at me. A genuine grin spreads across his face, and Bryant stands up.

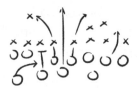

CHAPTER 38–BRYANT

"What are you doing here?" I ask, but I don't actually care. I feel like the bottom dropped out of my chest. It's heavy, like I might be having a goddamn heart attack.

His eyebrow raises. "What are *you* doing here?"

That's a fair question. This place—gay or not—isn't exactly my scene. I shrug. "Somewhere to go. Needed someone to talk to," I say, gesturing to my topless friend.

He looks even more confused now.

"Hey, you must be *the* Jack," Troy chimes in.

Jack makes a face, clearly picking up on the way Troy says *the* Jack. So it's obvious I've been talking about him.

He holds out his hand to the man I used to think of as Cowboy Jack.

"My name's Troy. This is my bar. Can I buy you a drink?"

I try not to laugh when I notice Jack trying to covertly wipe his hand off after shaking Troy's hand. He's always covered in fucking tanning oil, or whatever it is.

"Well, I don't know about Luke here, but Jack isn't twenty-one yet—" Wait. "Shit. It's your birthday today, right?"

Luke, who seemed surprised that I knew his name, looks up at Jack. "I didn't know it was your birthday. Happy birthday, man!"

"Guess I forgot," Jack says awkwardly.

Troy puts his hands on his hips. "How the fuck do you forget your own birthday, especially your twenty-first!?"

Jack shrugs, clearly not enjoying the attention. His eyes lock with mine. "Been preoccupied, I guess."

Despite Lynyrd Skynyrd playing on the Jukebox, the giggling woman currently riding the mechanical bull, and all the loud chatter of people around us, my attention hones in on Jack, and everything gets quiet.

He swallows, and my eyes break from his gaze to watch the movement. Jack looks down at Luke, who is nudging him.

"What?" He rolls his eyes. "Oh, for fuck's sake. Troy, this is my friend Luke. He's super smart and hates monster truck rallies."

"Ugh, who doesn't?" Troy says, and reaches his hand out to Luke, who doesn't seem to mind the oily handshake one bit.

"Alright, we need shots! Hey y'all! Shots on the house for my friend Jack's twenty-first birthday!" Everyone in the place—less than a dozen people really, cheer. People come up to pat Jack on the back as Troy leads him up to the bar to pour the shots, yelling out and asking who wants to do a body shot off the hunky football player. Jack hates every minute of it. And I love every minute of watching him squirm.

"You doing a shot, Daddy?" Troy yells over to me, and I shake my head.

"I'll drive," I say, and he nods approvingly.

One of the things I came here for—a fucking bar, of all places—was talking about giving up drinking again. Because I wanted to be clearheaded if or when the authorities come to talk to me about my statement. I didn't expect that Jack would want to file charges, but maybe after talking to the counselor, he'd feel differently. Or maybe that bitch Aniyah would cause more problems. Either way, I wanted to be ready.

And eventually, I wanted to be able to make a clear decision about what to do next. Most of that relied on talking to Jack, but I was still working myself up to reaching out. I don't want him to feel like he has to have anything to do with me, but I wanted to let him know it's an option.

"Daddy?" Jack says incredulously, sitting down at the table next to me.

I chuckle and shrug. "He's a character."

"Seems nice enough," he says quietly, his fingertips

reaching to skim my thigh.

"Oh yeah, he's real friendly. Maybe a little overly so," I admit with a laugh, wondering when I should admit that I almost let him give me a blow job because I was pathetically trying to pretend he was Jack. "You get used to him. He's a good guy."

"You come here often, then?"

"First time was the night I saw your engagement announcement. I was in kind of a bad way." Jack looks down and nods. "I almost—"

"I don't need to know," he says. "All I need to know is about now. And the future."

Troy comes over with an entire tray of fucking jello shots.

"We'll talk tomorrow, after you recover from whatever happens tonight," I say, laughing at the way Jack eyes the little cups of red gelatin. It doesn't bother me at all to be around the alcohol and people drinking. I nudge the tray towards him.

"I don't really feel like getting drunk," he says. "I just want to know that we're okay."

I smile despite myself. Uncertain, insecure Jack is almost cute. Scooting my chair back, I pull him over so he's sitting in my lap. The unexpected move, paired with the fact that we've never been in a situation where we could be together in public in any way, shape, or form, has him looking around the room with wide eyes. But no one gives a fuck here. There's zero judgment in this place. And I think it's the perfect place for us to try on this new version of us where we don't have to hide.

"Scared, baby bulldog?"

"Aren't you?"

"A little. But more than that..." I lean forward and whisper in his ear. "I want nothing more than to watch you ride that bull, and then I want to take you in the back and suck you until you can't stand."

Jack's ears turn red, and I watch his Adam's apple bob.

He thinks about it for a minute before he rolls his shoulders, reaching for one of the jello shots.

"Never could tell you no," he says before looking me right in the eye as he runs his tongue along the edge of the jello and then sucks it into his mouth. Troy whoops as he feeds Luke his second or third jello shot.

"Only the one," he says, holding a finger up towards Troy as if to warn him not to get excited.

Then he stands up and faces me before he pulls his hoodie and t-shirt off at once, throwing them in my lap. My cock woke up the moment I noticed him walking in here, but now I'm rock fucking hard in an instant. Everyone in the room turns to look, whistling. Troy rubs his hands down his own sixpack, muttering something about needing to work out more.

Jack's body is a work of fucking art, like he was chiseled from smooth granite.

Despite how much I know he hates the attention, he keeps his eyes on me, smirking when people start whistling louder as he makes his way to the bull and climbs on.

"I got you, Daddy," Troy says as he goes to mess with the controls. He turns the bull, so it's facing me, and then tells him what to do before he starts the ride. He has him ride it a little fast at first, although nothing like an actual bull ride, and then he slows it down. And just like I fantasized that first night I walked into this place, I get a front row view of every ab, arm, shoulder, and back muscle rippling and writhing as Jack tunes out everyone else and just looks at me. He rolls his hips so sinfully, I picture the night he got on top of me and almost cum in my pants. Finally, it all becomes too much. I look over at Troy, who gives me a knowing wink. "You got that one?" I ask, pointing to Luke. He nods and gestures me on.

Without any further preamble, and to the delight of the small crowd, I walk over to Jack and lift him in a fireman's carry. He protests, laughing and telling me to put him the fuck down, but I carry him out of the bullpen, past where our friends both swat Jack on the ass as we walk by, and into the back hallway.

"Where the fuck are we going?" He asks, laughing as he struggles, and I make my way through to the back of the building.

"Sucking your cock isn't going to be enough. I need to be buried inside you. Fuck, I might need *you* buried inside *me*."

Whatever we can do to get as close as possible, to burrow under each other's skin and know that we're both in this fully—that's what I want. The way he groans lets me know he's on board with that plan, and I all but start jogging.

I open a door, and we're both hit with the chilly night air. Especially Jack, whose hoodie and shirt are both still at the table in the bar. But it doesn't last long. There's a small duplex apartment back here. Troy lives on one side, and he offered to let me stay in the empty apartment, where he often lets drunk customers that can't get home safely stay the night. So it's where I've been calling home for the past two days since stopping by out of a lack of anything better to do. It wasn't likely that anyone would find me here, so it seemed a good place to go. I'm still not sure how Jack found me, but right now all I want to focus on is how happy I am that he did.

Jack isn't light by any means, so when I throw him down on the mattress, he hits pretty hard. I start to apologize, but he reaches up and pulls me down on top of him.

We fumble to take off our clothes, alternating between helping each other and tearing off our own clothes. Jack is naked in record time, considering he was halfway there, and he wastes exactly zero time pushing me down and swallowing my dick. I throw my head back and fist the sheets.

"Fuck, you're good at that," I grunt out, clenching my abs as Jack's throat ripples around the head of my cock as he swallows, then runs his tongue all the way up to tease around the tip. When the tip of his tongue flicks at my slit, my whole body jerks and my cock starts spurting cum wildly, like a fucking pre-pubescent teenager.

"I had a good teacher," he says darkly, pumping my cock until every last drop is spent. He starts lapping it off my abs. "That was so fucking hot."

"Use it," I say, pushing myself up the bed, and Jack understands my meaning. He swipes his hand through the mess of cum on my stomach and palms it over his cock. "Don't stop," I tell him, my voice coming out husky with lust. I watch him stroke himself, sitting back against the pillows and opening my legs. Gathering some of the mess I made, I start rubbing it around my asshole, lubing myself up for him.

Normally I'm the top, but there's something... I don't know, more intimate, about being the bottom, when you're normally the dominant one. By giving up that control, I feel like I'm giving him part of me.

And it also feels *really* fucking good.

Jack crawls up from the bottom of the bed, taking my half hard cock in his mouth. By the time he's licked and sucked all the remnants of my cum off my shaft, I'm erect and fucking ready to go all goddamn night. With his mouth full of spit and cum, Jack leans down between my legs and spits, rubbing his tongue around my hole before pressing a finger inside. I moan at the intrusion, and gasp when he takes me in his mouth again, adding a second finger. He alternates between sucking and fingering me, and spitting and licking my ass, until I can take a third finger comfortably. Then he lines up his cock and presses inside me.

He bottoms out, and then pulls out and thrusts back in a few times. He watches his cock move in and out of me for a while, before looking up at me with lust blown eyes. Pushing me back further on the pillows, he licks my neck and sucks at my Adam's apple before his thrusts speed up and his hands press on the back of my thighs. The angle hits me just right, slamming against my prostate. The bone deep spasm of pleasure that runs through me with every thrust has me yelling out his name, until he's thrusting faster and harder, until he's rocking into me and moaning as his cock pulses inside me.

"Oh fuck, oh fuck," he says as he cums deep in my ass.

"Oh fuck is right," I say, hovering at the edge of another orgasm.

When Jack pulls out of me, I flip him around and make him sit on my cock.

"Ride me like you rode that bull, baby." His hips roll and undulate as he works himself up and down my cock, grinding down on me.

I watch closely every time he lifts off my shaft and sinks back down, and when he starts to moan and whimper, I reach around and find him hard again for me.

He lays back against my chest, grinding his ass on my cock while I jerk him hard and fast. When he starts to get close again, our bodies dripping with sweat, he pants and leans forward, riding me in a reverse cowboy. I drive my hips up into him as he bounces up and down my cock while stroking himself. I can feel when he's about to come. His balls draw up tight to his body and his ass squeezes me harder.

Fuck.

"Come for me, Jack."

He cries out at the words, and spears himself harder,

meeting me thrust for thrust, until we're both erupting again, yelling out each other's names.

When we finally collapse, too fucking exhausted to even get up and wash off, I pull his back against my front and kiss the back of his neck, then his shoulder.

He's quiet, and I can tell by the silhouette of his eyelashes that he's awake, probably thinking too hard.

"Hey," I say, nudging him with my nose. "Overthinking is my job."

"I just don't know what's going to happen."

I think about it for a moment.

"Do you want to be with me?" I ask.

"Yes," he whispers, like the truth frightens him.

It frightens me, too.

"I want to be with you, Jack. For now, let's let that be enough. And we can figure out the rest as we go along."

He relaxes in my arms, and I watch him fall asleep. We have time to figure things out.

For now, we can just focus on learning how to love each other out loud.

EPILOGUE–JACK

"The first pick of this year's National Football League Draft, the Carolina Panthers select... Jack Perry, wide receiver, Groveton College."

Cheers go up around the greenroom, where other top draft picks are congregated around on couches and tables. Coach Sanders is sitting next to me, as well as my friends Luke and Troy. Both are dressed to kill and I'm not sure I've ever seen Troy in a shirt, never mind a suit. I did actually call my mom and invite her, but she didn't answer the phone or call me back. I wonder if she's watching it on TV in the diner she works at. Maybe because it's always been this way, I'm not hurt by her not coming. But there is a part of me that hopes she's watching, and hopes some small part of her is proud.

Sanders stands, and gestures for me to stand up, but I'm frozen in my seat. Despite working my ass off for this, despite dreaming about it and having a pretty good idea that it was really coming true—actually hearing my name is surreal.

"Come on, Perry, get that tight ass through those doors," Bryant calls from across the room. People around us laugh, and his proud smile breaks through my fog.

Bryant is making his way into a small conference room, where I'm going to be answering questions from the press and signing my first official NFL contract. First, though, they shuffle me through a set of double doors and over to a camera where I put a blue and black Carolina Panthers hat on. Then I'm walking up on a stage and shaking hands with the commissioner, and holding up a jersey and giving everyone my thanks. It all happens in a blur, and I'm not sure if it all takes half an hour or just minutes.

Before I know it, I'm being ushered into the conference room. I hold my new jersey over my arm as I enter the room to raucous applause, seeing Luke, Troy, and Coach Sanders in the front row. My new head coach steps up and shakes my hand, telling me he's proud to have me as a Carolina Panther, and looking forward to having me on his team. Some of the other coaches, including the offensive coordinator, whom I will be working with the most, introduce themselves and welcome me to the team as well. Then everyone settles for me to answer some questions.

"How does it feel to hear your name called as the first pick of the draft?" One of the reporters asks.

I chuckle. "I don't have an answer for that just yet."

They ask me a few more questions, and then I'm led to the table, where a folder with a Carolina Panthers logo sits at the middle seat. My name is embossed under the logo and I run my fingers over it. Lights flash and cameras click as I open the folder and look through the pages, knowing that everything is in order.

"You have a hell of an agent, Jack. I don't think I've ever negotiated so many details or signed a higher signing bonus."

On the last page, my eyes widen at the numbers. There are a lot more digits and commas than I ever expected. My eyes flash over to Bryant, who smirks and nods. He stands up and hands me a pen.

"Congratulations, Jack," he whispers, and pats my elbow. The touch is innocent, but it sends a wave of warmth through my entire body.

We aren't making any statements about who we are to each other, but we're also not hiding. We decided that figuring out a newish relationship was hard enough without the pressures of going public. So we're just going to live our lives, and do our jobs the best we can. In the meantime, Bryant is coming to Charlotte, North Carolina, and moving in with me. Now that he has his first successful rookie talent signed, he's going to spend a year learning the ins and outs of being a professional sports agent. So far, he's already the best anyone's seen, because he truly cares more about the player than the paycheck. And I know he'll be like that for all of his clients, not just me.

"Show us your jersey!" Troy says, and I roll my eyes at him, to which everyone laughs. Honestly, I'm impressed we were able to keep my surprise a secret.

After unbuttoning and removing my suit jacket, I stand up and slip my jersey over my head, avoiding Bryant's eyes until I'm ready to face him. Maybe this was stupid. I smile for the pictures before looking over at him. His mouth is open a little, and he has what looks like proud tears in his eyes as his eyes trace over my #88 jersey. I have to look away in case I start tearing up, too.

"I heard a rumor that you were able to choose your number, is that correct?" One of the reporters asks.

"Yes, that's true. I got lucky that the number I wanted was available," I answer.

"Is the number significant?"

"Very," I say. "It's the same number that once belonged to the man that changed my life."

THE END

THANK YOU

Thank you so much for reading *Head In The Game*! If you enjoyed Jack and Bryant's story, please consider leaving a review on Amazon, Goodreads, Bookbub, or any of your favorite bookish websites.

To learn more about the author and follow her on social media, go to Linktr.ee/RebeccaRathe

And if you're looking for fun book discussion, exclusive content, games, giveaways, and more, come join us in Rathe's Ratchet Readers on Facebook!

BOOKS BY THIS AUTHOR

Spark: Micah & Lukas' Story

They couldn't be more opposite of each other, the captain of the football team and the biggest nerd in school. It's almost cliché.

Yet somehow they work well together.

As Micah and Lukas explore a relationship that's almost too good to be true, they have more than just their self-doubts to overcome. Will their love be enough to survive societal and family pressures along with the looming threat of splitting up to go to college?

Or will it all be too much, popping the bubble they've created together?

Spark is an MM prequel novella that can be read either before or after The Progeny Duet, and does not contain any spoilers for the main story. This is a steamy romance story that includes mention of homophobia and death of family members.

Progeny

I don't know who I am or what happened to me.

I know that I've been running, but from what I don't know. And I know that the five men surrounding my hospital bed are important, possibly even precious to me, but they all swear they haven't met me before.

They say they feel it too, this familiarity, this connection.

So when danger comes looking, these five strangers take it upon themselves to hide me away while we put together the pieces of my past. What we find instead is darker. A twisted conspiracy that ties all six of us together in an unexpected and terrifying web of danger.

Progeny is a multi-POV contemporary MMFMMM romance with a sci-fi twist. Please refer to the author's biography for a list of sensitive content.

Retribution

I came to warn them, but instead I put them in the line of fire.

Now one piece of my heart is missing, while the other pieces are forced to leave behind everything they've ever known to protect me.

The truth about who I am and where I came from

weighs on me. Is anything real?

All I know for sure is that the people responsible for bringing me into the world are the very ones putting the only family I have ever known in danger. But I will stop at nothing to keep them safe. I will use everything they gave me against them and risk everything to take them down.

Little do they know, a reckoning is coming.

Retribution is the follow up novel to Progeny. The action and the spice in this sci-fi/ contemporary MMMFMM novel are turned up as Six and her men face the unknown. Please refer to the author's bio for any sensitive content.

Ignite: Tony's Story

Mara Wilson may look quiet and unassuming, but blending in is just one of her skills. She's lethal, taking down corrupt individuals and organizations that victimize innocent people, from the inside out. Sure that BioCere, Inc, one of the most powerful corporations in the world, is corrupting government officials, she finds proof of so much worse. They've not only got their claws in government officials, but they're doing medical experimentations and committing horrific human rights violations that are enough to turn anyone's stomach.

Determined to enact her own brand of vigilante justice,

she pulls together a team of the best hackers from the Dark Web. Tony Bartlett is already interested in taking down BioCere, Inc. To hook this infamous hacker, she has to draw him out by doing the impossible- hacking him. Rutherford Quinn, a programmer and expert document forger with a bleeding heart, is a little easier to convince when he sets eyes on his new partners.

The three of them make up the best of the best, and they'll set the world on fire in more ways than one. Their mission is to take down BioCere, Inc and expose their evils to the world, while also helping to save Tony's friends. Along the way, they find a burning attraction to each other as well as justice.

Ignite is a contemporary MMF ménage romance that contains dark themes and mentions of abuse, human imprisonment, and medical torture. This novella is a standalone accompaniment to The Progeny Duet. You do not have to read Progeny or Retribution to enjoy this story, however it does contain spoilers if you choose to read them in the future.

BOOKS BY THIS AUTHOR

Always Magnolia

A story about survival and second chances...

After years of suffering at the hands of her abusive husband, Magnolia Crawford escapes in the dead of night with her young daughter and finds herself back in the last place she remembers feeling safe.

A lifetime ago, she stood on this very property, in the shade of a magnolia tree behind her childhood home. Here, she made promises to the three boys that have held her heart since she was five years old. Circumstances beyond her control made her break those promises, but she never forgot Matty, Ryan, and Darius.

And they never forgot her.

Now that she's back, the guys are ready to do whatever it takes to help Magnolia find herself again and protect her from the darkness that threatens to break her. Can Noli find the strength to weather the oncoming storm and forgive herself? Or will the scars of their past destroy their second chance at love?

Always Magnolia is a contemporary MMFM (whychoose) second chance romance. Some material maybe be considered sensitive to some readers, as the main character lives through abuse both as a child and an adult. Please find an extensive list of sensitive content here: Linktr.ee/RebeccaRathe

BOOKS BY THIS AUTHOR

Revelations

Diya Steele, born of violence and condemned to the prejudice of heaven and hell alike, wanders the earth consumed by fear. Fear of the realms determined to kill her, and fear she will hurt innocents if she ever loses control.

The Dzhavo, a fearsome team of elite demons, are ordered to capture Diya and bring her in to face the Legion. Instead, they keep her for themselves, determined to get answers from her by any means necessary. Fighting through their lust with brutality, they discover nothing is as it seems.

With Earth caught in the crosshairs of a war between realms, Diya and the Dzhavo must find a way to work together to save the world.

How far will Diya go to save the worlds that branded her as an abomination? Will the Dzhavo be able to overcome the lies they've been told and trust the one person that might save them all?

Is a relationship built on fear and desire strong enough to keep them fighting for each other, or will their prejudices keep them from stopping the evil that threatens the world as they know it?

Revelations is a DARK paranormal MMMFM romance where five main characters, including monsters and demons, find love together. The path from enemies to lovers is a torturous one, and the story contains sensitive content. Please visit the author's bio to find a link to necessary content guidance.

BOOKS BY THIS AUTHOR

The Binding

Calista Batts lives a sheltered life, until the day she is kidnapped and used in a sacrificial ceremony meant to drain her of a dormant power she knew nothing about. When the magic inside her is unlocked, it nearly kills her, but not before calling three mysterious and powerful men to her side. Inexplicably drawn to the dying woman, they resolve to bind her to themselves-mind, body, and soul- in a desperate attempt to save her life.

Now Calista must learn to control her newfound magic and adjust to this previously hidden world, all while navigating the overwhelming effects of her new bonds.

As feelings intensify, all of them struggle in their own way- Draven, with his uncontrollable bloodlust. Seth, with his desperate need for touch. And Hawthorne, who is burdened by his past and guilt over the sacrifices made to save her. Together, they must harness their collective strength to confront the cult that nearly killed her.

Will they be able to accept their new bonds in time?

The Binding is a paranormal MMFM romance. Please refer to the author's bio for content guidance, as there may be subject matter that is disturbing to some readers.

Fractured Bonds

The anticipated follow up to The Binding!

The bonds that saved Calista's life are wreaking havoc on all their lives. Hawthorne's fate is unknown, Calista's severed bond with him making them all weaker and unable to tell if he's even alive. What she can feel is all encompassing pain and anguish, but she can't bear to allow her other bonds to help soothe her. Seth stands to lose his connection to the celestial world and his immortality, his body flickering between his solid and incorporeal form. And Draven succumbs to an uncontrollable kind of bloodlust that he can't control or comprehend.

They're confronted with mounting evidence that everything in the magical world isn't what it seems, and Calista's role might be more important than they ever thought. But can they really help save the world when they're spiraling into chaos themselves?

Eternal Bonds

The Binding Series Book 3

Made in the USA
Coppell, TX
13 March 2024

30091485R00207